DRINKWATER

ERIC HOPKINS

 ˈkræk.dʒə:

Crackjaw Publishing
Guelph, ON
www.crackjawpublishing.com

Library and Archives Canada Cataloguing in Publication

Hopkins, Eric, 1984-
    Drinkwater / Eric Hopkins.

ISBN 978-0-9782026-6-8

    I. Title.

PS8615.O653D75 2008   C813'.6   C2008-904732-X

CHAPTER 1

The trip hadn't been long enough to sleep through, but most of the passengers had tried anyway. Amber hadn't, because she was sitting back-to-back with someone who'd reclined his seat right away and left it that way for the whole four hours. She'd had to spend the trip leaning on her fist. She'd ridden in the middle seat, between her brother and someone else, an old man. Whenever he chatted up his friend across the aisle Amber could see his teeth; they were tiny and looked like little reeds, like the enamel was worn down to nothing. In the window seat was Guy; he was half-asleep with his head against the glass. He squirmed when the coach lights came on with the unwelcome of an alarm clock. He'd propped his knees against the next seat forward and probably couldn't feel them.

When they'd boarded the train in Ottawa it had been with pragmatism, as though they were just using a city bus. Amber hadn't bothered to get comfortable, so there was little they had to do in terms of gathering things up. They each had only two pieces of luggage, one bulky hockey bag and one backpack. Amber poked her brother in the side as they coasted over a river, approaching the loom of Toronto's downtown, the cluster of buildings much taller than all the others. The train at its slow urban crawl passed an open yard, and there it was: not all of Toronto, but the biggest part at least, the skyscrapers, the city's one neighbourhood where a twentieth floor was the normal thing. It was curiously finite, framed in the train window; to think, Canada was at its most high-risen in that little acreage right there. Even the CN Tower, the biggest tower in the world—you saw it, and then that was it. They didn't come any taller. From their eastern approach it looked isolated. Usually the Toronto skyline was depicted from the south, over the water.

The Union Station platform was a file of long piers, sheltered by high ceiling strips that were dripping water, like a storm had just

ERIC HOPKINS

ended. All over the wheel bays of the black VIA Rail engine were chunks of ferric-smelling dirt, thrown up from giant mud puddles.

The plan was to meet their Uncle Ian at the Harvey's at about 10:30, and they were fifteen minutes early. Amber had been there before, nine months ago, so she hadn't humoured her uncle when he tried to describe how to find it. It was in a tall, cathedrallike hall full of ticket windows. How could she miss it?

They followed the crowd down an escalator. There were signs directing arrivals, "To City / Ville," as though they might have missed it if they weren't careful. They continued through the departure hub and turned toward a wide ramp, there being apparently enough people in the group who knew the way. The ramp crested between two giant Christmas trees, and there was the hall they were looking for. "Here, Guy," Amber said to her brother, guiding him to a table in the Harvey's.

"What are we doing now?" Guy wondered.

"We're just waiting," Amber said.

"Is this where we're supposed to be?"

Yes, it was. Guy was sitting straight-backed, like he expected to be flying off any minute. His parka had a hood, but he never put it up in public.

"Amber?" her brother piped.

"What?"

"Is that him?"

Amber looked. It wasn't.

"It's not even half-past yet, Guy."

Her brother made a sound and looked toward the counter.

"Can we get dinner?" he asked.

"No."

"Why not?"

"Because it'll cost a crapload."

Dinner on the train had been twenty dollars for these tiny sandwiches. Guy had his own money, and he was free to blow it on food if he wanted, but whenever he did he always made Amber buy something too, and she couldn't afford stuff like that. She was paying for school.

"When we get to Uncle Ian's he'll probably feed us," Amber told him. "Or at least buy us doughnuts or something."

Guy hummed, undoing his coat.

4

Amber could smell the hamburgers, sweet and greasy. Inevitably they made her hungry; they were supposed to do that. And Toronto was a new place, and she still felt the tourist's inclination not to let any indulgence slip away, even just something like eating familiar fast food. But she'd all ready made a big deal about waiting until they got to Ian's. She could show some self-restraint, this time.

So there they were, waiting for their uncle at a table in Harvey's. The trip was almost over, as well as the chapter of limbo when nowhere felt like home. Once they got to Ian's they could put down their things and start working out a normal life again. They could finally take a break. Looking forward to that was what had kept things in perspective.

Amber smiled at her brother. It was to let him know they'd almost made it.

On the floor was an empty bottle, right side up like someone had carefully set it down that way. Amber's wristwatch said it was midnight. Guy was close to sleeping, stretched out on a bench, on his side so he could spring back up at a moment's notice. He hadn't taken his coat off; neither had Amber. She wandered in a lazy circuit to the front doors, to the security gate across the Harvey's, and back to their bench. After half an hour she'd succumbed and bought a cheeseburger, and then the place had closed.

At that time of night the station was serene. There was a sound like wind and occasional beeps from a guard's walkie-talkie or the Scotiabank ABM. An announcement about a departing train flared from the walls and ceiling, echoing, the list of destinations like an incantation. It was repeated in French. The information desk was abandoned at midnight, but it had laser barcode readers that stayed on, drawing roses on the counter. Amber held her hand under one, watching the shape twirl around in her palm. The first time she'd tried to call her uncle was at 11:00; there'd been no answer. She'd tried again every twenty minutes. What could it hurt to give it one more shot? If no one answered, again, then she'd get her quarter back, and their Union Station sleepover would go on just a little longer. She went to the bench and removed her backpack from under Guy's legs, while he pretended not to notice. Maybe it wasn't very wise to have a catatonic fourteen-year-old in charge of watching their luggage.

The phones were in a group of four on the sidewalk, mounted in black old-fashioned pedestals that were supposed to go along with the whole Edwardian theme of the train station. Amber was conscious of her opportunity to start observing Toronto buildings, and she observed the Royal York Hotel across the street. It echoed the station's old-fashioned style, with concrete walls and tear-shaped windows. But there would surely be better times to observe buildings, when it wasn't after dark and there wasn't a wet breeze gusting over everything. It wasn't cold, but it made Amber squint viciously. Something about it just bored straight through her jacket and made her want to get indoors. No rain or snow, a tolerable temperature, but it was miserable weather anyway.

That made it all the more vivid to think about the guy with all the plastic bags wrapped around his ankles. Amber tried not to look at him, and she was glad to see his face was in his hands. In Ottawa, once, she'd done the right thing. She'd walked past a bum in front of the Hockey Hall of Fame, then fished a twonie out of her wallet, stolen back and threw it in his little cup. "God bless you," he'd said, and Amber had turned away, face flaming, startled at how petty she felt. The sidewalk had been full of people, and they'd all seen her.

Amber had her uncle's phone number written down in her grade twelve homework journal, which she still used even though grade twelve was behind her. She'd started filling it with phone numbers in her last year of high school and, even though high school was over, she didn't see any reason to buy a new address book when her journal still worked fine. The first few times she'd called Ian that night she'd had to look up his number, but now she discovered that she had it memorised. She started dialing but didn't finish. Hanging in the air before the last digit was the ragged end of her fingernail, which had just broken. She'd already been through this four times, she reminded herself; she'd press the receiver against her ear, staring over the phone at the VIA Rail sign, she'd listen to her uncle's phone ring for five minutes, and then she'd hang up and report to Guy that he still wasn't answering.

Then it was 12:00. So it had been an hour and a half, then. After so long, Ian's absence started to acquire a presence of its own, the fact of his not being there congealing like a smell, and she'd decided that, all along, somehow, she'd known there would be some kind of fuck-up. The minutes piled up, the clocks on the departure schedule gradually advanced into the morning, and all she could do was kiss her teeth and wait some more.

He couldn't have forgotten entirely and gone out someplace; there would be actual legal consequences for that. This pick-up had been orchestrated by the social worker, Janelle, a woman from whom Amber had heard a lot over the last few weeks. Ian didn't own a car, but it was still decided that he would be at Union Station to meet them and escort them through the subway. As soon as they were safe and sound at Ian's house, Amber was supposed to call Janelle and give the all clear. Perhaps it would have been right to call her number that very minute to tell her about this latest happening.

But Amber decided to finish dialing her uncle instead. She leaned against the phone as the ringtone twittered. There to the south-west, twelve hundred feet up, the CN Tower gallery floated. When the clouds moved, it looked like it was falling over.

They could always get to Ian's on their own. Amber had made the trip herself in fact, earlier that year, when she was attending an open house at University of Toronto. There had been things to do on Saturday and things to do on Sunday, so naturally the prudent thing had been to spend the night with their relative who happened to live in the city.

Her high school had applied to three programs for her. She'd stuck with universities in Ottawa so she wouldn't have to travel, since nothing interested her enough to tempt her elsewhere. Carleton University and University of Ottawa were the obvious choices. As for the third option, her mother had tried to get her to apply to a college, like Algonquin College where she'd taken an apparel design course, but Amber was sure she'd get into one of her first choices. She'd put down University of Toronto as a throwaway option; she didn't seriously plan on moving to Toronto.

Amber was sure she could remember the way to Ian's on her own, but what if when they got there they banged on his door and he wasn't home, considering he wasn't answering his phone? Then, instead of a bench in Union Station, it would be the hill in front of his house. Amber couldn't think of any plan that was better than what they were already doing, so she'd be as well to give up and sit down.

There was a chance, though, that she could make use of an invitation that was extended to her in March, when she'd gone to the Toronto open house. She hung up the phone; her quarter danced into the coin return. It had been just a little social brush on the campus walking tour, chatting while a girl with a bullhorn showed them around the student centre. Carrie Sykes had decided to dress entirely in blue denim that day, a jacket and skirt and white sandals. She'd introduced Amber to the fact that place names in Toronto had short forms: the city was "T.O.", and the university was "U of T." At one point the itinerary had taken them to a brand-new computer science building, and there was a gallery on the top floor with a panel of windows overlooking a court. They'd watched as an apparently miserable young man tried to get people to take interest in the neon pink pamphlets he was handing out. From their vantage they could watch the fate of most of those pamphlets, to join a bright pink dump on a newspaper rack nearby. They'd both had a big laugh and went for lunch together.

After the tour their relationship had basically ended. Carrie had given Amber her phone number and implored that she call her up if she was accepted into "U of T" and would be coming back to "T.O." Amber *was* accepted, indeed, but had declined in order to stay in Ottawa, and she'd never seen a reason to talk to Carrie Sykes again.

But she was coming back to T.O. now. And she was attending U of T after all.

So Amber dialed Carrie's phone number, still written in the girl's own handwriting in her grade twelve homework journal. Someone answered with a much older voice than Amber expected, and she realised she'd just called Carrie's parents. The voice was gravelly with sleep, and it explained that Carrie no longer lived at home. *Duh.* Amber bristled as she asked where in the world Carrie did live, imagining that she could have gone off to another province or country—the voice told her that Carrie had wound up at York University instead, which was in Toronto but so far north that it almost wasn't. The subway didn't even go that far up, but Mrs. Sykes said there were buses that did. She even provided the phone number for Carrie's residence, which was kind, considering that Amber had just woken her up after midnight.

She hung up and was about to call Carrie's new number. Then, for an instant, she broke out of her dialogue with the phone to notice the guy with plastic bags on his ankles moving around, blinking and cringing. She placed the call and looked away from the street, up at the train station fresco, feeling a prophetic heaviness in her gut that no one would answer. Someone did. "Hello?"

"Carrie?" Amber asked.

"No... You want Carrie?"

"Yes, please."

"She's not... She's out... I don't know."

It must have been Carrie's roommate on the line. The way she said "Out," she barely offered a vowel that could be heard over the Front Street traffic.

On a trip into Ottawa Amber's family had gone to a cafeteria. The server had a foreign accent, but Amber hadn't been old enough to notice whether he was Indian or Hispanic, Greek or Columbian, Chinese or Georgian or Filipino. All she remembered was being short enough to look straight on through the servery glass. The man had listed off vegetables. "Some onion?" he'd asked. "Some tomato?" To each query Amber had answered *no*; she'd wanted her tuna sandwich extremely plain. To her astonishment, the man ignored her and went ahead adding everything.

From then on she'd never been able to deal with people with accents. Fighting through bad English was exhausting, and as soon as she identified that tentative, halting quality in the roommate's voice, Amber stopped expecting a real conversation. The roommate proved unable to provide information about Carrie Sykes; she didn't know where she was or when she'd be back. "Never mind," Amber said and hung up. And that was that.

She stared at the phone, deciding whether to try Uncle Ian's number one more time before trudging back into the station. Suddenly she noticed that the plastic bag guy was watching her. Amber turned around, slowly, not even a real turn, she just yawed her head enough to catch him in the corner of her eye. A bad spine made his head jut forward; he had that intense look that only homeless people had.

"Hey there," Amber said, as though they'd bumped elbows.

He said he had to call his son, and if he'd had a choice he certainly wouldn't have wanted that blob of drool to splash on his jacket

9

when he said it. "Yeah, sure," Amber muttered, carefully holding her wallet so he couldn't see how much was in it, digging out a quarter that disappeared into his fist. He thanked her, nodded his head theatrically and walked away, slowly, probably still with that look on his face and drool on his jacket. It was obvious he didn't really have to call his son; Amber cross-examined herself, trying to remember whether she'd actually believed him for a second. Just to put the moment behind her, she tried her uncle's number once more. She was amazed to find that she hadn't quite given up hope.

Finally she went back inside, looking to make sure her brother hadn't been kidnapped while she was away. Guy was still there on the bench, as expected—in fact, he was probably the least likely person in the building to become a kidnap victim, the way he sprawled there in his old black coat, surrounded by fraying luggage, looking like a street kid himself.

Amber kicked the bench to make sure he was awake. "We're leaving," she told him.

Guy sat up in a trance, but with a hint of purposeful energy. He dutifully shouldered his bags and then asked, "Where's Ian?"

"He's not coming," Amber said.

Guy looked at her strangely; he thought she'd woken him up because their uncle was there.

"Just come on," Amber urged him. "We'd be waiting forever."

"Why's he not coming?" he demanded.

"Do I look like I know?"

"So where are we going?"

Absolutely nowhere, Amber thought. Uncle Ian was a dick, and the whole world was conspiring against them. She marched right back out to the payphone, kneading in her head the words she'd say to Janelle, but then at the last minute—

"Is Carrie there yet?" she demanded when the roommate answered again, but it was really just a salutatory remark; it had only been five minutes since her last call. "Look, my brother and I need a place to stay tonight," she said. "Carrie would know us."

"Uh..."

"Really, she would," Amber went on. In residence at Ottawa there had been a residence orientation meeting, whereat a police officer had dealt out plenty of terrorising security instructions, foremost among which was never to let strangers into the building. Since Amber was no longer living in the boonies, she had to appreciate the dangers faced by young women in the city. And now Amber had decided to try and talk this barely-anglophonic person into letting some friend-of-a-friend in for the night, not just into the building, but into her own room. Still, Amber was sure that if she presented herself as brightly and benignly as possible, as very clearly *not* the sort of person who would lie about being in trouble (like the guy who'd just suckered her out of a quarter)... The girl gave in eventually, muttering a weak 'okay' that was probably only another grunt of incomprehension, but it was the best they could hope for. Amber hung up hard, hoisted her bag and ordered Guy to follow her, quickly, so she couldn't pore over how badly the whole night could end if they got there and couldn't get in. As for how to get to York, it was a bus ride from the north-westernmost subway station in the city, at least an hour's travel from Union, and that would have been during the day when buses and trains were more frequent. But going anywhere was better than waiting.

Amber ran down the subway stairs and twisted her ankle at the bottom. She dropped her bag and fell like she'd been pushed. "Slow down," Guy said, and she barked at him to shut up. So he did; he resolved not to say another word for the rest of the night. They'd been on trains for twenty-four hours, and this extra traveling was brutal. His sister had complained to him about how much she hated waiting, but while she'd been striding around all evening like she knew what to do, he was stuck on a bench watching their things. And that was worse. If she was going to tacitly put herself in charge, then it was her fault.

"Looks like we're not meeting Ian tonight," Amber remarked, ten minutes late, when they got on the subway and slumped into seats. Guy had heard that tone of voice before, from their mother. He didn't answer her, as per his resolution, but Amber went on explaining, just the way Mom did, that they were going to stay with someone she knew. Guy didn't know where they were going, and station after station went by outside the windows until he figured that they were going to the very end of the line.

Even after they tromped up two stopped escalators at Downsview, the last station, Amber said, "Now we've got to catch a bus." At that time of night, buses came with half-hour waits, and they'd just missed the last one.

So by the time they actually set foot on the campus, it was 1:30 in the morning. Guy didn't say anything after the bus pulled away; he just stood there, silent treatment in full swing. The bus had left them on a lane by buildings that looked like a mall, and no one was there to meet them.

"Now we've just got to find her residence," Amber remarked.

Guy watched his sister carefully, satisfying himself that she didn't know what she was doing and that she expected to find her friend by luck. It was perversely enjoyable to see her failure keep them up hour after hour; he understood that the fault was entirely hers, and there was a lot of it to take. There were other people around occasionally, but Amber didn't look like she was about to talk to any of them. Guy finally broke his snarly silence to ask why she didn't get directions from somebody. Amber told him to shut the fuck up, and Guy knew that pretty much guaranteed that she'd do anything at all *except* get directions now. Nevertheless, she finally found an unthreatening girl walking by herself and asked, "Could you tell me where to go to get to the residence building?"

"Which one?" the girl said.

Amber got her to list them all, and said, "Yeah, that one." The girl's directions sent them to the other side of the campus, which was longer across than a city block. The residence lobby was locked, but there was a speakerphone in the antechamber.

Amber had basically lied. She didn't know which was Carrie's residence, and both Mrs. Sykes and the roommate had seemed content to just refer to 'the residence' at York. How was she supposed to guess at these things? As it happened, the phone wasn't even willing to cooperate. Amber dialed Carrie's number and waited, and there was no ring. Her brother watched her critically. She dialed again, in case she'd made a mistake, and the same thing happened. It wasn't even a real phone, just a number pad and a speaker on the wall. Pressing a silver button had started a dial tone, so it should have been straightforward. Then she saw that it was all explained on a little poster: she had to press five followed by the last four digits in the phone number. They always had to make things as complicated as possible. Well—the roommate's voice cracked as she sighed hello; she'd been asleep. It was so inconsiderate of Amber to be disturbing her in the middle of the night, but alas, it was an emergency, wasn't it?

"Sorry," Amber said. "Can you let us in?"

The speaker was quiet. Maybe she was still asleep. She made only a pip of confusion.

"Actually, can you just remind me which residence you're in?" Amber asked.

The roommate told her. The odds of guessing right had been one in eight. Phlegmatically Amber asked where it was, and when the roommate sounded confused, Amber raised her voice and started spelling things out like she was talking to a baby. She was in the wrong residence, sorry, she needed to know how to get to the right one. She was too frustrated to care, although she was profuse with apologies after she had her directions and was about to hang up. And why shouldn't the right residence have been all the way back across the campus? Guy had to make some comment about making them walk all over the place, and Amber had to hit him for it.

Once they were in the lobby of what was hopefully the right building, after clomping around all night, there was one more call to make, the final security violation. Even if that roommate of Carrie's had been a pushover so far, that didn't mean she'd be easily convinced to march downstairs and actually let them in, especially after having been woken up so many times.

In fact, as the phone rang and rang, Amber considered that she'd decided to stop answering altogether. It was what Amber would have done. It was after 2:00 in the morning, and they would be stuck in the entrance. Already her mind was cutting the cables on sanctuary with Carrie Sykes, brainstorming alternatives—find their way to Ian's house after all? Somehow, after all the buses and subways had stopped?

Then, the roommate answered after all. "Hello?" she said. Her voice was getting worse with each call.

"We're downstairs," Amber said simply.

Again, as usual, the roommate seemed totally confused. And then, abruptly, she muttered, "I'll be a second." Amber heard sheets rustling.

"Are you coming down?" Amber asked, making sure they were on the same level.

"Yah, yah," the telephone said. They bade each other extremely polite farewells.

"So there," Amber announced to her brother. The residence lobby, still sealed behind the locked glass doors, was still for a minute. The lights made yellowish squares on the floor.

Finally, a girl in black jeans emerged from a doorway. Amber tried to narrow her down from general pan-Asian, but didn't really care. She hesitated in the doorway and eventually noticed Amber and her brother, like the epiphany of a bad dream.

She opened the door just a crack. "Hi," she mumbled, eyeing them doubtfully.

There weren't any more speed bumps in terms of getting inside. The girl was supposed to sign them in with the porter, according to the rules, but the little booth in the lobby was dark and empty. Her name was Ginger, she said. She wasn't keen to talk, and Amber mainly stared at her back, following her up the stairs. They got to her floor and went down a thin hallway with soundboards in the ceiling and green carpet that could scour rust off pots and pans. It was very narrow; two people could barely squeeze past each other, and it smelled like detergent.

"This is the room," Ginger announced and fumbled with a set of keys. She'd locked her door for a sixty-second trip to the lobby. Amber brushed her hand over her brother's shoulder; he was facing the wall, eyes closed, like he was sleeping standing up. He looked like he'd been sleeping on train station benches for years.

Ginger turned on the room lights as an afterthought.

The masonry walls on Carrie's side looked wildly cracked, but after an instant Amber realised it was just the effect of fifty metres of Christmas lights strung around, clinging to the wall with squares of duct tape. It wasn't that Carrie had a zany and flamboyant style of decorating; rather, she seemed to have no style at all. She put things on display because she had them. The posters over her bed couldn't have been more random in their subjects: one was a painting, one depicted cartoon characters, and the last was one of those gloomy, mostly-black pictures of a band. And everywhere there were the Christmas lights, zigzagging between it all like black lines on a map.

Ginger's side was plain by comparison. There was nothing on her walls. Ginger walked to the head of her bed and turned around, a half-hearted presentational gesture. Amber had clawed and scratched her way into this room for the purpose of passing out, but the consequence of the clawing and scratching was that there was an edge of unwelcome that kept her on her toes, stiffly courteous. She wouldn't have been surprised if Ginger were terrified. They'd sure built up the suspense for her, when she thought about it; phone calls first, around midnight—*Hello there. Are you home alone?*—and then announcing that they were coming over and that there was nothing she could do to stop them as the hour got later and later.

"So," Ginger said, wringing her hands.

"We just have to sleep here," Amber stated once more, dropping her bag. "On the floor is fine," she added.

Ginger nodded but still looked nervous. Amber made a bland remark about the Christmas lights, just so she could mention Carrie again and remind Ginger of their common acquaintance.

"You like to sleep?" Ginger asked.

Amber nodded and glanced at her brother, as though that final offer had been a great accomplishment. She looked down at the carpet; it was covered in grit. *Oh well.* Amber pulled some clothes out of her bag and fashioned them into a pillow, demonstratively, for Guy's sake. Then she excused herself to the bathroom, soliciting some very general directions from Ginger: walk down the hall one way or the other until there was a door with a bathroom behind it.

She went out and found a room enough like a bathroom to satisfy her. The light buzzed, and the paint was peeling. A brown stain twisted around the floor drain and the hand dryer looked like it would fall apart if she touched it. There was a row of sinks under the mirror, and none of them was stopped properly, being packed with mildew. They all dripped. There were two toilet stalls; Amber could see shoes inside one of them, and the other one wasn't flushed.

After washing her hands and drinking from the sink she stared at her reflection, deciding not to brush her teeth that night. She didn't think she had the energy to squeeze a toothpaste tube. It wasn't as if she relied on her smile anyway. Her teeth were like carbon paper; according to the whitening guide that came with her toothpaste, they were off the chart in the yellow direction. And her incisors tried to occupy the same space at the same time. Her dad had offered her braces years ago, but she had declined. Braces seemed a bigger bother than a few bizarre teeth.

It didn't seem like it was over yet. They'd spent all day travelling, transferring between different trains... She remembered how she'd felt at the stations, constantly checking her watch, tramping between the platforms and ticket windows, barking at Guy to stay near her, never so much as sitting down lest lethargy smother her like a heavy tarp. It had been pointless exertion, she knew. They'd had only two trains to catch, one to Ottawa and then one to Toronto. But still, until she and her brother were safely aboard, even if there were still a good twenty minutes, she'd felt an almost physical pain in her gut knowing that there was somewhere they needed to be and time was slipping by; and she still felt that way. To take off her coat now, to just relax and forget about getting anywhere... It would be like standing on the platform and watching her ride pull away.

Granted, they were in a completely different place than they'd expected to be that night. But that shouldn't have mattered. She planned precisely what she'd do in the morning:

- Call her uncle again and find out what the hell happened. Then he'd pick them up, and it would be back to plan A.
- As per plan A, she'd then call Janelle, laugh over this incident, and apologise for any worrying that she might have caused.
- As per plan A, her stuff from Cantley would be delivered in the middle of the week.
- Then regular life would resume. At the moment regular life mainly involved her physics notes, since she had an exam next Monday, in just over a week.

Wouldn't it be a hoot if Ian had actually showed up at Union Station two minutes after they left. Served him right. The guy in the bathroom stall hadn't moved or made any noise since Amber had been there. She left him and went back to Carrie's room, leaving the faucets dripping.

CHAPTER 2

Ever since dedicating her career to designing buildings, Amber had started to deliberately observe buildings she saw, the idea being to assemble a mental library of techniques that she liked. She could say, "You know that big hall in the SITE Building," or, "They have this look on Elgin Street..." At the moment her aesthetic was coarse; she latched onto certain buildings, deciding she liked them without knowing why. Her experience was also limited to only one city: Ottawa, Ontario. Moving to Toronto was no substitute for actually travelling the world, but it still appealed to her like getting a new box of toys.

It didn't bother her to be ignorant, though. That was the best way to be at the beginning of a university program. Architecture was such a nebulous area of design. There was psychology involved when people had to spend eight hours a day working in a place, or when crowds had to walk through a lobby without jams or confusion. This was in addition to general artistic care, and of course it was all constrained by math, the fact that a million tons of stuff had to stay up by itself.

What it came down to was that whenever she was among tall buildings, she always found herself looking up, squinting appraisingly, behaving as though she could divest at a glance every design trick that went into them.

Carrie's residence building at York University, for example, wasn't impressive. It was bland, flat-roofed, made of brown bricks, with teeny-tiny windows and full of asbestos. Amber's impression was that it was one of the oldest buildings on campus, based on the bricks. Bricks were old-fashioned.

When Amber had woken up she'd been too uncomfortable and too worried about calling Ian to stay there on the floor, so she'd gone for a walk to the bathroom, checking the shower stalls and deciding to wait to wash up at Ian's. Her shirt and underwear felt clammy after sleeping in them. She'd even left her shoes on all night.

There seemed to be nothing less lively than a university residence on a Sunday morning. All the doors were shut up like heavy eyelids. Across from the bathroom was a staircase down, and Amber decided to walk outside. At every landing a bulletin board announced this or that upcoming event; Amber was used to ignoring them. The main conceit of every special event in a university was drinking, and if she were to show up and decline, as she would, she'd discover that there wasn't much else to do.

The stairwell led straight outside, to the edge of a courtyard. The sky was that strange white colour that it turned in winter, as though a paint were made from clouds and spread from one end to the other.

There were no people to be seen, anywhere. Could it be true? Amber walked all the way around the building. There was absolutely no human life, as far as she could see. The campus was empty, the buildings sat like quiet stones, silent cars sparsely occupied the parking lot—like it was only the model of a university campus, all-inclusive except for the people. Amber had to allow herself some satisfaction. As much as students wilder than her prided themselves on their party lives, come Sunday morning they were all dead to the world.

It was fine with her. She enjoyed the privacy. Everywhere there was the thick smell of fungus. It was still too warm for ice, but a tiny layer of standing water was spread on the ground, as if rehearsing for when the temperature dropped. There was a scattering of yellow and black leaves with curled-up points. The trees were like buildings without siding, balancing in iron grates.

That was enough. Amber squinted and went back the way she came. The stairwell door clunked stubbornly in its frame, and right away it occurred to her that these doors were always locked, that there wasn't even a handle on the outside, just a keyhole.

Well, that was dumb. At least you slept in your clothes, Amber thought.

She walked around the building, checking every one of the entrances. She'd imagined that one of them would be unlocked or propped open. They weren't. And no one was likely to come around to help, seeing as she was the only one conscious within a mile or two. Amber waited at the lobby door, looking in every direction. She resolved that if she ever wanted to do anything illegal in broad daylight, Sunday morning in a university would be the place for it.

Ten minutes passed quietly before Amber returned to the speakerphone in the lobby and dialed Carrie's number, picturing the scene way up there, the telephone going off in the quiet room that smelled like beds and people. Amber let it ring, three, four times—maybe they were just ignoring the phone, waiting her for to give up.

The ring was cut off. "Hello?"

The voice sounded strange, even for being groggy with sleep. "Ginger...?" Amber asked.

"This is Carrie," the speaker mumbled. And then, "Hey, who is this?"

Amber stared at the green light.

"Do you want to talk to Ginger?" Carrie asked.

And then Amber remembered waking up that morning, coming to the point where she'd decided to get up—the bed on Carrie's side of the room being occupied. But her brain hadn't fired its cylinders yet, not enough to realise—so she'd come back early in the morning, had she? Unlocking her door and stumbling in to find a pair of strangers curled up on the floor. *Surprise!* But supposedly she'd assumed they were Ginger's guests and let them lie there, stepping between their arms and legs.

"Hey, Carrie," Amber said. "How are you?"

An accusing pause came from upstairs. "Who is this?" Carrie asked again.

"This is Amber. Remember? From last spring."

"Who?"

"Amber Drinkwater."

Further silence.

"We talked during the tour, remember?" Amber felt like it was last night still, like she was bargaining on the phone again. She had to start all over.

"Really?" Carrie mumbled. "What tour?"

"Last spring—you said I should call you if I was ever in the city, right?"

"Amber?" Carrie gasped. "Why the hell are you here?"

There was noise under her voice. Everybody was awake now.

"Kind of a weird story. Uh..."

19

"Did Ginger let you in?"

"Yeah."

Amber heard a burst of words away from the phone. Ginger covering her ass?

"Where are you?" Carrie asked.

"Down in the lobby, actually." Amber raised her voice like it was fabulously interesting information. "I've kind of locked myself out."

"Really?"

"Yeah."

"Why did you go out?"

As though she needed an excuse. "I was just going for a walk."

Carrie sighed into the phone.

"Okay, one sec."

She hung up. Amber felt the chill of chastisement down her neck, and she spent the next few minutes pacing between the speaker and a row of mailboxes, hating how she'd said "going for a walk". It sounded so precious and geriatric. She should have thought of something better. Eventually Carrie emerged from the stairwell door in a housecoat and sandals; and since she'd just climbed out of bed, of course her hair was messed up and her face was weak and miserable, yet Amber couldn't help but understand that getting called out of bed by someone who'd unnecessarily shut herself out would in itself make a person miserable. Amber hadn't seen Carrie in six months; she hadn't really expected ever to see her again.

Carrie looked back and forth, like she hadn't learned which way the doors were. Amber stared like a caged puppy until Carrie opened the door.

"What are you doing here?" was the first thing she said.

"My brother and I just needed a place to crash."

"Why?"

"I don't know why," Amber told her sullenly. "We were supposed to be going home last night, but no one picked us up."

"Picked you up from what?"

Did that matter? Amber had used the word "crash," a term she drew on very consciously; it was used by people too drunk to find their way home, people who needed pity. It was Guy, probably. The fact that she had a fourteen-year-old family member with her was suspicious.

"We were waiting at the train station," Amber said simply, and that seemed to satisfy her springtime acquaintance for the moment. In spite of her questions, Carrie was moving to go back upstairs. Amber felt somehow that it was her duty to provide space-filling chatter, but nothing occurred to her.

The sunlight in Carrie's room was full of swirling dust. The roommate and Amber's brother were heaps on the bed and the floor. Carrie went back to bed in her housecoat.

"Can I use your phone? I've got to call my family," Amber said.

Carrie mumbled assent. The phone was on the wall, accessorised with a sticker of emergency numbers. Amber wondered if she could remember her uncle's phone number from last night; she sat in Carrie's chair and gave it a shot. She was prepping herself for whatever sort of conniption her uncle would throw when he learned what had happened. He was probably scared and embarrassed, etcetera. But the phone just rang and rang, like last night. Amber waited, losing count of the rings, affected by a sort of apathy that gave her unending patience; she could sit and listen for ten minutes.

An hour later she woke up with pain in her spine, having fallen asleep in the chair. Maybe she wasn't that different from all the hung-over people after all. The angle of the sunlight had changed, and not much else. Guy was curled up in a ball under the mantle of his black coat. It was 11:00.

Dimly Amber remembered that the last thing they'd eaten yesterday had been Harvey's cheeseburgers. Accordingly her guts were sitting in a dull pain that sometimes went away if she moved. It was overpriced, of course, more than fifteen dollars for both of them. But it was because she'd thought it had been only reasonable, that there was a ride on its way for them, that in a matter of minutes the trip would be over, and when would there be an excuse to eat fast food again?

Carrie had a bar fridge under her desk. Amber opened it with her foot. There were cartons of milk, ginger ale, a closed bag of potato chips, and six wine coolers on the door—nothing she could skim without Carrie's knowledge.

Ginger had cereal bars sitting openly on her dresser, in gleaming green foil. But Amber had set herself up as Carrie's guest, so by some kind of logic it was only Carrie's side of the room that she could steal from. Very carefully she stepped over her brother to Carrie's closet. It wasn't that she was *really* going to chow down on whatever she found. Of course she would ask first, but that meant waiting until Carrie pulled her face out from under the pillow. Amber imagined how her brother would feel when he woke up; he would be hungry too. They would probably wind up buying breakfast on campus.

"What are you doing?" Carrie asked.

Amber closed the closet door carefully. "Just waiting for my brother to wake up," she said.

Carrie sat up. "Oh." She reached to the windowsill for a hairbrush.

Amber squirmed on her feet, sensing resentment. "He's like a slug," she said, to get attention off herself.

"Are you leaving as soon as he wakes up?" Carrie asked.

"I guess so."

Carrie brushed her hair, sitting in bed, her eyes flickering aimlessly around the room, or perhaps not so aimlessly, since Amber's eyes were doing the same thing, making testy searches of Carrie's face. Carrie replaced her brush on the windowsill, arching her arm oddly, as though she didn't usually brush her hair before getting out of bed. "So what the hell brings you here?" she said.

Amber didn't think Carrie really wanted to know. And Amber didn't want to try to explain it all. After asking that question she'd laughed, a fake nervous laugh, just a huff of air through a fake, nervous smile.

"Well," Amber said. "My uncle was supposed to pick us up at the train station. He didn't show." Then Amber did the fake laugh.

"Last night I was so pissed," was what Carrie said instead. She got up and went to her closet, describing her experience. Her boyfriend had taken her to a "great little restaurant" in the middle of Kensington Market that had turned out to be closed, after which he'd insisted on making her walk halfway across the city to go to another great little restaurant. It hadn't been worth the corns on her feet, and the date ended badly. Listening to Carrie talk was better than the eyeball tag from before, even though Amber hadn't had the chance to tell her own story, skipping over everything, how late it had been, how long they'd held vigil on the wire bench, the torrent of phone calls, every oath she could remember uttering that evening, condensed into *He didn't show.*

Carrie said she was going to have a shower. "Do you want one?" she asked. "They're free."

Amber said no. She wanted to wait until she got home.

So Carrie left. Amber drank some ginger ale and woke up her brother. Amber asked how he was doing. He said fine.

"So Uncle Ian's still not answering," she remarked.

"Why not?" Guy asked. "What if he isn't there?"

"Then he isn't there," Amber said.

"But what then?"

"Then I don't know."

"Does he think it's today, maybe?"

"I talked to him a thousand times. He knew it was supposed to be yesterday."

"But he didn't come."

"I know. What do you expect me to do about it?"

Guy looked out the window.

"He couldn't completely forget," Amber went on. "He's not stupid like that."

But her brother was quiet now.

"At least we can go someplace good for breakfast," she added. She hoped to lift his spirits a little, like it was still just a vacation. A fun adventure.

Both of them had visited Uncle Ian before, but only Amber had been to his present address. He'd lived there less than a year. Ian had been there to meet her at Union Station—during the day—and he'd shown her through the TTC, since he didn't own a car, to a neighbourhood called Silverthorne. Ian had taken her on a bus, and their stop was just over a railroad bridge. "It's a walk from here," he'd told her, and she'd nodded, adjusting her backpack—the very same backpack she had now, in fact.

Ian then walked her through a cluster of streets that seemed incredibly European, writhing left and right and going up and down grades, very unlike the graph-paper streets downtown. The houses were small and detached, and they all looked different. Finally they arrived at Ian's house, and Amber remembered feeling incredulous that out of all the houses in Silverthorne, he'd managed to snare that one. It was made of grey stone, and its height was a surprise; you had to crane your neck to look at it from the sidewalk. It was at the intersection of two streets taking off at inclines, called Silverthorn and Dunraven Avenue, magical-sounding names, and Ian pointed out that the district name, Silverthorne, had an 'e' on the end, but the street name didn't. He didn't own the whole house, though. Wouldn't that have been nice. There were three floors, and each floor was a separate property; Ian rented the second. To get in they had to climb a hill—a narrow cement staircase curved around the corner of the house—and enter through a door nestled below the third-floor balcony. The bizarre, almost secret entrance and the sense of vertigo-inducing elevation over the street, as well as the convoluted borough around the house, made it feel titillating and secure.

And now, what had happened was that the third floor had become vacant, and Ian had offered to rent it out for his niece and nephew. He was confident that he could get a deal, renting two floors and having a good rapport with the landlord.

So imagine that, a place of their very own. The view from the third floor would be even better than from the second.

Now she had to remember the way to the house by herself. The first step was getting to Eglinton West station; after that, she remembered the position on the bus platform where she'd waited with her uncle, all those months ago. Getting off the bus in the right spot was trickier. Amber's attitude fluctuated between confidence in her memory and a thudding fear of being on the wrong bus entirely, particularly when they passed a cemetery she didn't remember. The railroad bridge was unmistakable, though; not acting in time, nervous about pulling the stop signal, Amber missed the stop and wound up riding all the way to the corner of Keele and Eglinton. Amber jumped up and told Guy to follow her.

Between the Keele intersection and the stop they should have used, Eglinton Avenue was a giant hill. The flat roofs of all the stores were stepped in a way that reminded Amber of a small town. As they walked up they passed a sign, faded and flaked away rustically, depicting a lighthouse and the caption, "Newfoundland: The Happy

Province," and in front of a pharmacy there were two grey-bearded men on the steps, smoking in wet-looking jackets. If it weren't for all the Caribbean restaurants, it would have seemed even more like a small town. It was in front of a pizza joint that Guy said he wanted to get lunch, but Amber told him to wait.

At the top of the hill was an apartment building. It soared beyond twenty floors and must have been visible for blocks down the hill, were anyone to look for it. It was probably populated by the owners of all the Caribbean restaurants. A bunch of black kids loitered in front. Amber didn't pay it any attention; it and the kids were on the other side of the street. Guy pointed out, though, one of the ground-level businesses, called "West Side Rehab." How convenient for all the alcoholics just upstairs, Amber remarked. They laughed about it. On their side of the road was a line of garages. Guy also pointed out, a bit further on, a porn shop among them. Neighbourhood conveniences, eh? They laughed some more.

After climbing the hill on Eglinton West they went straight back down, as the first leg of the walk to Ian's house started with a downhill that would be perfect for amusingly dangerous bike rides. Or at least, it would have been when she was Guy's age. The icy street wiggled back and forth, and Uncle Ian's strange house was at the very bottom.

"It's a cool looking place," Amber told her brother. She climbed up the stairs to the door under the balcony, now hemmed with icicles, and knocked.

Amber looked down to the sidewalk, imagining what it would be like to see that view of the street when she left for classes in the morning. The tree on the hill was bare of leaves; it jutted diagonally over the sidewalk, mingling with a telephone pole. In the spring it had been covered with green and brown buds and had masked part of the house, for even more of a sense of security.

Amber looked at her brother, vaguely expecting him to turn to her with vengeance and try to play it all up as her fault, and she had plenty of time for it, since Uncle Ian wasn't answering the door. There was a window that allowed a view into the second floor. No lights were on inside except for one at the other end of the house, but something about it seemed desolate, a light left on when the house was empty. It looked like Ian had cleaned up for them, but not thoroughly. There were piles of things, an out-of-order newspaper, and clutter on the kitchen counter.

It wasn't so much that it was a complete surprise, Amber decided, but she'd just been in some sort of denial. Obviously, if Ian was being so bizarre as to let the phone ring and ring, could she really have expected everything to be normal again if she just showed up at his door? What sort of excuse had she expected him to make? But in spite of all her premonitions and gut feelings, she'd gone ahead carrying her luggage here because, well, no reason at all. She'd planned to do it, she'd arrived in the city intending to march to this door, and she'd done it.

Now the door's empty rectangle was like an impersonal hand shoved in her face. So Amber wound up sitting on the hill with her brother, the grass pale and crunchy, looking over Silverthorn Avenue.

When his sister had come home for Thanksgiving, Guy had planned a poem to recite to her as she walked in the door:

Amber, Amber, home at last!
Those two months were all but fast.
Are you cold? Here, take my vest.
Of all sisters, you're the best!

Obviously this greeting demanded that he wear a vest, and he spent all afternoon in a brown cotton vest that he owned but had never worn before. Mom was cooking: roast beef in mushroom gravy, sweet potatoes, stuffing and green onions, bean salad and cranberry sauce. Guy was in the bathroom when his sister arrived with Dad. He washed his hands and ran out—and crashed into her, heading for the stairs. She shoved him into the wall and told him to screw off.

She was staying the night, then going right back to Ontario on Monday, since she had work to do. At dinner Mom and Dad asked her, of course, how it was going, and she said that she was only in classes for three or four hours a day, but that the amount of homework was immense. Each week was a new chapter of physics. Guy listened, feeling both inspired and terrified.

That night the two of them sat in the den watching TV, finishing the coffee that had been on since morning. Amber had a thing for the short film channel, and they were showing an Italian movie with a husband and wife seducing people and then butchering them. Guy struggled with whether they had used real corpses for the butchering parts. The footage was gated like a music video but without any hint of a camera trick.

"So, how do you like university?" Guy asked.

"Crisp," his sister answered.

"I like my University Crisp!" Guy exclaimed.

The butchering scene was over, and it went back to the couple at a party, seducing another victim. But the standing-and-talking scenes were boring.

"Remember those commercials?" Guy asked.

"Obviously."

Amber got up to refill her coffee. She kicked Guy's ankle.

"Bring me some too," Guy said.

"No, you're not old enough."

Amber went back to Ottawa the next morning. And Guy didn't see her again until that day just two weeks ago when he was eating Kraft Dinner that he'd made himself, not getting up from the TV couch even when he heard the front door and knew it was her.

Now they were wandering back up the hill to the mall beside the giant apartment building, since there was a coffee shop there, and it might have been a Tim Hortons. The mall was called Westside Mall. "I guess we're on the west side," Guy remarked.

"You'd think," Amber replied as they ran across the street.

Back in Cantley, the closest Tim Hortons to their house had been beside the high school, not exactly walking distance. And they hadn't been of age to control any money either, so doughnuts and stuff had always come down from above. Most of the time they had to settle with a little no-name bakery in Plaza Point Nouveau, a plaza near their house. The very month Amber started high school, though, a Tim Hortons went up in Point Nouveau. What happened was it stopped being so special and became a part of weekend routine. Their neighbours would always say, "Let's go to Point Nouveau," meaning they would go to the Tim Hortons and buy Iced Cappuccinos even if it was December, then retire to someone's house and keep doing whatever they were doing before.

In spite of those visits, Guy had never bought plain old coffee in his life. And neither had Amber, until she went off to University of Ottawa. They had a Tim Hortons there too, but they also had other coffee shops, and she lost her brand loyalty.

Maybe they should have knocked on his neighbours' doors, Amber supposed at one point. Maybe whoever lived on the first floor of the tall house knew what the problem was.

But that would have to wait until they were back there. Amber and her brother had gone walking down Dunraven Avenue, thinking they could see Guy's high school from the house, but it had turned out to be an office building beside the school. They'd reached the school itself, looked at it, but not gone in. Then, carrying their bags, they'd walked down the street to the south. At least, Amber had figured it was to the south; she'd come to Toronto under the impression that the CN Tower would be visible everywhere, a half-kilometre-high compass, and it wasn't.

At the next intersection was a 24-hour Tim Hortons, and it went without saying that they were going in. It was a delightful find; it was even closer to their home than Plaza Point Nouveau had been in Cantley.

A group of Italian people filled one table, and an old woman with missing teeth complained loudly about how hard it was to do such-and-such because she didn't speak English. Complaining in English, though, she sounded eloquent enough. Amber and Guy were both very quiet when they ordered lunch, and just as it had gone without saying that they'd enter, it went without saying that they weren't eating in.

Thus they wound up walking down the street again, draped with their luggage and eating take-out. A bunch of guys passed them, and Amber was obliged to comment to her brother that they probably looked really stupid, trying to manoeuvre bagels and hot chocolate to their mouths without dropping anything.

In truth, Amber wanted to walk around and get started ogling architecture like she'd intended. It seemed she was in the wrong part of town for it. None of the buildings here were taller than two or three floors, except for the apartment buildings. Across from the Tim

Hortons was a fairly eye-catching specimen; it looked like it was made for children, big and blocky with primary-colour balconies. But she really wanted to be back downtown; that was why she gently guided her brother in that direction. It became evident that walking downtown would take hours from where they were, but not before they'd gone so far that heading back would be just as hard. And of course it had been then, once they were an ordeal and a half away from Silverthorne, that it occurred to Amber to talk to Ian's neighbours.

The bag-carrying and walking was tiring them out, so they looked for a place to rest. Naturally, it was another coffee shop. And they couldn't go in without buying something. Amber made a brash "eenh!" sound to acknowledge the irony. Then she asked Guy, "Do you want to go downtown and see my university?"

That started an argument, since apparently Amber hadn't "let" Guy look around *his* school. Fine, Amber said, Guy had to go there anyway to set up his schedule, but that wouldn't be until tomorrow.

Slugging their bags had made them both bitchy, but where did they have to put them? Amber considered hiding them somewhere near the house; but outside, where they would get rained on? Could they rent lockers indefinitely at a bus station or a gym? Even if they could, where would they find a place like that? Downtown was a better bet; Union Station was the best bet, in fact, it being one of the few places they'd seen so far. Amber didn't recall any lockers there, but seriously, it being a train station...

The other issue was that Amber quite simply didn't know where they were. She'd had the standard field-trip survey of the city during school; theatres and museums, fancy stuff along the lake and the food court in the Eaton Centre. She imagined that eventually they would get to some place she recognised.

The street they were travelling ended at a railroad junction. Amber said, "Shit, I think we're just more lost." She chuckled. Guy didn't buy the levity. He snarled something, and Amber told him to go fuck himself and find his own way back, and then she hopped the railroad tracks and kept going. She knew he'd follow her, if at a distance now. Where else was he going to go?

After that the street seemed to go on forever, the railroad on one side, block after block of meaningless houses on the other, Amber wanting to look back to make sure her brother was still tailing

ERIC HOPKINS

her. There was a slight curve to the street, making it impossible to
see far ahead, making the stretch seem even more endless, going nowhere. It took Amber by surprise when she came upon a subway station with a parking lot and a McDonalds attached to it.

She waited for her brother and paid his fare. She looked at the
subway map and was startled to see how far out they were—Dundas
West station, at least a half dozen stations away from her university,
and any part of Toronto she'd recognise. She and her brother had
been drifting through space. If she hadn't happened upon this station,
how far would they have gone, where would they have wound up?

It was an arresting thought, but immaterial, since this put them
safely back on track. Amber had hoped to put her bag down while
they rode but, horribly, the train that pulled up was packed.

Yes, she'd come down to the University of Toronto for her
own benefit; she wanted to look for herself. Her brother's presence
was an accident. The only thing Amber could placate him with was
food. She told him there were lots of restaurants and stuff on the
campus, some right in buildings where she had her classes. They
went down St. George Street, past the smaller departments based in
old houses. Amber pointed to the Arts and Sciences building, in-
forming Guy that there was a cafeteria in the basement. After thus
building it up, taking him all the way in and downstairs, logically,
the cafeteria was closed because it was Sunday. It sure wasn't Guy's
day.

The U of T campus had galleries of older buildings around the
two main commons, and they had all the Neoclassic trappings:
arched doorways with dark, dusty corners, rusticated walls, rows of
latticed windows and huge volumes of climbing ivy. One building
even had a tall bell tower. It was cause for sentiment to consider that
buildings like those would never be built again. No architect in the
21st century would ever humour so much block and mortar in place
of metal, or try to commission wood carvers to embellish every railing and doorframe with stripes and diamond patterns.

Inside, the lecture halls were small, built before microphones
existed. Amber had briefly seen one on the tour in the spring. Instead
of being long and deep to accommodate a large class, there was a
second level of seating on a balcony, connected to the first by a narrow wooden staircase. It was so antiquated, like a room from another
world, but this other world was disciplined and cozy.

The real attractions, for Amber at least, were the engineering buildings across the road, giant, generous edifices with names like Galbraith, Walberg, and Sandford Fleming. There was no point going in; there would be nothing to see but locked doors on a Sunday, nor could Amber look for her winter classes, since she didn't have the info yet. It was fine just to show the outside of the buildings to her brother, point them out the way Dad had pointed out his warehouse the first time: *Look, that's where Daddy works.*

But Guy wasn't dazzled. She'd promised food, and he wanted to eat. Fine, there would be no university cafeteria food that day, but there were still restaurants on College Street. Not until after Amber had paid and they'd sat down with footlong subs did she say, "Well, I guess I made you do a lot of walking today."

"That's for sure," Guy said, but he couldn't be angry since Amber had just paid for his dinner. She'd planned it that way.

She suddenly added, "Shit, I was supposed to call Janelle."

It couldn't have been a big deal, considering the strangeness of their situation—but no, Janelle would have called Ian's herself in that case. And if she did, she would probably have got the same response, the ringing phone, the silent rooms. And it probably would have been her opinion that this was a problem; however, instead of just calling again and again like an unimaginative child, she would have done something more official, and a flutter of panic fired in Amber's spine. Suppose she'd called the police?

Amber looked back and forth, expecting an officer to be watching them, a man to leap over the Subway counter. But no, it was only 1:00. All she'd promised was to call "tomorrow," "when they got there." That was open for interpretation.

It was afternoon already. People were walking their dogs. That posed a more concrete problem anyway, another hellish evening over the crest of just a few more hours' time. Would anything be different if they went back to Ian's, back home? That was the usual comfort for kids in the city: just go home at the end of it all, have a sleep, and anything could be suffered through. But what happened when the home was suddenly locked and empty?

Suppose there was an actual search party out for them, that very minute. They'd done nothing wrong, so they couldn't get in trouble. They'd waited at Union Station, they'd delivered themselves to Silverthorne. If there was to be any embarrassment or recrimination for this, it would be someone else's, not theirs.

She asked Guy, "What do you think of the campus?"

"It looks just like a street."

"It is a street. What do you think, we use cable cars?"

"I don't know."

"D'you think we use ziplines?"

"Okay, I get it."

"D'you think the professors snowshoe to your classes?"

"Shut your face."

He got ready to bite his sub again. The fact that she'd paid for it did the trick a second time. To calm the waters he asked, "What are we going to do now?"

"What do *you* want to do?"

He didn't know.

Money was a consideration as always. Amber took cash out at a bank machine and saw that her balance was just over $600, enough to last for a while, at least. Although, already that day she'd spent ten dollars on subway fare alone.

Guy waited for his sister, again. It had been three hours since they'd arrived downtown, and the sky was getting dark, the streets lit and cold-looking. They'd walked around a little and not done much of anything. They'd discovered Chinatown and went into a computer hardware store, without any plans. They'd walked down streets full of stores, making a running joke about how every single store in Toronto sold nothing but shirts and pants. And yet Guy had kept faith in his sister, since she always seemed like she was waiting for something, like something proper was just around the corner, like every idle moment was just in anticipation of something perfectly sound and useful.

Presently Guy waited on the sidewalk as Amber used a payphone. She'd said she was going to find them a place to stay. After a long time on the phone, she came back and said that Carrie would let them stay at York again, but she was just on her way out to see a movie. And they'd been invited along.

Guy didn't want to see a movie. He wanted to get somewhere where he could put down his bags.

The movie was happening at a big fabulous downtown theatre. There was a giant diagonal TV on the roof. They met Carrie, the girl from the other night, in the lobby, with another guy who was her boyfriend. He was fat, one of those big orange-shaped people who wore poor boy hats, and Guy had to think, good for him for having a girlfriend. Guy never had one. And his sister had never had a boyfriend.

The movie they were to see was already decided on by Carrie and Jesse, since this was a date of some kind upon which his sister and he were last-minute intruders, though Jesse expressed only delight at the extra company. He made a joke about the two of them moving into the cinema, referring to the hockey bags, really incongruous things to bring to the movies. Amber laughed it off and said something dismissive, but Guy was humiliated. Jesse was right. It *was* ridiculous to be barging into the movies with their bags.

He stood there with a surly attitude, even when Amber paid for his ticket, then they went up a giant four-storey escalator to the concession. There was a lounge where you could get alcohol, and Carrie made remarks about it, wistfully. If that happened, Guy would be the underage one who had to wait outside the velvet rope—or else forcing that on him would be too awkward, and no one would go in even though they wanted to. Once he'd gone to a music festival with his friend's brother's friends, who were all over twenty, and it had been a situation like this. The older guys had abandoned him, and it had become a disaster. Fortunately, the plan of drinking never gained momentum. Amber bought popcorn to split with him, grouching about how expensive it was.

The girl taking tickets made them open up all their luggage and root through it to prove they didn't have video cameras. Humiliation, again. At the end of the movie they all found love and wandered back outside at about 11:00 pm.

Jesse and Carrie kissed. The girl had to crush herself up against Jesse's gut to reach his lips. "And over here," Guy intoned, "shirts and pants."

It was the joke he and Amber had laughed about riotously that afternoon. Now Amber just sneered at him like he was an idiot.

Well, fuck her. She had one way of behaving when they were alone, but now in front of her friends she was this high-and-mighty cunt. *Fine, then.* Guy wasn't going to say anything for the rest of the day.

Jesse drove them to Carrie's residence in his car, dutifully kissed her, and left.

Carrie opened the door, and they hauled their bags up the stairs a second time. She unlocked the door to her room and turned on the lights, and they all walked in on Ginger in bed with someone. Amber was in the middle of taking off her coat. The Asian girl and her boyfriend had clothes on, on top of the covers. "We're just sleeping," Ginger explained.

"Sorry," Carrie said anyway and fussed with things on her desk a little. Amber let her coat hang around her arms. Carrie asked if they wanted to go get a coffee, and Amber said sure, but first she adamantly threw her bags on the floor and made sure Guy did the same. Carrie casually turned off the lights, and they all filed back out.

The place selling coffee in the Lanes was still open. Carrie didn't know the time that it closed, but they'd clearly made it. Lots of people had made it, in fact; the line went out of the store. Amber heard one of the servers bellow a request that everyone please come ten minutes earlier next time. And the line seemed stuck in place. Amber peered ahead; the servers strolled around lazily, poking at the steamer and the cash registers as though they were about to start their shift rather than end it. But eventually, inevitably, they did reach the counter. With distaste Amber pulled out her wallet and stared into the coin pouch, prompting Carrie to offer to put it on her meal card. Amber shook her head, saying she was fine for cash, and offered her brother a hot chocolate. She asked the server if they were still allowed to sit down. "For a minute," he sneered, and went to close the security gate.

The tables and chairs were all stylishly taller than regular tables and chairs, or awkwardly taller, considering Amber's feet could touch the floor but not loosely enough so that she could lean back. They sat there with their paper cups, and there was pressure to talk, but they weren't a group made up for talking—Amber, her little brother, and a friend she hardly knew, out for coffee not because they wanted it, but because of that dumb thing that had happened in Carrie's room.

Carrie brought up the Uncle Ian situation with, "Any idea what you're doing about...?"

"Nope," Amber said.

"Where can you stay 'til he turns up?"

"Well, here," Amber said with a simper.

Carrie didn't simper back. Guy drank his hot chocolate and looked away. He was trying to put on airs of someone older, blending in with the university crowd.

"Well, you can stay here today," Carrie went on. "But not forever... In fact, there's a limit of two nights in a row to have guests over, actually."

That limit sounded made-up, but the message was clear: move out. "I have no idea where we're going to go tomorrow," Amber said, a weak complaint against Carrie's admonition, and in all sincerity it wasn't even true, since tomorrow was Monday, and first thing in the morning she could call... someone.

Carrie asked what Amber was going to do about exams, considering it was exam time. Amber had ordered hazelnut-raspberry coffee, and she sipped a little, it tasting like neither hazelnuts nor raspberries. She could have gone on and filled the air with details of how the plan, worked out meticulously with Janelle the social worker, was to petition University of Toronto to let her join up with its first-year students in the winter term, after Christmas, based on her mid-term grades and a variety of performance evaluation forms she'd had to shuttle around the Ottawa campus. Toronto was letting her join the Civil Engineering core classes in January, as long as she made it back to Ottawa one week Monday for her last outstanding piece of business in that city, the fall physics exam.

As for Guy, they'd chosen George Harvey Collegiate Institute for his high school because it was the closest one to Ian's house. At least, Amber wasn't privy to any other considerations that had gone into the choice. Guy also had a deadline for the upcoming Monday: that was the day he had to be back in class. Even though it was almost time for Christmas break, it was important for them to re-establish a routine, Janelle had confided.

Someone told them it was time to leave. They nodded, climbed off their high chairs, and went back to the residence. As they drew near Carrie's room the girl laughed and talked needlessly loud, and fumbled noisily with the door handle. The light was on, and Ginger was at her computer. The other guy was gone.

At 2:30 in the morning Amber was still wide awake, torturing herself. She couldn't stop thinking about what she was going to do tomorrow. It was an oscillation of confidence; one moment she would be masochistically listing off all her uncertainties, and then she'd reassure herself that life didn't end just because one uncle wasn't answering the phone. So she hadn't actually called her social worker that day. It didn't matter; she'd call tomorrow, once she had answers about Uncle Ian. Wouldn't it leave a better impression if she could supply information that she'd gathered herself, rather than just calling up to shrug her shoulders? Naturally. It was Janelle's job, after all, to make herself unnecessary, to make sure Amber could take care of herself.

For the hundredth time Amber shut her eyes and ordered a stop to her internal monologue. There was a hollow rectangle of light in the seams around the door, since the hall lights were on all the time. The streetlights outside made orange shapes on the wall, as well as a little colourful Milky Way in Carrie's Christmas lights.

Carrie kept her window open, even though it was the beginning of December. Otherwise the room got clammy, she'd said. Amber could hear a group of students outside, drunk. They were talking in that unchecked, giggly way drunk people talked, the girls hurling fucks and shits, the boys exploding with football stadium laughter. Someone screamed one of those top-of-the-voice exhortations that drunken people were always looking to scream, and there was the sound of running and a smashing bottle.

Amber thought, at least Janelle could be happy she wasn't like them.

CHAPTER 3

Carrie said, "Do you want to get up? It's ten o'clock."

She was standing. It was a harsh perspective at which to see someone, from the floor, first thing in the morning.

"Okay," Amber said. Immediately her plans for the day flew into her head. She stood up and saw Ginger, still asleep. More for ritual than anything else, she called her uncle on Carrie's phone, listened and listened, and put it down, satisfied once again.

She hadn't washed or changed her clothes in three days, and neither had her brother. She didn't remember what colour the shirt under her sweatshirt was. It was sweaty and stuck to her back. It was like they were still on the train.

For the hundredth time, Amber shrugged her backpack into place and lifted the strap of her hockey bag into that sore position over her shoulder. Once Guy was up, Amber tempted him with promises of breakfast, and they left without saying goodbye.

As soon as Amber stepped outside she knew it was below freezing; the coldness in the air was submerging, lung-filling. Any snow that fell would stick around. Unlike Sunday morning, there were actually people to be seen. Amber wondered if anyone at York was starting to recognise her and her brother, the two of them and their baggage.

As for the route from York to her uncle's, there was probably a way to get there without transferring onto the subway and off again. The fact that York and Ian's were both skirted by the same street, Keele, was a clue. But right then she didn't feel like exploring or innovating. They had to get to Ian's easily, without confusion, so she could talk to his landlord and get it over with. She paid her bus fare and her brother's, and they moved to the seats at the very back, where their bags would be the least obtrusive. It took an hour to get to Silverthorne. There were the same turns, the same walk down the twisty hill, and her uncle's door beamed down at them as it always had.

"Aren't we going up?" Guy asked when Amber ignored the stairs to the second floor, going instead to the first.

"He won't be there," Amber declared, but she invited him to go up and check for himself.

There were three mailboxes lined up beside the door, one for each floor. Amber peeked into the second one; there was a pizza flier and a couple humdrum letters from companies. There wasn't enough accumulation to suggest that Ian was in trouble and hadn't been home for a long time. The last time Amber and he had spoken was when she called him Friday evening, confirming Saturday's plans, making sure he'd be there at Union Station.

Amber peeked through the first floor window. In front of the door was a little green mat that looked like it was for indoor use; the colour had faded and leaked onto the cement. Amber looked at the doorbell, not knowing what she was going to say. So instead she joined her brother on the hill. "What's the scoop?" she called.

"No one's home. What did those guys down there say?"

"They're not answering the door either," Amber told him. She squinted at the front window, looking deep in thought, thinking about how she'd just lied, and she had to go back down there and actually ring the bell this time. And she did, allowing Guy to watch from the grass. A man opened the door, wearing a white dress shirt with thin blue stripes like a sheet of notebook paper. He said hello by raising his eyebrows.

It was finally time to inquire about any messages Uncle Ian might have left, a paper trail that would explain everything. But as she started to ask, Amber felt a sort of premonitory disenchantment, like at school assemblies when they started to give out awards, and she knew in her gut she wouldn't be getting any. The man looked confused at first, even a little amused and suspicious. He thought it was a trick. He shook his head slowly, grinning and muttering shakily that he didn't know anything about the man on the floor up, except that he always walked around in his shoes. Amber said, "That's okay, thanks anyway," as he closed his door. She wandered back to the sidewalk.

It was almost brutal to step out of the little entranceway and discover the street so immediately. The yard associated with the house was to the side, the grassy hill and a flat bit at the top, so between the front door and street was just a patch of tar as wide as the sidewalk. Amber stepped right into street. She was carrying her bag over her elbow, which was probably the least comfortable way to carry anything. She hated it; she wanted to throw it in a river, but of course she couldn't because it was all her stuff. She just wanted a place to put things down, storage space, any kind of space, just so that she didn't have to hang all her possessions from her shoulders.

Of all the crap she'd brought, only one thing was actually valuable. Upon graduation from high school her parents had bought her a laptop computer with a CD-ROM drive. She remembered the afternoon it was presented to her; there had been a family gathering around the dining room table as her dad figured out how to start it up. The power cord stretched in a dangerous arc between the table and the wall; they finally located the little white button and gave it a brush, and the screen's little prisms lit up.

Amber had been very conscious of her brother being extremely jealous; he'd hung around the table the whole time, watching over Amber's shoulder as she tried to use the touchpad. Maybe their parents had noticed too. That was probably where his iPod had come from. Other than that, she'd really only brought clothes with her in the big bag. In her backpack were the books she'd need to prepare for Monday's physics exam. Everything else that she owned she'd left behind for the movers.

She looked up to the second floor of the house, Uncle Ian's floor, with a plaintive, melancholy feeling as though she was seeing it for the last time. The door was a puzzle with which she was finally exhausted, it seemed, a locked box too intricate to open, that she'd toyed and fussed with for many more hours than it deserved. And now she was past the point of intensive study and reduced to simply staring, from the street.

She remembered a discussion in English class about how, if they ever invented a way to go without sleep, nobody would need homes any more. Such an invention hadn't yet come to be, but still, up until then she'd just assumed, somehow, that Uncle Ian was ultimately the only source of security now that they'd moved, which was why it was so crucial to find him. But that wasn't true—since they weren't exactly moving in with him anyway. They were getting a different floor, a different property entirely.

It had been a dim idea in the back of her mind for a while. Ever since she'd started mucking around with university forms almost a year ago, she'd had the idyllic notion of living in the big city in a tiny room with two or three other girls, with a living room and a kitchen with shelves and furniture—not lavishly huge, but reasonable, or maybe a bit less than reasonable, uncomfortable enough to be memorable. And she'd have to walk a block to the grocery store, and every month they'd all groan about paying rent.

Of course, she'd been stuck in an on-campus residence for her first year in Ottawa, which wasn't quite the same, but it was a natural first step. By her second or third year she'd be out, and that was when she'd expected that buoyant apartment life to start.

But then she lifted her gaze just a little higher, to the third floor, to the For Rent sign in the windows. She'd just call up the landlord and ask for the room herself, matter-of-factly, as though it was just a normal, everyday request, which it was, and when her uncle caught up to them he could take over if he wanted. There was probably a down payment to make. But she had money in the bank, about $600, which was enough for that at least, and her children's benefits would help. That was what they were for. On top of that she'd obviously need a job, but there, again, that was just another normal, usual thing, one of those basic chores that everybody in the world shared.

Suddenly the weight of her bag didn't bother her as much. She knew she wasn't lazy; she could hold down any job she wanted, within reason. Of course it would be something like answering a phone, but, shit, everyone started like that. And for someone in her first year of university it was perfectly appropriate anyway to have a boring, awful job. That was just another part of the package, coming home exhausted and ruing her next shift—although it occurred to her that her social worker likely wouldn't approve of her having such ideas without a consultation first.

She still had to make that phone call.

But Janelle would only try to discourage her. Amber just had to wait until it was too late for that woman to do anything about it.

Amber went back up the steps to see where her brother had gone. She tested her uncle's door and found it familiarly stubborn. She even tried knocking. That was when she spotted Guy, sitting in the corner of the yard, against the garden shed.

"So he's not here," Amber remarked.

"No?"

"Okay, look." It was time to take charge again; with Guy there she had someone to dictate to. "We can't keep staying with Carrie Sykes." She paused cautiously. "Do you want to just move in by ourselves?"

"You mean up there?"

Amber nodded.

"Can we?"

"Sure."

Immediately Guy demanded, "Why?" Amber figured it was just a grunt of surprise, but he had a sneer on his face that pissed her off very quickly. "Why don't you just call Janelle?" he asked.

Why, indeed. Amber looked over the street as though the black-haired woman were right there, observing. Guy wanted that nod from authority, from someone three times his own age. He was afraid of being in trouble, taking things into his own hands. She'd said, "on our own," as though he would be in charge of bringing in an income too, which was not true. He probably thought she'd be sending him out to the street with a squeegee. Of course he'd just be going to school as usual, and maybe she'd expect him to be in charge of cleaning up at home, considering she'd probably have to work a lot of hours…

And, what the fuck did she think she was doing. There was no fucking way she could make a down payment on an apartment by herself. Perhaps if she dropped out of school, but that just wasn't an option. It wasn't like they were a pair of landed immigrants who'd have to toil and sweat their way up from the bottom. Dropping out would be a step down for her.

So at that moment, reeling from sudden shame at her overzealousness, she hated Uncle Ian more than she'd ever hated anyone else, in that fiery, adrenaline-swamped way like when she was chasing her brother through their house to beat the shit out of him. It was all Ian's fault. They'd done nothing wrong, but because of him, there they were, standing there in front of his locked apartment, impotently, day after day, all because of his disappearing act. She didn't care if he was dead; even if he were right then decomposing in a culvert, she didn't pity him. He was responsible for them now, they had a future to worry about, and it was his job to give them security until then, and if he wouldn't even be there to answer the phone...

All that happened in about three seconds after Guy mentioned their social worker. All her brother had seen was her looking away, across the street, and then her lips had probably done something tight and fidgety, so perhaps he understood that he'd annoyed her.

"Because," Amber answered, "she'd just point out all the shit we did wrong."

"So what are we going to do?"

"I don't know what we're going to do," Amber snapped. "What do you want to do?" She stared at him. That was how *she* always felt, having to come up with stuff. Guy shrugged. Relenting, Amber decided, "Let's go visit your school now."

"With all this shit?" Guy said, meaning the bags.

"Maybe. Shit." Amber swayed her bag distastefully. "What do you think we should do with them?"

"Stash them somewhere," was Guy's answer. Amber pressed him for any idea of where, exactly; "I don't know, let's rent a locker," he said. Amber harassed him for details, in what she hoped was the same fashion that he harassed her, until he spat, "How the fuck should I know?"

"Well let's just go and do whatever."

"Even before we see Uncle Ian?" Guy went on, which confused Amber at first because she didn't see a connection there. No, Amber told him, they didn't need to talk to him first. Everything was already set up at his school. Guy just had to present himself in person and sign a thing or two.

Settling on a course of action lifted Amber's spirits, but Guy got gloomy and resentful, since she'd just made him do something. So Amber made a big thing out of falling down the hill and rolling to the sidewalk. Physical humour. Her brother snickered appreciatively, because she hardly ever did things like that.

In Cantley they'd had to ride a bus to school. Perhaps if Guy got miserable about George Harvey Collegiate Institute, its relative nearness could be used to cheer him up. The front entrance was behind big arching trees, brown with tall thin windows, reminding Amber of a dentist's office.

At the beginning of December, the teachers would be pushing end-of-term assignments, portfolios and essays measured in hundreds of words. Amber didn't recall what sports would be in season. When she'd finished her last year of high school she'd thought that her teachers would miss her. As she discovered in June, returning for commencement, it was more true to say that she was missing them. She remembered finding her physics teacher, Mr. Scurlock, during the reception in the gym, basketball nets hoisted up to the ceiling. He'd written a glowing letter of recommendation to get her into University of Ottawa. Apparently Amber had expected some sort of extravagant reunion, since she remembered feeling bewildered and disappointed when he only acknowledged her with a little cordiality, staring out over the crowd, clearly having more important things on his mind. Mercifully she hadn't made an idiot out of herself; she'd finished what she was saying and gone away to find her parents, wearing this glitzy champagne-coloured dress that she'd never worn before, that her mother had pulled from her closet that afternoon.

After all, every year there was an entire generation of students cycled out and replaced with new ones while the faculty stayed, retreading the same courses year after year, and even if some students stood out in their time there would always be others just as exceptional, the next time and the time after that, and anyway teachers were just regular people. It was childish to imagine that their lives revolved around the kids they taught to the degree that they would pine after them when they were gone. Life lesson.

And now her brother was part of the incoming year—not any more, since he'd just moved across the province. He'd have to start over again. But he would, and once he did, finished and got out of there the same thing would happen to him. It just happened that she felt suddenly nostalgic, seeing linoleum floors and bulletin boards, hallways lined with those thin, squeaky lockers.

The front doors of George Harvey Collegiate Institute used double-jointed hinges that caused them to open in an unexpected sort of arc. That style of hinge was usually used only on ultra-modern doors made of solid glass, since solid glass couldn't be trusted with a regular hinge. But the doors of George Harvey weren't solid glass; they had thick metal frames. The more she thought about them, the more Amber figured the frames were added as an afterthought, since glass doors wouldn't last very long in a high school. They probably hadn't. Maybe it was that sort of neighbourhood. There was a policeman hanging out in the lobby, after all. Amber wondered if he was waiting for them.

A sticker on the door informed her that she'd be charged with trespassing if she didn't report to the main office, so that's where they went.

Guy was beside her, wearing his black parka unzipped and the hood off. He was suddenly walking in a different way, trying to look on top of the world. Amber forgave him. There were two secretaries behind the office counter, a line of students in front of each. Amber picked one arbitrarily, or not so arbitrarily, since the other one looked like a slut, blonde, eyeballs sunk into deep black craters of eye shadow. When Amber got to the front the woman was on the phone.

"Excuse me," Amber said.

The woman held up her hand. Amber shut her mouth. Her fingers perched over the edge of the counter like flower pots. The receptionist wasn't saying anything or doing anything, as though it was a cold compress in her hand instead of a phone, like she wasn't listening but just holding it against her cheek. Finally she hung up, and the next thing she did was peer up at Amber and ask, "Could you tell I was on the phone?"

"I thought you were on hold," Amber said.

The woman wrote on a pad. "I'll be back in one minute," she said and got up. Amber leaned against the counter. If Guy were beside her she'd have glanced at him and widened her eyes in comment. But he'd moved behind her, as though to pretend they had nothing to do with each other.

The other secretary, meanwhile, who was not bothered with silent phone calls or errands away from her desk, was busy writing up late slips for a line of guys with short hair who were obviously only polite with her because she looked like a whore. After a minute Amber's secretary returned, settling into her grey chair. "Yes," she said.

"I need to sign up my brother," Amber told her.

The secretary looked at her questioningly.

"This is Guy Drinkwater," Amber said, reaching back to make sure he was still there. "He's supposed to make an appointment for this week...?"

Still the woman waited.

"He was just enrolled here," Amber added.

"You need to make an appointment?"

"I mean, it should already be set up, we just needed to show up and set a date or something like that."

The secretary looked between them. "So you have an appointment, or don't you?"

"Yeah," Amber stuttered. "We do, but that's what we need to find out, when it is."

What the fuck had she just said? Why couldn't she put two words together?

The woman pondered a minute more, asked for their name again, then turned away to consult her computer. So the story was that she knew she had an appointment of some kind, she just didn't know what, or where? In a fit of flaming terror it occurred to her that perhaps a date and time *had* been picked, and they'd already missed it. What she'd just done in her flustered state was try to pretend that their reason for being there, all along, was... She'd assumed, somehow, that all she had to do was show up, send her brother's name across the counter, and everything would work itself out. Amber had no idea what the woman was doing on her computer, but she desperately wished that all she had to do was to look them up in the system, that it would spit out in plain words exactly what they had to do next.

But the secretary clicked and clicked, staring at her screen with a grimace. Amber knew it was taking too long. Somehow she could sense that although this woman was double-checking and triple-checking to avoid missing something, there was nothing to be found. Amber watched as she abandoned the computer and turned to a prism notepad on the desk, turning page over page. At what point would she give up? What would she recommend to them when she did? Then she glanced over her shoulder, like she thought someone was watching, and she said, "Guy Drinkwater."

Her voice inflected like she'd found his name on a list. Amber felt a flutter of relief, prematurely, since for all she knew—

"Guy?" said the woman, looking past Amber to her brother.

"Yeah," Guy replied, stepping up.

"You're here to choose your courses?"

"Yeah," Guy said again.

"We've already received a signed enrolment package?"

"I'm pretty sure."

"Here you go," the secretary said. She scribbled out a note in unreadable penmanship and handed it to Guy. "What you need to do is go straight across the lobby to the guidance office," she said, pointing with her pen. "Talk to Ms. Reuben at the desk, and she'll find a time slot for you."

"When?" Guy asked.

She just said Ms. Reuben would decide that, idiot.

"You may have to wait an hour or two."

The woman's face looked so much different when she was looking through Amber and not straight at her.

"Okay."

"Thank you," Amber said.

Her brother echoed, "Thanks."

And that was that. Having tied up that secretary for ten times as long as anyone else in line, they went back through the lobby. Amber finally took off her hat. Her forehead was sweaty.

At first, in the main office with Guy hanging behind her like he didn't want to be there, she'd thought she'd be doing all the talking, but her brother took over very readily when they got to the guidance office—so readily, in fact, that Amber thought he was showing off. He charged through the door in front of her and barked a greeting at the woman who was probably Ms. Reuben, an old woman in a silk shirt. In spite of the secretary's talk about waiting an hour or two, Guy was sent in right away to see one of the counselors, a man in an office full of binders. They left the door open, and Amber waited at a table in front of a wall full of potted plants and a gamut of pamphlets about AIDS.

After fifteen minutes Guy came out with a piece of paper. "Our parents have to sign this," he said, holding it up to her.

Amber looked at the sheet. It was a form with Guy's classes listed out. She carefully skimmed the course titles as though to make sure it met her approval. There were two lines at the bottom: one for his own signature, which he'd already supplied, and one for the parent or guardian, for the older person in charge of their wellbeing.

"Here," Amber said. "I'll do it."

"What?"

Amber snatched the page from him, inciting from him a shout of dismay, which Amber considered to be an awful over-reaction, conspicuous in the quiet office.

"What are you doing?" Guy asked.

"Being your legal guardian." Amber had seen a pen five seconds ago. Guy watched her nervously. He'd be wondering, could she really do that? Amber realised she was wondering the same thing herself. She stared at the empty line, frustrating like a blank face.

"But you're not my guardian," Guy said.

"They don't care."

"He told me to get it signed by my parents and bring it back."

"And how do you plan to do that?"

"We might find Uncle Ian today."

By calling his number again, by going back to the house again?

"We'll check his place again if we have time," Amber said. Of course they had time. It wasn't even noon yet, and this school business was the only thing they had to do. Once this was done it would be yesterday over again. She held a pen an inch above the page, above the black line, the parental permission line. "Shit," she said.

Her brother was still watching her.

"Well, shit," she said again. It was her only comment. She looked around the office, at Ms. Reuben in her cubicle. "Okay," she sighed. "Let's go then. Let's take it home." She didn't know what they'd do with it once they were there—and of course, she didn't know what "home" meant, it really just meant she would stick the page somewhere and carry it around until they got to some point, some point where it would be clear what they had to do.

Amber's jacket had large flap pockets at the waist; if she carefully folded the paper into quarters it would fit into one of them, nestled up beside her wallet. Guy watched her do it, concerned at first, then seemingly making up his mind to not give a shit. They went through the lobby and straight back out the glass doors to Keele Street, since there was nothing there to stop them.

It was 2:00 by the time they returned to that familiar bus lane, so Carrie's class may or may not have been over. In the time Amber and her brother had spent in transit to Silverthorne and back Carrie had been slouching in a room over coffee with sweetener, learning Japanese. What Amber didn't know was whether the Japanese class was two or three hours long, or longer, or whether Carrie had any other plans for afterward, or if she even planned to go right back to her room after all that. So the point was, basically, Amber didn't know if Carrie would be there when they arrived.

It was such a familiar theme since they'd been in the city. Sure enough, nobody answered when Amber called Carrie's room from the speaker phone, a rehash of the first night's fiasco. She clucked her tongue, a show of isn't-this-typical. So there was nothing to do, once again, but loaf around the campus until Carrie returned. Amber asked her brother, wasn't it wonderful being an unexpected guest three days in a row? But they weren't carrying their bags one second longer. After a ten-minute wait with Amber wondering if she should sit down on the grass, a guy came by who opened the front doors, shrugging indifferently at her apologies. There was an empty study room at the other end of the lobby, acceptably shady with the blinds drawn. She and Guy wedged their bags underneath a carrel in the corner, and that satisfied them.

Walking felt luxurious without luggage attached to her body. They started by going back to the mall, for which York was infamous among students at U of T, then they just walked around, not looking for anything in particular; the exploring was an end in itself. If they ran into something interesting, like a coffee bar or a fifteen-foot-high confusion of bright orange girders—"Look, it's art," Guy remarked—then that was something.

They could tell when they got to the edge of the campus, because there was absolutely nothing past the edge of the campus. It was a lot different from downtown. Here, there'd be a parking lot, then a four-lane highway, and then factories or a bleak apartment building. There were no shadows of office towers beyond the severe grey buildings, severe and grey in spite of upper floors that stuck out, thrillingly, farther than the lower floors, in spite of jumbly orange installation art.

Amber offered to buy her brother a coffee. It was because she wanted one herself, but Guy had hissed and complained that he was running out of money. Guy went on that he'd never drunk coffee before because it was gross, but Amber went ahead anyway, knowing. Looking savvy, he tried to open the sip latch on the plastic lid, but wound up tearing the whole thing up in a triangle. He flicked the bit of plastic into a garbage can and tasted it, then bemoaned that it was too hot, with a disinterested frown as though he'd been drinking coffee for years. "Don't complain about everything," Amber said.

She'd got coffee for herself too; she didn't like it. It was a flavour called amaretto, and she knew she'd never be trying it again. It tasted like black liquorice.

They passed through the designated set-up-tables-and-hassle-people spot on campus, a corridor with tables along either periphery, serious-faced people standing around in those half-pleading attitudes, handing pieces of paper to anyone who wandered too close. Up ahead they were in for an even better treat, though; the corridor ended at a large rotunda and, wouldn't you know it, there was a full-out protest. The entire rotunda was packed with students in winter coats, faces turned up to the balcony. They were complaining about the cost of tuition. *What a surprise.* Tuition was *always* too high, and always would be; that was the nature of anything that cost money. When you had to work for a living, everything in the world seemed a bit too expensive, and making a spectacle in a university rotunda wasn't going to change that.

Counting on the premise that Carrie was bound to go back to her room eventually, Amber kept calling every fifteen minutes. Statistically, the more often she called the more likely she was to catch her. She felt dull about how overdone the routine was; she'd spent practically her entire time in Toronto with a phone in her hand. Walking around the campus had been a way to pass the time, but now they were parked at a table in the mall food court with all patent activity stripped away from the fact that they were just waiting for Carrie, at her leisure, to return to her room and answer. Once, when Amber had come back from another failed attempt, Guy had tried to play it all up as her own fault they were sitting around, bored and famished, and Amber told him to go fuck himself and buy his own food if he was such a pig.

She wondered, what had they *used* to do with their time? In high school, almost all the time she didn't spend in class was idle. She'd come home on the bus and have a whole afternoon with a bit of homework and no real plans. She'd waste hours in her room with nothing to show for it; furthermore, she'd spend the whole school day in anticipation of this time, that moment skipping off the bus and walking through her door with nothing to do.

Carrie didn't have a cell phone, Amber thought, but since she didn't have one either she couldn't complain. Perhaps Carrie had just decided, like herself, not to bother getting one, since she didn't need one. That went for credit cards too; Amber didn't want to be like the idiots in high school who threw away all their money because it made them feel older.

Their social worker had offered to lend them a cell phone for their trip. No, she hadn't offered so much as just mentioned it in passing: "I can give you a cell phone if you like," Janelle had said, "so you can reach me if something comes up...?" But her attitude had suggested that she didn't really think it was necessary. She had confidence in Amber. So Amber had declined.

She tapped out the now-familiar number with quiet, mechanical movements. The laws of probability paid off; Carrie actually answered.

"Where've you been all day?" Amber asked immediately.

She'd been lots of places, Carrie explained. Then she realised where Amber was calling from.

"What the hell happened?" she cried.

"Nothing," Amber said flatly. "He's still not there."

"That's terrible! Did you get to talk to the super?"

"I don't think he really has a super."

"What do you mean?"

Meaning he clearly *did* have a superintendent of some kind, and Amber should have thought to track him down, but she just hadn't had the inclination (and why the hell hadn't she?). After getting nervous in front of Ian's downstairs neighbour she'd given up. But what the hell was she supposed to say? *Hey Carrie, I didn't do it just because, now let me in.*

Carrie was wearing open-toed sandals that looked cold for December. Amber went to get their bags from the shadowy study room, even gloomier than before with the passing of hours. They went upstairs. They put their bags in the accustomed place. Carrie had a word processor on her screen, Christmas lights on the walls. "I was doing an essay," she said.

Amber said to go ahead and keep working, but Carrie seemed to feel like a hostess. Not having any plans for them, she spent a few frantic moments sitting on her bed. Amber felt a bit of cruel fascination, watching her squirm.

"I like your posters," Guy said.

"Thanks. Do you guys have to stay here again?"

"I don't know," Amber answered, and they faced each other stubbornly. Amber was annoyed at Carrie's coldness even though see could see the girl's point of view, that she and her brother had been, basically, annoying interlopers all weekend. With each new interruption Carrie's scant hospitality had frayed a little more. There was no chance of banter, no skipping out for coffee this time. Carrie closed on her computer and moved the mouse around. She was pissed.

Well fuck her. What did she expect? It was all Uncle Ian's fault.

"It's just, like, you can only get, like, the maximum time that you can have people stay overnight is two nights in a row."

"So, what, I should go?"

"Well, it's just the maximum time that people can stay over is two nights in a row, that's all."

Silence, stubbornness. It was great to see Carrie putting out. *Fine. What a calibre of friendship.* Amber was ready to stand up, say sorry and leave, to let her have the peaceful evening she'd planned for, because, fuck, what was she supposed to do, stamp her feet? So she thought. The world didn't end. It occurred to her, they could sit in the food court, sleep with their heads on a table.

Instead she swayed on her feet, stupid and out of place, Guy an awkward appendage in the doorway, Carrie pretending they didn't exist. She'd dropped it, not enough of a bitch to actually force them to leave, so Amber leaned on the wall, not at home but not leaving either. And it was silence that prevailed, ridiculous, long-standing, until Guy said, "So...?"

It was a comment useful for nothing but shaking up the impasse. Carrie uttered something about where her boyfriend lived, talking like a sleeping person, and Amber had to dig into her like one of those fucking annoying people who wouldn't shut up with their fucking prying questions. But eventually Carrie surrendered that her boyfriend Jesse lived in an actual house, renting a room from a family, so there probably weren't all these rules over there. Amber asked, was the implication here that they should go stay with him? Carrie said they could do what they wanted. Could they call him? Carrie said sure. Amber then had to request the phone number, and Carrie slammed it down on a piece of paper, shoved to the corner of her desk, and the final thing was that Amber had to borrow her telephone, but then she didn't even bother to ask.

Out of the deep fryer of Carrie's dorm room, Amber and her brother waited for Jesse by the road. The first thing Jesse said when he got out of his car was, "So, what's going on?" Carrie's pissy mood about questions had put Amber in a similar mood, especially for questions like that. Guy got in the back seat, and, for some reason, Amber did too. As soon she started in she realised what she'd done; Jesse would be alone up front, like a taxi driver. The whole trip would be passed in suspense, watching the back of Jesse's chubby jowls. And she was already feeling so fucked, it didn't help that there was a bubbly song on the radio about how high school was dumb and the liberating thing was to realise that the real world didn't matter, sung by a guy who'd probably got caught shooting up.

Jesse's house was down Steeles Avenue, a street that defined the north end of Toronto. Amber had just noticed *Canadian Street* on the Markham side, getting her wondering how they came up with street names in the first place, when Jesse turned into a neighbourhood of duplexes with below-ground garages and sloping driveways. Jesse wove a bit and arrived at a dead-end street called Lowbank Court, one of those wide courts for turning around, and he parked at the curb. "Here we are," he announced.

It being dark out, the streetlights were on, and there only seemed to be one in place to light the end of the road, frail in a chilly wind that stirred up the leaves into cyclones. Jesse's house already had Christmas lights up, on the spruce in their lawn as well as along the wrought-iron porch railing.

They could hear piano music as Jesse helped them get their bags out of the trunk, coming from one of the houses around the court. Jesse's house wasn't a three-storey tower; in fact it had only one floor unless you counted the basement. It was a duplex like all the houses in the neighbourhood; on Jesse's half there was a basketball net above the garage door. They didn't get rooms at the very top with battlement windows. In fact, when they went in the front door

Jesse veered hard toward the basement stairs, opposite the rest of the house, a living room and a kitchen, the fabric smell of other people's things, chairs and tables and empty bowls in front of the TV. Down to the tiny basement they went, a room across from the furnace, smaller even than Carrie's half of the little dorm room. It had one window in a well, and a ceiling light in a simple round diffuser that wasn't quite bright enough.

Imagine living in there, the room barely more spacious than the window well outside, crammed with more implements of life than should ever have been together in one place, the mattress on the floor with unmade sheets, a desk barely big enough to support Jesse's computer monitor and a coffee machine; on the floor a ten-inch TV, piles of video games and an electric guitar, the patch cord making its labyrinthine path to an amplifier, boxes of Coke and cold pizza, and many, many plastic crates keeping junk off the floor, and smelling, God, like a person who never washed.

If only it had been her own room. She would have loved to live in squalor like this, surrounded by her *own* cold pizza, at least for a little while. She would if it were her own apartment, and she didn't have to walk on glass, and she'd probably clean up a little more than this, but hell, it would be at her own discretion.

Or even her old room would be nice, the one back in Cantley, where she'd slept for the last time over Thanksgiving, not knowing it would be the last time of course.

If they were getting the floor, again, there might not have been room, even if all the junk and shit were cleared away. Jesse got to work moving things, mostly papers and little white boxes. Amber looked at the thin carpet, wondering how it would feel. If they were any older they'd be getting back pains—well, that was why she'd do all her floor-sleeping now, during school.

She and her brother sat down obediently on the edge of Jesse's mattress, careful not to touch anything. The boy settled into his computer chair with a guttural creaking of metal. Like his girlfriend, he'd been in the middle of something. It didn't look like an essay, though. He was happy to put it aside; he turned on his PlayStation or Game-Cube or whatever the one was that he had, and announced, "Well, this is what I was going to do tonight."

Amber looked at her watch. It was only 6:00. Assuming bed-time was midnight, they had six hours to watch Jesse play video games. Wasn't there anything useful to do? If Uncle Ian was still out there somewhere... and if he wasn't, well, she would have to arrange something herself, and quickly, since twenty-four hours later they would be right back there, the same place, another night with no place to stay.

The moving people would be trucking up all their shit from the old house on Wednesday, and it was already Monday evening.

Fuck.

Well then, tomorrow would be a big fucking day.

- Go back to Uncle Ian's house, and don't leave without answers, get a key, say they have to move in or else, whatever the hell it took.
- Then call the goddamn social worker already, let her know they weren't lying in a ditch.
- Wednesday: be there to receive their stuff.
- Then she would actually open her physics notebook for the first time. She remembered she'd wanted to start studying the very evening they'd arrived in Toronto.

The problem was that anything she thought of doing could only be done during the day, during working hours when the world was up and running, like calling the number she'd seen in the window of Ian's house, the third floor window, in *their* window, or even roughing up the guy on the first floor. But now it was the evening, and she'd wasted the entire day, she realised, walking uselessly around York University.

All she could do then was just resolve to be more productive next time, to hammer out her list of chores over and over, to grind it into herself and make sure she didn't fucking forget it.

- And she wanted to find a job. She didn't need one, but she wanted one. She had a résumé on her computer; tomorrow she would print off a few, and then if they wound up downtown again she'd drop them off places. Any place at all would be fine; waitressing, selling shoes. She didn't care.
- And her brother had to be set up in school. He was supposed to be in class by next Monday, one week from today, the same day she was to return to Ottawa

for her exam. She had to make that piece of paper bear one of their parents' signatures. Somehow. Magically.

All of this was impossible to do at 6:00. It all had to be put off until tomorrow.

Why had she wasted the whole fucking day?

Meanwhile, Jesse was hitting it up with her brother on the video games. Amber was sick of being a guest. When she wasn't pacing around the city, killing her feet on the pavement, she was having to exert herself anyway, grin and chit-chat like a normal person. It was wearying. What Amber wanted was for everyone to shut up a moment; she wanted an excuse to leave the room and flop on her stomach and do nothing at all. Alas, in spite of there being an entire house upstairs, she wasn't allowed out of this room. That was the rule of being a guest.

There was an excuse, in fact, which presented itself to her with such forthrightness that she wondered why it hadn't occurred to her long ago. What if she just called Janelle right then, the woman with the scary hair who was in charge of their wellbeing, in spite of having nothing to show for her three days of procrastination? It would be Janelle's home phone number, of course, since it was after hours, and not her real number either, but one that rang in a special way so she would know it was a client calling. And then? Amber would just tell the truth. Her legal guardian had disappeared off the face of the earth, and it wasn't her fault. She'd been staying with people and keeping her brother fed and trudging back and forth to Ian's house day after day. And she'd been putting off this call, why? Because she'd wanted to get everything straightened out herself. Because she persevered that way.

"Can I make a phone call?" Amber asked.

"I guess," Jesse said. "But the only phone is upstairs."

He said it beseechingly, as if to ask, did she *have* to make a phone call? The phone was up in the kitchen, deep in the territory of a strange family. And now it was dinnertime too, when everybody was home and dressed down. He shifted in his chair, pneumatics groaning. Was there a problem? Are you allowed to use the phone? Am *I* allowed to use the phone? Can I right now? Where is it?

"Just don't take too long," Jesse admonished.

Amber took her grade twelve homework journal and excused herself up the basement stairs. The lights were on, but the house seemed empty; the TV and computer were off; a quiet shape of yellow emerged from the bedroom hallway, the really private part of the house. Well then, that was better; there'd be no friction with the family if the family wasn't even there.

The kitchen had a peninsula table, covered with mail, plastic bags and a strange little machine that looked like a soda fountain. There was a smell of ashes, like something was burned on the stove, and the phone was a black cordless one on the counter. The message-waiting light was on, messages for another family, to remind her once more that she was invading another family's home. Maybe she was being too paranoid. But imagine being caught there, a stranger in the kitchen, using the phone.

Amber picked it up, intending to figure out how to work it, when she remembered that Janelle was based in Ottawa. It would be long-distance from Toronto, and that changed everything. It made everything worse, even less acceptable. And then sound exploded through the kitchen, a clatter of metal beats, the handle of the back door, the weather seal smacking wetly. The door had barely opened, and it was a pair of boys, both younger than Guy, but the older one in a dark blue sweatshirt and the younger one in a colourful sweater, warm and cottony outfits. Their trajectory through the kitchen faltered when they saw Amber.

Amber smiled at them, relieved that it was only children. As if. Everyone had been outside, having some family moment in the backyard. Amber had of course prepared all kinds of shame and chagrin to spill over her for just such a happening. Mommy and Daddy had been in a good mood, laughing. Guilty, conflicting feelings, wanting to run, knowing it was too late. Caught, after all. At first they were bizarrely phlegmatic, looking at Amber, still smiling about what had made them so happy before.

The children ran into the living room. Amber tried to say something disarming: "Hey, I just asked Jesse if I could make a call."

"Okay," Daddy granted. "Did you make it?"

"Yeah," Amber said. She put down the phone and walked out of the kitchen. Soon she was back at the entranceway, the stairs to the basement. But who knew, she didn't care to be down there, like in a trap, easily available in case there were words to be said to Jesse about his stupid friends. So instead of going down, Amber walked out the front door, still in her shoes but without a coat or hat, and she knew as soon as she was on the porch that she'd made a mistake. Amber Drinkwater, why did you do that? But it was too late to change her mind; she skipped down the steps and walked around Lowbank Court with her hands in her pockets.

She'd run away, a bizarre and juvenile thing to do, to escape having to explain herself. She had to go back inside before it got even weirder, before she had even more explaining to do. But how? Still walking down the street, shivering: how? How the fuck were these things done?

At least, outside in the cold, she'd finally found some time to relax.

CHAPTER 4

There was an easy way to imagine contacting Ian's landlord: calling him up and talking. But first they had to find out the phone number; that involved another trip to the house, to read it off the For Rent sign in the window. Then she had to find a payphone, and then she had to drudge up the words to ask what had happened. The anticipation might have kept her from making the effort, were it not for the fact that waking up on Jesse's floor had felt like waking up on a sidewalk. She'd lit up her watch in the dark and discovered it to be 6:00 a.m., still way too early to face the dizziness and cold sweat of the morning, but she knew she wouldn't be getting back to sleep again, the room smelling like dirty laundry, humid, her brother's legs touching hers, Jesse snoring away on the mattress. Jesse might have been willing to hold onto her luggage so she wouldn't have to manoeuvre it onto the bus again and carry it from her sore shoulder, but it was moot because she didn't want to have to come back later. She'd made sure Guy went with her as well. "Can I get a drink?" he asked.

"If you give me millions," Amber told him.

"I'll be your slave."

"You already are my slave."

The real question was, of course, would Amber give him money for a drink. She suspected that he didn't want to have to blow the last little bit of his life savings on pop and food.

For the third time they walked down the twisty hill. Amber noted the phone number in the window, and for the third time their exit route was not back up the hill, but out the avenue to Keele. At the corner was one of the little no-name convenience stores with a bland red-on-white sign. It was a tiny place, the kind that made Amber feel sorry for the owners. That was, in fact, why she'd decided to check it out. Behind the counter, framed by rows of cigarettes, an Indian woman was reading some novel with a white cover, and the

space in front of the counter was about the same as her little area behind it. More stuff was packed into the tiny room than seemed possible. The only flat surface that was empty was on the counter between
them, over the lottery tickets, the aisle for money.

The woman patiently stashed her book under the counter when
they entered. "What do you want?" Amber asked her brother, lower-
ing her voice. The woman's waiting and the size of the store made it
seem inappropriate to speak loudly. They both picked drinks, and
Amber added a couple of Bundt muffins, since this was supposed to
be a meal. This had been their diet for the past few days: snack food,
coffee and sport drinks. No, it wasn't healthy, but they were hardly
in a position to be decadent. It was only until they got Ian's shit
sorted out.

Speaking of money, she didn't have any quarters for the phone
call. It would have been smart to get some change at the convenience
store, but no, of course she hadn't thought of that while it counted.
So that meant, basically, stopping for food again, more Bundt muffins, at the next one down the road.

Between her and her brother, since of course she was paying
for both of them, that had been twelve dollars right there on convenience store junk. At least there was a payphone right outside the next
place, and she called the number from the upstairs window, the number that was hopefully Ian's landlord.

A woman answered and, as if she hadn't hit enough bumps already, Amber realised she didn't know her name. Her greeting was
rather bizarre: "Hi… Do you…? Do you…?"

"Huh?"

"Do you own a… a house? For rent?"

Quiet.

"I'm calling about your house, that you have a sign up…"

This woman was clearly not an English speaker. It wasn't as if
Amber was doing any better, though. What she had to put together
was:

- Was this the right number for the house in Silverthorne?
- What was the status of the second-floor tenant, and
  had he left any instructions concerning taking pos-
  session of the third floor?

- And could someone come by and let them the fuck
  in?

"Sorry," Amber said. "What's your name?"

Not that she'd provided any reason for this woman to trust her with her name.

"I'm supposed to be moving into your house, that you rent?" she ploughed on. "I'm the niece of Ian's...?"

"Oh, you're calling for renting?"

Thank you.

It was the landlord's wife, Mrs. Goto, and she wouldn't say much over the phone, perhaps because she couldn't. Her mantra was, had Amber talked to Mr. Goto? Her husband was at work. Did she understand a word Amber said or not? It was a good question; the way Amber strung words together, she could barely understand herself.

"Like, all I need is, just, to get in."

"So you want to look at the renting house."

"Well yeah, but... no, like, we're actually *there*, to stay."

"You are at the house right now?"

"No, we're not *at the house* right now. But we just need to get in, when we go back to the house."

"So you want to look at the renting house."

"No, not just looking at it, though. We're supposed to be staying there, already. Like, it's supposed to be paid for."

"So... What do you want?"

Good God. The conversation veered around to Mrs. Goto having spare keys where she lived, the suggestion being to come over and pick them up. Perhaps she thought Amber was a tenant and had just locked herself out? That was close enough to the truth. The address, then? Some street she'd never heard of. Directions? Oh boy. Amber changed her mind about not being at the Silverthorne house. It would be easier on everybody.

The Goto residence was further west on Eglinton. They had to walk all the way past a park and under a bridged road called Photography Street, so-named because it only existed to communicate with a Kodak factory. The Gotos lived on an L-shaped street called Brownville Avenue. It was an old street, old and weedy, packed with tiny houses, some only as wide as a single room, with a spider-web-like accumulation of low-hanging hydro wires. As Amber and her brother walked down the sidewalk, they kept noticing old people sitting on their porches. Brownville, that was funny.

The house with Mrs. Goto's address was flat-roofed, and the front of it was made of some material like stucco. Also, the windows and doors had arched tops; it looked Mediterranean.

"Tum te tum," Amber said as she rang the doorbell. It was in reference to the number of times they'd been in that position over the last few days, outside a door or on the phone, waiting for attention. They waited once more, and in truth Amber didn't even know if there was going to be an answer, because it wouldn't have surprised her if she had the address wrong completely.

A woman opened the door, in the middle of paling her face.

"Hi, I'm Amber," she introduced herself. "I called you...?"

What were the odds that most of Mrs. Goto's neighbours understood her fine? How offensive would it be to ask her to repeat just about everything she said? Clustered over all that like bushy moss, remembering that this woman was grown up, she didn't need pity or sympathy.

"Hello," Mrs. Goto said. She didn't smile. Maybe she wasn't supposed to smile, to keep her face clear. Her palm was on the screen door, as though she wasn't used to seeing people. Her face powder was unnerving.

"So, I called you, just now," Amber repeated, waving vaguely to the east. "About the house that you rent out the floors of...?" It had occurred to her, naturally, *naturally*, she'd ring the wrong doorbell. It seemed easy in theory to correspond an actual building with an address, but then, Ian obviously hadn't found it easy to correspond Union Station with three nights ago.

"Okay," Mrs. Goto granted.

"The thing is," Amber started, and pretty much repeated the conversation from before. She forgot half the details, got the other half all out of order. She managed to make the problem sound stupid, not worth the time of explaining it. Mrs. Goto listened nervously. The Asian make-up made her look nervous, at least. Amber went on, "Is it okay – can we be let into the third floor? Just so we can leave our stuff there?" She said it as though they just intended to drop off their things and go. It was a fresh addition to the story, and a lie.

"Oh," Mrs. Goto said. "Wait." She retreated from the door. A little Chinese girl in sweat pants appeared, staring up at Amber in that stand-there-and-stare thing children did from doorways. Amber smiled. Then the door whooshed open farther, and Mrs. Goto handed Amber a silver key.

"Oh," Amber said.

"This is good?"

"Yeah. Thanks."

Mrs. Goto shut the door. Amber felt sorry for her altogether, for wearing that make-up, for staying home on a Tuesday, for having non-North-American customs, for being foreign-born. It was a torrent.

Supposedly. Presumably.

Anyway, as soon as the door was shut Amber said, "Hey, look," jingling the key at her brother. It was on a keychain with a card that said '3'. "We've got our place now."

Amber Drinkwater hoped her brother was happy too, after the painful walk back to Silverthorn Avenue, to put down his bags in the third floor of the tall house, right inside the entrance, as though they were loath to carry it even one more step. The arrangement was a living room to the right and a dinette to the left; obviously a dinette because there was a light on a chain that seemed meant to go over a dining table. Off the dinette was the little kitchen, an aisle with a fridge and counter space on one side, a sink and oven on the other.

The place was empty, suspenseful, the hardwood floor crunching with a vague echo because there wasn't any furniture. Straight forward was the hall to the bedrooms. It went without saying that Amber would be getting the master, with its own bathroom door. Guy's had a hardwood floor, like the entrance, and wallpaper on three sides with little pink flower petals. For some reason, the fourth wall had a different kind of wallpaper, with naked women and sunflowers suggested in moody pointillism.

"Nice wall there," Amber remarked to him, crunching the hardwood as she walked to look out his window.

"What wall?" Guy said. "Oh. Nifty."

"You're going to put your bed there, aren't you?"

"Fuck you."

As for the master, it had icy blue carpet and splotchy primer on the walls; it was the only carpeted room, actually, and it came with a bed. Amber sat on it, swung her feet up. Guy asked her what she was doing. She told him she was resting, and why didn't he do the same? He asked her, were they allowed to just stay there? Of course they were. Finally. Amber told him to just do whatever the fuck he wanted, they were home. But there was nothing *to* do, he countered. They didn't have their stuff. Then go be bored, Guy.

She'd spent three days getting him in here, and he was still complaining.

If the place came with a bed, then she obviously didn't need her old one from home. What would she do with it when it arrived tomorrow? Maybe she could have two beds. There was probably enough space. Her new bedroom spanned the house. Until now they'd only owned as much stuff as would fit in their Cantley bedrooms: one each of beds, dressers, desks, squeaky desk chairs, a tall and thin set of shelves. They'd had the liberty to choose any furniture in the house they wanted to keep, before the rest of it went off to whatever, and naturally they'd zeroed in on the area around the television, the grey fuzzy couch, the TV cabinet, even the coffee table, and a wicker end-table that had always stood by the couch. Uncle Ian had said it was so old and cheap, the wicker fraying, that there wasn't any point, and that he could get them a new one from Ikea. The computer desk for the living room, maybe, but Amber told her brother he could just *have* the family computer now that she had one of her own. She knew he'd have no complaints. It would be like an early Christmas.

There were also boxes of stuff, their own stuff, cheap shit, and the little bit that Ian had urged them to keep, as an investment. The painted plates, they could be worth something. So they'd packed the painted plates. But, seriously. Vases? Little statues? Amber had invited her uncle to take anything for himself, if he wanted, if he was interested in appraising it. He'd grinned and said that wasn't his prerogative.

Amber lay on the bed for maybe fifteen minutes, then she was bored too. Guy had ambushed her laptop in the living room. She thought about looking at her physics notes, but there was another thing they didn't have yet: food. Amber looked through all the kitchen cupboards, just in case. She was starving. All the convenience store muffins in the world just didn't matter after an hour or two. And, hell, moving in was something to celebrate, so Amber suggested they order a pizza. Guy acted indifferent as usual. Except, did they have a phone yet? No, they didn't. So they put their coats on, Amber locked the door, tested it, and they went back out to the street, for the first time having somewhere to return to.

They remembered a 241 Pizza halfway up the hill between Keele and the Westside Rehab apartment building. When they got there, Amber noticed that it was probably the only the store on the street that wasn't selling Caribbean or Asian food. And here were two white kids who had gravitated to it without a second thought— but there was no point in being paranoid. Amber brightly consulted her brother for his opinion about toppings and looked out the window. Were there *any* other white people? Well, they'd passed those old guys the other day who looked like fishermen, on the steps of the pharmacy.

And then they had to do the walk, back down the street, the walk home with food, which was always a long one to begin with. Let's just eat it here, her brother had joked, on the sidewalk. Ha ha. Just as soon as they got back to the place, mounted the steps and locked the door behind them, then they could relax, bust out the pop and pizza, play computer games, eat the leftovers cold.

When they got back there was a minivan at the curb. A worried-looking Chinese man was hurrying down the stairs. He didn't raise his voice, threaten, insinuate, or any of that, but for the life of her, why weren't there three or four simple words that could justify what they were doing, slumming in an empty flat that wasn't rented out? No, of course not. See, people would be coming by to look at the place every so often, so there couldn't exactly be a pair of kids lounging on the floor eating pizza, could there? Obviously not.

Well, when you put it that way...

So Amber and Guy searched for a spot in the neighbourhood where it would be socially acceptable to sit and eat pizza out of the box, in public, with their bags.

Any time Amber used a bank machine, she never got out more than the minimum twenty dollars, and she always printed out her balance, frowned over the print-out thoughtfully and stuffed it into her wallet with the cash, where it would stay until her wallet was packed with little bits of paper and she threw it all out. Her balance was always a little bit less than she expected it to be, because of using debit. Wasn't that a great idea, letting people spend money with cards? And she'd been using bank machines pretty often since coming to Toronto.

When she and her brother had left Cantley she'd had $700 in the bank. It was plenty, considering it was only supposed to pay for the train ride and a few odd things to help them settle in. And it was all her own savings, as well as principal that had come, under the direction of Janelle the social worker, from the pension their parents had left for them. She and her brother each would be getting around $150 every month, as long as they were students. Guy would need it especially, considering he'd saved only about $100 in his life, and he'd blown it already. Chips and donuts added up. Well, he'd be a student still for twice as long as his sister, so that counted in his favour.

Normally Amber ignored advertisements of any kind, but those computer-paper things taped to telephone poles got extra helpings of her apathy, since they were always full of stupid shit, like the word *sex* in giant letters just to get people to look, since the thing itself didn't have enough merit.

Today she looked at one. It mentioned employment for students. Well, that was important. It was time she seriously looked into that, by way of calling the phone number—but Amber had already passed it by then. She hadn't wanted to stop and trawl a pen and paper out of her bag, not on a city sidewalk with other people all around, watching her every move.

She also looked at another one, taped up in a bus shelter. Someone owned an apartment with two empty rooms, looking for tenants. Straightforward—she and her brother were two tenants, looking for rooms. Another number, another thing to look into as soon as they settled down a bit, and it was the right time. The street number of the building was 2468; the pattern seemed to make it more special.

Although, settling seemed to be out of the question for them, apparently, Amber having surrendered the key to the apartment, having told Mr. Goto over and over that she understood and that she was happy to cooperate and wasn't looking for trouble, and if it was trouble for them to be there, well, that was what she wasn't looking for.

She'd clucked her tongue at her brother in a that's-the-way-it-goes sort of way and with weary humour packed her things up while Mr. Goto swayed on his feet in the doorway. Yes, he knew Ian, but no, there was nothing on paper about him renting out the third floor for his nephew and niece. Once they were out he locked the door himself, and the movements somehow translated through his body to make the deck and the stairs shake.

It gave Amber occasion to feel even sorrier for his wife. He was probably going to go home and yell at her.

Once, eating at restaurants had been a rare and anticipated thing; since they'd been in Toronto, it had been their only means of dining. When Amber had taken out cash out for pizza, her account had stood at under $500. She'd stared at the little piece of paper resentfully, listening to traffic drive past.

But hell, she was buying food for two people, from convenience stores and restaurants, four or five times a day. It would be modest to imagine that adding up to $40 daily; it was probably more. And then there were all the bus and subway fares that piled up, as well as convenience charges every time she used an ATM, and the cost of that stupid movie they'd seen on Sunday, with overpriced movie snacks—since when could they afford to go to the movies?

But there was no going back; her account had sunk under $500.

Since when could they afford pizza?

At some point in the future they were switching to the grocery store. They'd start eating like actual people, who lived in houses.

Unfortunately, they'd neglected to consider drinks when buying the pizza. Actually, the guy had said, "Any drinks?" but Amber wasn't falling for that, and she had said no. She was thirsty now, after eating pizza that started out lukewarm and cooled quickly once the box was open, in her lap on a park bench in her winter coat and hat, then pounding creases into the box so it would fit in the garbage drum. She was thirsty, so she asked her brother if he was thirsty and, it being cold out with hats and coats on, their destination would be a coffee shop. Like that one, Keele Donuts, named after the street it was on.

Inside Keele Donuts: bar stools; a soap opera on the TV near the ceiling; a little hall straight to the back door. Amber thought there was a back room, but her view was blocked by the man standing in the hall, a black man, fat and bald, and saying on a cell phone, "The fucking plasma screen TV, he took it to fucking Newfoundland, the fucking plasma screen TV. He tells me he fucking took it to New-foundland. With the fish and fucking Labrador."

Behind the counter was an old woman, an older version of Mrs. Goto. The only other person in the store was a white woman with wavy brown hair and sweat pants that ballooned around her hips, smoking a cigarette.

The black man said: "It's saved on his fucking computer and he took it with himself to fucking France, to fucking France."

Coffee, requested Amber.

The old woman had a kerchief tied around her hair and a man's shirt under her apron. "*Shit*," she snarled. She was having dif-ficulty charging coffee to the cash register. She called someone out of the kitchen, younger, with longer hair, probably her daughter. There was a very young girl there, too; three generations were repre-sented in Keele Donuts.

They got donuts too, apple fritters that were giant, swollen, looking like a steal for eighty cents.

On the TV: "You had a nice story the last time you tried to kill me. What's it going to be this time?"

And the white woman smoked.

What Amber concentrated on was not looking fucking scared of everything, of the man running a stolen-goods business on his telephone. Amber had only met one other person who swore like him, her roommate at University of Ottawa. Everything she did or saw was fuckin'. She fuckin' did fuckin' that. She never sounded like she meant it; it was more like she'd taught herself to talk that way, for image. Coming from another white girl her own age it was pitiful; coming from this black guy it was terrible, vaguely crushing too that he was *actually like that*. She couldn't let the locals know how she felt. She didn't want her brother knowing, either. If she put on a guise that nothing was wrong in neighbourhoods like this, that black men weren't to be feared, even though, frankly, she didn't be-lieve it, maybe he would believe it, learning from his big sister, thinking she knew the way of the world. The Chinese grandma handed over their donuts in a bag, and Amber gently urged Guy to-ward the door as though it had been understood from the start that they weren't staying.

The black guy had left and was hanging out in the parking lot by a van with a bunch of kids. Amber didn't make a move on the food until they'd got the hell out of there.

"That was weird," was her comment.

Guy had none of his own. He was too ashamed to talk. And the donuts were half-baked.

Amber suggested, jokingly, that they go to a coffee shop for food, for a treat because they had some free time—jokingly, because they'd just come from one, and they had nothing but free time. The joke wasn't even funny any more, since that had been consistently the first and only idea that came to mind over the last three days whenever they found themselves like that on the sidewalk, between destinations, useless hours still arrayed between then and the end of the day, time for doing things but with nothing to do.

They looked so sad, in public with all their bags, so that Amber considered, well then, they should just get on a bus and... what? Anything would be better than what they were doing—walking, on the street, a street they didn't know but walking anyway, because it was either walking or else it was sitting on the curb.

They were going south, Amber figured. A truck drove by, spreading road salt. They came up to the Tim Hortons at the corner, and Amber made a joke about going in and getting donuts. Guy had nothing to add.

Across the street was that really weird building, boxy and flat, gray with primary-colour balconies. It might have been meant to look ultra-modern, but it looked more like they'd just needed cheap and fast building plans. It was a parking garage for four storeys, then it turned into apartments. "Let's check it out," Amber said.

An unfortunate feature of the place was that that the paint was severely weathered, with enormous stains reaching down the outside walls. One balcony on the top floor had a giant banner with the building's phone number; Amber wondered if those tenants got compensation for having that there. The public entrance faced a Value Village and a utilities enclosure with a "Danger: 47,500 Volts" sign.

"Would you want to live here?" Amber asked.

"Looks like a piece of crap," her brother answered.

She hadn't actually meant for him to speak honestly, but she let it slide. "That's the point," she said, surprised at her own coolness. "It'll be cheap as crap."

Guy slipped back into his sulking and silence. Yes, he would stop voicing his complaints, but the way he glowered, avoiding her eye, meant the complaints were still obviously there. He was giving up on her, being passive-aggressive, trying to blame her for everything. Just let him try.

There was nothing special about this apartment building; it wasn't bigger or smaller than any other of the thousands jutting above Toronto houses. It had been peculiar enough to draw Amber's attention; other than that, it was simply the one in front of them at the time. Maybe she'd have preferred one closer to University of Toronto—but no, it had to be close to Guy's school. It wasn't fair to expect him to commute instead of her. She was looking for cheapness, and that meant getting what she could pay for, roaches and holes in the walls. She wasn't a princess.

And anyway, there weren't roaches or holes in the walls. The place was cheap all right, but cheap in a wash-and-wear kind of way, unadorned, every corner in plain view and in reach of a mop. There was a rec room with a bar and billiards by the entrance, plain, shallow carpet, everything made of materials that could be cleaned with spray and cheesecloth. There was an office down the hall, the sound of adult voices emanating like a fog. There were two women at a desk, chuckling about which of them was going to plan a birthday party. Amber waited politely in the doorway, ignoring the black couch—vinyl, stain-resistant. Apparently, these two women were the only ones who bothered planning birthdays in this building, and since both of their own birthdays were in the same week, who would be doing the work? And how much longer would they yap before they noticed her there? She wasn't going to speak up, not after that sneer from the secretary the other day. *Could you tell I was on the phone?* She wasn't going to have these women bitch at her too.

"Hi," Amber said. The one sitting down acknowledged her by raising her eyebrows. Suddenly Amber didn't remember what she was there for. Then: "We're looking for a room," she said, "and we'd just like some information about what you have...?"

It was a completely simple, pedestrian request. The woman probably heard the same thing a dozen times a day. Duly she delivered a spiel about the different tiers of rooms and suites they had and asked a few questions like whether Amber needed a parking space.

"How many?" she asked.

"What?"

"How many bedrooms?"

She glanced at Guy as she said it; she shouldn't have brought her brother in. What would the secretary think if she found out it would be just the two of them?

But wasn't it was none of her damn business? "Just two," Amber said.

The woman explained that there was one basic double bedroom they had, "with bathroom en suite," pointing out the item on a laminated sheet. Broadly declared beside the picture was the monthly rent: $840.

"What about single bedrooms?" Amber asked, holding the edge of the desk.

"They have bathrooms too," the woman said, guiding them to the appropriate item with her pen: $725.

"Okay," Amber said.

The desk woman prattled for a while. Amber leaned over, nodding and handling the pages. She was afraid to look up. Finally it ended, and Amber made remarks to the extent of having no further questions. She thanked the woman, said that she was still looking around, and so on, working through the nuances of breaking off and leaving. Guy anticipated her intentions and stepped out in front of her; she followed him to the parking lot.

"So, yeah," Amber said. "Nothing special."

Guy stepped up on a cement parking block and bobbed on his toes. Amber counted the other buildings in view, a half-dozen, rising like sentinels, the Value Village across the parking lot. They were all basically the same. There was nothing to pick and choose between, really.

"Are you bored?" Amber asked her brother.

He made a sound to convey that he wasn't.

"Go back if you're bored," Amber told him. "I don't care."

"But I thought we're not allowed there," Guy said.

"Yeah well, I'm going to be doing this." Amber gestured off into the distance, as though to call attention to some particular building. She meant all of them in general.

Guy kept going up and down, slowly and methodically, staring at his toes like he was trying to get the movement just right.

So what was there to do? Check out other apartments, compare prices. Amber considered personally visiting each of the buildings closest to George Brown Collegiate Institute, but she was stricken by a sense of futility. They would all be basically the same. The prices she'd just seen were the normal ones. It really didn't matter if they settled on this apartment or that—as long as she had a job. The urgency of it exploded inside her. She needed a job, as did everybody. Children's benefits weren't enough to live on. Nothing mattered until she had a job, and even the delay of a few hours, eating pizza and thinking, was life-threatening.

What kind of job? Anything, whatever there was to do, awful, tedious, insulting work, whose only reward was a smatter of cash. That would be just fine. In light of that, there was no point in touring all these other buildings on sore feet. She wouldn't find any new solutions.

They could waste time in a coffee shop instead.

Amber said they were going to forget it. Guy replied by banging his knee against his hockey bag. Amber returned to the student employment poster she'd seen and wrote the phone number in her grade twelve homework journal, and the name of the business. It was called Origin Marketing.

Amber gave Jesse's door handle a turn and found it locked. Everybody was out. The guy's car was there, though. Amber peered through the fogged front windows, looking for any kind of movement; there was only the static square of the window at the far end of the house. Amber knew she'd have to ring the doorbell to know for sure, but she felt paralysed, like a grade-schooler selling cookies. How on earth would she explain herself?

Guy made an annoyed sound in his throat, a plosive huff of breath, and that made it a lot easier, in a way. Amber jabbed the doorbell, listened to the muffled sound inside. She waited thirty seconds and rang it again.

"I guess no one's home," Amber pointed out.

"Where's Jesse?"

"Not here, obviously."

They stood on the porch. There was a piercing squeak from a bus out on Steeles. A pile of green willow branches steamed in a neighbour's yard.

"What time's he coming back?"

"I don't know."

"You could've asked him," Guy muttered.

Amber's response: "Shut up."

"You could've asked him."

"Well, I didn't." Amber stomped back down the steps and walked. Down Lowbank and around the corner was an elementary school, echoing with after-hours hollow. It adjoined a park and a playground—a sand pit with a wooden perimeter, wooden swings, wooden jungle gym, and a giant blue octahedron full of rope webbing. The playground was empty. It was December, after all, and practically getting dark. It seemed like Amber had spent an entire week at this time of day, when the sky was luminous but everything else cold and blue. The sand looked damp but safe for running shoes, and she sat in a swing.

Guy had followed her, loyally, and he climbed onto the swing next to her. They gazed over the skyline, Amber spotting more apartment buildings. She'd never noticed before just how many of them there were. They were everywhere. The focus of Guy's gazing was anyone's guess.

So, big surprise: they waited again. And this time they didn't even have a phone number.

Probably they should have been waiting where they could watch Jesse's house, instead of down the road and across a field. Watching something was exhausting. Amber was getting hungry again, too. It was ridiculous to be hungry so much.

For some reason she thought of a time in grade seven or eight when someone shoved a piece of paper into her hands while she got off the bus. She unfolded it, standing on the strip of grass beside the bus lane. "Dear recipient: You are one of the ten lucky persons who have been chosen blah blah blah..." She read the entire thing, as solemnly as if it were a class assignment, including the block-letter admonition about what would happen if she threw the letter away. She looked up and spied the kid who'd thrusted it at her, standing forlornly at the edge of the playground, looking for more takers.

There was a time limit: the letter explicitly laid out twenty-four hours for her to carry out its instructions. By 9:00 the following morning her fate would be sealed. She considered copying the letter out by hand, onto lined paper, but that would have been horrible and tedious. She couldn't photocopy it, either. When she got home she tried slyly asking her mother to use the family computer, but of course Mom could tell something was up, and she coerced Amber into blurting out her intentions, which, as it seemed Amber had known all along, were very, very dumb, whereupon she'd retreated to the last bastion of a teenager's non-dignity and burst into tears.

She and her brother finally started swinging, legs doubled up on account of the equipment being sized for little people. There was the hint of a breeze, just enough to make a sound in trees, and there was the soggy smell again, the smell of leaves. A damp film made everything a shade darker than normal, especially the playground sand, even the dulcet chains on the swing set, squeaking along.

"It's starting to snow," Guy said.

At first Amber didn't believe him, but then she could see a very slight texture in the air.

She checked her watch. It was 4:30. She left Guy on the swings to watch their stuff while she went to check the house again. And, of course, Jesse was there. He'd been there the whole time, why couldn't he hear the doorbell? Nothing could be simple for her. She ran back to the park, moreover, to discover Guy gone, and his bags gone, hers unattended where she left them. He'd gone strolling, apparently, down a trail into the woods, and he was perfectly fine, but of course first Amber had to stand there, pissed off, listening to the leaves and snow falling. When he came back she demanded a reason why he'd walked off and left her stuff in the middle of a park, and he called her a raging bitch. So she ran after him, forcing him to drop his own bags, and he got pissy about how it was all broken. She left him there and marched back to Jesse's by herself, granting that he could come back whenever he felt like it.

"I guess you're here again," Jesse said.

"I guess we're here again. *Fuck*," Amber huffed, daring Jesse to ask what had gone wrong this time. And yes, they could sleep in his basement again. He didn't make her beg or fight; he just wearily turned his back and went on down the stairs. Well, good. Amber had hoped to make it clear that she didn't want to talk about it, and he got the message.

Amber pulled a folded sheet of paper from her coat pocket, not quite remembering what it was. It had developed a vein-like pattern of wrinkles: it was the permission form for Guy's class schedule. The line at the bottom was still empty.

"Hey, can I have a Coke?" Guy asked, standing on the bed.

Jesse threw him one. The chair groaned as he leaned toward his DVDs. Amber rooted for her pencil case, happy that they were distracted with each other. She'd forged her parents' signatures on things before, things that had seemed like big deals at the time, like her practice record for music class. She remembered she'd tried to write her mother's initials, pretending at a loose, natural style of penmanship, and the result had been pathetic, but she'd meekly handed it in anyway. Guy's schedule, however, was actually important. If they discovered it was forged, they probably wouldn't just sigh and let it slide, like her music teacher had.

It would have to be a *good* forgery.

And it would have to be her uncle's signature, too, which Amber had never seen. Did he write out his name, or just initials, or what?

She opened her grade twelve homework journal and found a bit of empty space. She tried drawing the 'I' first, making a row of little squiggles. The letter started to look lazy, just a loop. That was fine; it was realistic. Because capital 'I's in script were disjointed, Ian probably never bothered to finish his first name, so Amber left it, and tried Drinkwater the same way: a 'D', a wiggly mound, the 'k' a spike upwards like on a seismograph. All the letters after that diminished into just a line. And that was it.

Would it pass for her uncle's?

They probably already had things from him on file.

But they wouldn't care enough to check this signature against any other ones. This paper wasn't *that* important; it was just to force kids to show their schedules to their parents so they couldn't take gym five times. The office person would just glance at the paper and then throw it in a drawer somewhere, never to see it again.

Amber scratched a few more practice runs into her journal then spread out Guy's schedule. She tried to hold the pen gingerly, and then she jumped into it—her tendons clenching, she made a mess of everything, flew over the cliff of the 'k', and then it was over.

Well, it looked like a signature. Mistakes were fine; people messed up their own signatures all the time.

She had no way to know if it looked anything like Ian's.

She could always say she lost the printout, ask for a new one.

Guy and Jesse were absorbed in the TV, some obnoxious show she didn't care about. Amber stashed the schedule in her backpack and turned her attention to the other business, the new phone numbers she'd duteously added to her journal. She asked Jesse if she could use his printer to make some résumés.

"Sure. Finding yourself a ball and chain, eh?" Jesse said.

"You bet."

Amber hooked his printer up to her laptop. Her résumé had the filename "Nice n' Desperate".

"Jesse," Amber said, "can I put my phone number as here?"

He looked away from the TV. "What are you talking about?"

"Can I use your phone number on my résumés?"

"Why do you need my phone number?"

Because I don't have my own, Amber thought.

A cell phone would have been useful right about then.

Jesse didn't care much about *why* she wanted to use his phone number. He said he'd gladly let her use it, except that it wasn't really his. The phone belonged to the family upstairs; whenever someone called for him, it was their phone that rang. The Dundases probably wouldn't like it if they started getting all kinds of calls for someone who didn't even live there.

"Okay, that's okay," Amber said, looking down.

"Okay?" Jesse echoed her, and went back to the TV.

So what the fuck was she going to do for a fucking phone number?

She licked her lips and typed in Jesse's after all.

Other than her name, it was probably the most honest piece of information she'd be printing out. Her employment history was a big zero, but she'd worked out impressive ways to describe babysitting and mowing lawns for neighbours: "child care;" "operating ride mower on irregular terrain." She printed three; Jesse noticed and invited her to do more. She could print two dozen if she wanted. Amber didn't know what she'd do with two dozen résumés but printed them anyway, weighed them in her hands when they were done.

So the paperwork was over with. Amber put the stack of pages, still warm from the printer, up against Guy's schedule in her backpack. The right thing would have been to get up right away, head back into town and spread them around as soon as possible, but her feet weren't interested. If she tried to relax for half an hour, it would turn into an hour, and then another, and by then it would be too late, and the whole thing would have to be put off another day.

"I might go out again pretty soon," she said to Jesse's back.

"Yeah?" he muttered.

Amber was still wearing her coat, and she idly stuck her hand into the front pocket. *How about now?* she thought.

But she felt a terrible disinclination. Apparently, she was too tired to dial Origin Marketing's phone number, as though to do so would take the same gathering of strength as to personally walk across the city. She turned her homework journal over and over, thinking, *I don't want to do this.*

She'd had a substitute teacher one day in the tenth grade, one who held whole-class discussions instead of following a lesson plan. She'd said, sitting on the edge of the teacher's desk, rolling one ankle around and around: suppose they were each given $86,400. What would they do with it? She guided the discussion toward the distinction between *spending* money and *investing* it. When spent, it was gone; it was a fleeting convenience that sizzled into the air and disappeared forever. But an investment never left you, miraculously. Everyone knew that investing was the better choice.

Then came the button on the end, the moral of the story. There were 86,400 seconds in a day. And what was the difference between *spending* those seconds and... yeah she got the point. So Amber got to her feet, stepped around Guy and excused herself to use the phone again.

It was time to account for the family in the house. One of the brothers was in the living room. The TV was on, but he wasn't watching it; he was sitting with a mess of magazines on the floor, going through them with a pair of scissors. There were voices from the kitchen; it sounded like Mommy had a friend over. Amber lingered at the top of the stairs, weighing the situation. Maybe she could get away with just nonchalantly strolling to the kitchen and asking.

Amber smiled thinly at the boy on the living room floor and trailed her finger along the sideboard. She took in the scene in the kitchen: Mrs. Dundas faced her at the kitchen table, leaning on her elbows with a pile of toast in front of her—four pieces of toasted white bread, nothing on them. She looked up. "Yes?"

"Hey," Amber said in a cardboard voice. "Can I make a—" She stuttered and bit her lip. "I need to make a phone call."

Mrs. Dundas looked like she thought it was a confusing request. Across the table was her friend, a woman wearing several necklaces, calmly concentrating on a mug of something that smelled like really rich coffee. Amber's appearance had caused an impasse; teenagers walking in always made adults stop in their tracks.

"Is that okay?" Amber asked.

Mrs. Dundas nodded slowly, perhaps unsure. Amber tried to reach the phone without having to step into the kitchen, leaning forward ridiculously, cantilevering one leg way up into the air, realising how dumb it looked while she was still doing it. The phone was cordless, and she was happy for the opportunity to vanish with it. Gently she pivoted around the corner while dialing, out of sight, trying not to panic.

The person who answered reminded Amber of the business' name, Origin Marketing. She called herself Tanya.

"Hey," Amber said. "I saw this poster, for student work..." What was she talking about? Her mind was blank. "Could you tell me what that's about?" she asked.

The first thing Tanya said was, "Are you a student?"

"Yes."

"And you say you found an announcement on a poster? Where about?"

"Just on the street," Amber said. "Uh, I forget where."

"Was it at school? Was it at Old Mill...?"

"I don't really know... I haven't been in Toronto too long. It was a poster. Near where I live."

Tanya launched into a speech that she'd probably given hundreds of times before; it started with more pleasantries, then got into details about the job: "You set your own hours and work wherever you want in town. It's *not* canvassing," she stressed, "and it's *not* telemarketing."

"Okay."

"So, we need to schedule an interview if you're interested?"

"Yes," Amber said, heartily.

Tanya hummed a moment. She said, "Could you come in today?"

"Today?" Amber echoed.

"If you can do it, could you come in today for five?"

One of the pictures in the hall was a wicker basket full of cone-shaped flowers. She stared into it like a mandala, thinking: she had nothing else to do that afternoon. Yes, it was sudden, she thought, and she hadn't wanted to go out again, but she'd never get a job, she'd never achieve anything, if she backed down from opportunities like this. 86,400 seconds. She said, "I can do that."

"All right," Tanya said pleasantly. There. Amber had a job interview in—she checked her watch—two and a half hours. She had to write it down, she had to note in her journal, "5:00 – Origin Interview." But her pencil case was downstairs, and she couldn't fumble for a pen on the kitchen counter because she was a stranger in the house, not able to just grab and use anything she found. So she dashed back to the entrance and downstairs, holding the phone against her ear. She burst back into Jesse's room; Guy was still on the bed, now lying on his side. Amber stepped over him.

Tanya was describing how the find the office. "Just a minute," Amber said while rooting through her backpack, squeezing the phone with her shoulder. Her pencil case was there, faithfully, and she whipped her journal open to the present day. Taking great care, Amber was sure to repeat each direction back to Tanya as she gave them, and then she repeated the whole sequence after it was done, and the two of them shared some delight that Amber had heard it all perfectly.

Amber wondered if her brother had figured out something important had happened.

"So," Amber said. "That's it?"

"Just let me tell you a few things about the interview," Tanya said. Amber nodded. What a thing to do while on the telephone. "First, there's a form to fill out, so be sure to be there about fifteen minutes early. Bring a notebook and something to write with."

"All right."

"And the interview process may last for up to ninety minutes. Would you be prepared for that?"

"That's fine."

"And it's going to be in a business setting," Tanya added, "so make sure to come in *business attire*."

"Okay," Amber said. The idea of a ninety-minute interview was serious, but with a dress code it was momentous, especially since there wasn't anything crammed in her hockey bag that could possibly pass as business attire. She tried to conjure up whatever the latest incarnation of business attire was: something made of dull-coloured fine-gauge fabric; a jacket with a big lapel and a knee-length skirt. How on earth could she draw something like that from her hockey bag? "You mean like…" she said.

"Business *casual*," Tanya clarified.

Did that just mean "nice" clothes, without pictures on them, pants that weren't blue jeans, a matching purse and shoes? Did it mean just not looking like a slob?

It seemed that was everything that needed to be said. The two of them exchanged goodbyes, and then Amber mashed the off button.

"What was that about?" Jesse asked.

Amber mildly remarked, "I got a job interview later."

"Really?"

"Yeah." Amber turned the telephone over and over in her hands. So she needed business clothes for a ninety-minute interview. She thought of asking Jesse for help, but she did a visual scan of his room first, and… Never mind.

Maybe a nice sweater would count as business casual. The nicest sweater she had was probably the one she wore right then. It was uniformly maroon, sewn down the trunk and sleeves into a raised pattern. It was halfway fancy, although in the past she'd slept in it. She'd slept in it for several days now.

She also owned one bowling shirt, white with yellow marks along the collar. Unmarked bowling shirts probably counted as business casual. That and her most decent pair of pants…

At 4:15 Amber was on a westbound bus, wearing both the sweater and the polo shirt. At first she'd pulled the shirt collar up through the neck of the sweater, but after a few minutes in public she'd decided it looked goofy, like a science teacher, and she stuffed it back down.

The bus was taking far too long to get where it was going. Standing in the aisle—it was rush hour—Amber kept compulsively checking her wristwatch. It being 4:15, she had only forty-five minutes to get to the Origin office. And that was not counting the fact that she had to be fifteen minutes early. Every time the bus stopped Amber cursed whomever had decided that they had to slow the trip down for everyone else, knowing, however, that if she wanted to get there earlier, it had simply fallen to her to leave the house sooner. She should have given herself a good ninety minutes. Instead she'd left Jesse's house at 4:00, a mere hour before she had to be there. And it hadn't helped that, just as a bus arrived, Amber found herself stuck on the other side of the intersection. She watched everyone at the stop get on, taking their time, and she was sure the light would change in time for her to dash across and get the driver's attention. At that intersection, though, the signals were stacked against her; they held and held, and the bus finished loading and idled and pulled soundly away, while Amber watched, desolate, wondering if the driver really wasn't obligated to look around for people like her, people obviously waiting to cross the road. All she could do after that was wait for the next one.

She couldn't be late, not for this. Yes, she'd had the grace to accept a same-day interview, but that was no excuse. Tardiness was a pointless problem, the hallmark of deadbeat employees who didn't care for their jobs much. If she stumbled into the office even five minutes late, it wouldn't matter how well she'd dressed.

And there was nothing she could do about it, ferried along by the bus, the pace entirely out of her control.

She wasn't familiar with the route either, so she couldn't reassure herself with knowing exactly how much further there was to go. Sometime in the future the bus should have been turning into Finch subway station. She then had to take the subway to another station called Islington. When she got into the subway and looked at a map, she was mortified to discover that Islington was way out west on the Bloor Line, almost as far west as you could go—so far out that it took her a minute just to find it on the map. When she got to the platform there weren't any trains in sight, and again she had to wait, again time was slipping by, and she ordered herself to stop looking at her watch as though it made a difference.

At that point she had to reach Islington station in only half an hour to entertain any hope of being on time, and she was discovering that the subway map placed all the stations deceptively close to each other. There was probably a whole two minutes between each one. She was full of ridiculous, indignant fury. At 4:45 she was just getting onto a Bloor train.

Imagine being early, striding into the place ten minutes ahead of time. What discipline. Inevitably, of course, Amber looked through the train window and saw the name of Islington glide past, carved into the wall. Many people in the car rose. At that moment Amber indulged herself to check the time once more: it was almost 5:10. What did bosses do while waiting for late people? She didn't want to think about it. Hell, it was a same-day interview. They could do it in eighty minutes instead of ninety.

Emerging from the subway, Amber felt as though she'd come up in the middle of a secret government facility, if there were such thing in Canada. It was a group of enormous plate-glass skyscrapers around a set of equally-proportioned residential buildings—and nothing else around. At least, it seemed like nothing, the buildings along Bloor Street being no bigger than two floors; it was that and suburbs. It seemed as good as nothing compared to the lonely monoliths that wished they were downtown. Amber had never been here before, but she could imagine the furor it must have caused with the old-timers, these buildings going up in their neighbourhood.

Were they designed gracefully enough, perhaps, to appease the nay-sayers? Amber decided they weren't. They were too flat and functional, assured of their own existence. It was good that she was thinking that way; those would be the challenges facing someone with a career in civil engineering.

And here she was, ten minutes late to her first job in that career, a job involving… she didn't know yet. Tanya hadn't told her.

Origin Marketing didn't have an office in the big buildings. It was in one of the two-storey strips along Bloor, above a store. Tanya had directed her to find a staircase around the back of the building; it was a wooden thing, like the one outside Ian's Silverthorne house, from the second-floor door to the third. At the top was a door that said Origin Marketing behind the glass. She was there.

As soon as she entered, she was no longer in a hurry; she forced herself to be perfectly calm, looking around at the place. It was a waiting room, with chairs around the walls, many of them already populated by other people, most of them dressed better than her. She was surprised; for some reason she'd thought it was going to be just her tonight. She saw a woman in a navy blue long-sleeved dress, and a man who had worn an entire burgundy suit. But it seemed there were also many others, like herself, who had just thrown together something "nice." At a desk facing the room a woman leaned on her elbows. She may have been Tanya, the woman from the phone, but she wouldn't have answered it from that desk, since there wasn't a telephone there. In fact, it wasn't much of a desk, just a cheap pre-fab bureau like her teachers had in high school.

Tanya made a general inquiry as to what program everybody was in, and for a moment Amber thought no one at all was going to answer. Then burgundy-suit spoke up, haltingly, to say that he was in business administration. One at a time, a few more people offered information, and Tanya said, "Uh huh." Amber located an empty seat. The floor creaked as she walked to it and sat down, gathering her backpack in her lap. There was a big white clock behind Tanya's desk; she'd arrived thirteen minutes past the hour.

"Excuse me?" Tanya called to her. Amber looked. "Do you want to fill out one of these?" She passed Amber a paper on a clipboard.

It was the form. Amber said thanks. "So sorry I'm late," she breezed. "I got here as fast as I could, but I thought…"

Tanya waved and placated her, saying it was okay, they were still in the middle of initial interviews. Adjoining the waiting room was a row of offices with sound-proof windows. Inside one of them Amber could see, at a desk facing the door, a big man in a dark purple suit, standing up and shaking hands with someone.

Up from Amber's clipboard stared a whole jungle of white boxes for details of her three most previous employers, and at least two other personal references. That was a bit optimistic, Amber thought. She moved the form over a little to look at her résumé. Her employment history was pathetic. She basically didn't have one. She had no personal references at all. Might Janelle count? Well, no. She didn't want them calling Janelle, not before she did herself.

She'd work with what she had. Teenagers' résumés always looked like crap, she reminded herself. Employers knew that, so her mother had reassured her, even though they sometimes did things like demanding several years' experience. Amber wasn't going to agonise over it; she simply copied her résumé into the form as it was, leaving spaces blank when she had nothing sincere to put in them.

The man in the purple suit came to his door and saw her. He raised his bushy eyebrows. "Miss, are you ready?" he said. He had a bit of a lisp, a weak 'r' in "ready".

Amber said yes and followed him into the office. She carried her backpack in one hand, low to the floor, and leaned it carefully against the wall. The man sat behind the desk. Amber hoped she was standing right. She hoped she was holding her hands right. She experienced a brief crisis over whether there were rules about her sitting down as well, whether to wait for an invitation—but she ploughed ahead and took a seat facing him. She tried to be completely alert, to herself, to purple suit man, to everything. Job interviews were governed by a lexicon of rules so vast that no one could hope to learn them all; she'd learned bits and pieces from different sources, and it was startling to suddenly have to remember them, like not tapping pens or fidgeting, not crossing the legs, making eye contact—she had to be on edge and have answers ready for every question, including silly riddles about jelly beans or manhole covers—"case questions" were apparently popular in job interviews, so she'd heard. And on top of all that, she had to appear perfectly relaxed, like it wasn't any effort at all, like she wasn't really doing everything she could to please this man. It was her first job interview.

"Well, Amber," the man said, reading her name. He ignored her personal résumé, studying only the Origin form. "Welcome to

Origin Marketing." Amber nodded and smiled a little. Then came his big hand across the table. Another of the big important things; Amber took it and measured a few shakes, hoping they were strong but not unnatural.

"My name's Mike," he went on, hissing the soft consonants.

Mike, not Michael. He didn't say anything else, examining her form in silence, so Amber thought it would be appropriate to respond, "Hello."

Mike made one comment: "No references?"

"No," Amber replied, grinning like there was some amusing reason for it. Miraculously, an excuse presented itself. "I wasn't sure you wanted my references," she said. "They're all long-distance numbers."

She really *wasn't sure* if *they wanted* long-distance references. She tried to force the blood back out of her face. It was her first lie in a job interview.

Mike didn't press the issue.

"Okay, Amber," the purple-suited man said, sitting up in his chair. Amber realised she'd been leaning over the desk, reading along with him. "So, how did you hear about Origin Marketing?"

"I saw a poster."

"Whereabouts?"

"Downtown. Uh…" Hadn't Tanya already asked her that? The thing was, she knew exactly where it had been; she could have taken Mike to the exact spot. But she didn't know how to describe it, the names of the streets. She said, "I guess I don't quite remember."

Mike wrote "poster" on the corner of her application. "Are you looking for part-time or full-time work?" he asked.

"Well, I'll be going to school starting in January," Amber said. "Until then I'll be able to work full-time. But when my classes start I hope I can do fewer hours, just because I'll be going to classes…"

"Oh, that's fine," Mike assured her. He didn't move his head at all; across the desk he looked like a talking pedestal, his gut filling out a purple sphere in his suit. His lips were big and limp; they wouldn't co-operate with his 'r's and 'v's. "You know that we let employees set their own hours," he went on. "So if one week you have a lot of schoolwork—" and he went on to describe meticulously exactly what it meant to set one's own hours. Amber nodded and said, "Okay," a lot.

"All right, Amber," Mike said at last. "You've passed the initial interview."

Amber smiled.

"What's happening now," Mike went on, "is I'm going to give a presentation that will last about an hour. Then there will be one more personal interview, and then we'll let you know whether we have a spot for you. You'll have an answer before you leave."

"Okay," Amber said. "Great."

Mike stood up; Amber rose in tandem and excused herself back to the waiting room.

About then Tanya told everyone to take the chairs from along the wall and arrange them in rows facing the desk for the presentation. Amber was surprised again; they didn't have another room? But she worked with everyone else, wordlessly co-operative, the floor creaking as they turned the waiting room into a presentation room.

And then Mike came out to give his talk. He brought with him a white board and a box of props. He mentioned that everyone could take notes if they wanted; Amber took it as an imperative. She pulled a white notebook from her backpack, the one she'd used for physics class, the one she should have been studying from, in fact, for her exam.

While Mike oriented himself she found an empty page and wrote down the date, considered a moment, and underlined it. In lectures over the last few months she'd developed an obsession with note-taking trappings like headings, indents, bullets and diagrams. When it came time to review, she figured, nothing could have been more wearying than having to face pages full of ragged notes that all dangled insignificantly from the left margin, pages like those some of her classmates had been scribbling out. In her physics lecture, Asian kids behind, beside and in front of her, Amber had been able to peer straight over the shoulders of the students in front of her, and very often she'd seen one of those horrible pages, pages with an entire lecture crammed into one run-on sentence. That was the sort of stuff Amber never intended to be faced with when it was exam time. And indeed, in a little less than a week it *would* be exam time.

Mike didn't have to work to get their attention. No one there knew anyone else; there was no chatting. He welcomed them all and said that he would be watching for audience participation while he talked. He outlined the segments of the presentation then began: the history of Origin Marketing. Mike described when and how the business was started and what its principles were—Amber wondered, was that important to write down? She made a few trite notes, in case name-recognition was necessary in the future.

At last, Mike started to broach the subject of what the job actually was. He approached it obliquely, however; he launched on a narrative about Origin Marketing's mission statement, building up a series of principles about mark-up and the value of a sales approach that focused on personal contact. Mike introduced a job title: the Independent Contractor. That was the suit she'd be wearing, a sales associate who promoted the product directly to consumers, not via ads or phone calls but privately, in person. Mike restated what Tanya had said on the phone, what the job was *not*; it was not canvassing, it was not telemarketing. The product was a set of knives from another company. "What are some of the benefits of selling products this way?" Mike asked. There were several right answers; anyone with a little sense would know about eliminating retail and getting more personal with clients, and in fact the obviousness of the answers made Amber hesitate. But, he'd said he would be watching for participation, so she'd participate. Mike fielded a few responses before Amber suggested that clients would feel more in control of the transaction if they were on their own turf instead of in a store. Mike nodded supportively.

He had a presentation kit. It was full of knives, an entire set, all different sizes, as well as free bonuses like corkscrews and scissors. Mike had them in order to demonstrate the sort of presentation all the Independent Contractors would be giving to their clients— after putting down a deposit for their own presentation kit.

The knives were pretty fucking awesome, as Mike demonstrated. He stoically exposited on how the handles felt, then he called upon members of the audience to try cutting through pieces of rope with different brands of knives. Amber passed on volunteering, in spite of wanting to do all the participating she could. She didn't want to go too far and be an attention whore. The woman in the navy blue dress was called upon to try cutting the rope using a blade of this patented design that combining the best of both straight-edge and serrated blades. It didn't cut the rope. Mike had to instruct her to try pushing down *and* forward—and she let out a vindicating gasp as the blade sliced through with one stroke. Everyone chuckled appreciatively. This was something they'd get their clients to do during their own presentations, first with their own knives. Mike asked, why would you get clients to use their own knives first? So that the Origin knives could then dazzle them with a superior performance. The knives did the selling for them.

Mike had some other tricks too; he borrowed a penny from an audience member, promising that he'd get it back, and he used the scissors to convert it into a corkscrew; again, everyone responded with chuckles as Mike handed the coin, mutilated, back to its owner.

The system was that Amber would have a number of prospective customers to choose from at any time, and she would call ahead, then arrive in person to repeat the pitch Mike had just delivered. Whether or not she actually made a sale, she got a commission of $22.50 just for making the pitch; however, if she did make a sale, she got a percentage, or the $22.50, whichever was higher. There was "a floor to stand on, but no ceiling," as Mike said. "You know that that twenty-two-fifty is there whether or not you make a sale, but the most you can make is..." He trailed off speculatively.

"Infinity?" Amber suggested.

Everybody laughed.

"Theoretically," she added, with a wan smile.

Soon Mike mentioned their first customers would be their family members. Amber looked up from her notebook. In their experience, it was a necessary part of the training. Why was it a good idea to start with family members, Mike asked. Because she'd have to practise the pitch; her first few tries were probably doomed to stuttering, awkward failure, so of course they had to be made to a sympathetic audience. Who could fill that role? Anyone she knew? The scant acquaintances she had in Toronto probably had little need of a new set of knives.

Origin Marketing would charitably supply phone numbers of the first few clients for her, mostly restaurants, or else old retired people with money to throw away. Each time she visited a client, Mike explained, she could slyly throw out the question, whether or not she made a sale: did they know anyone else who might be interested in learning about these products? If so, she'd ask the client to call them up—Mike asked, why would it be helpful for the client to chat up the product to his or her friends before the contractor visited them? Because friends trusted each other. They'd be more receptive if they first heard about the knives from someone they knew. And even if each client could only supply two other prospective clients, what kind of pattern would develop over time? Mike took the time to depict it on the whiteboard; if the first two clients each recommended the product to two others, then at the next iteration there would be four! And so on. She was assured that at some point she would find herself able to pick and choose from clientele, and then she could structure her sales so she'd never have to travel far from home, or whatever she wanted.

Amber squinted at the whiteboard, the way she'd scrutinised lecture notes that she didn't understand. It seemed a bit idealistic to think that every single person she showed knives to would give her two or more clients, as reliably as chemicals in reaction. She couldn't really picture people dashing to the phone after her presentation, the way Mike described it, bubbling with excitement about new cutlery.

In fact, Amber found it a bit far-fetched to imagine anyone even agreeing to invite her over in the first place. Who would ever respond to a phone call from someone itching to barge into their home or business to sell something? Amber did her best to ignore ads in general, muting the television during commercials, willfully resisting second looks at billboards and posters; who would ever concede to sit through a half-hour presentation? She wouldn't.

Nevertheless—it wasn't like she was selling knives to herself. Not everyone was like her. Amber's pen moved over her notebook, marking down promontory points in the discussion.

At length Mike wrapped up. Everybody clapped. He announced that he and Tanya would begin calling them into the offices for the final interviews, and they would indeed know, before they left the office, whether they had a job. The atmosphere in the room relaxed a little, but still, no one knew each other. Everyone waited in their own private space. Mike retired into his office, and Tanya reappeared, instructing them all, all the men and women in business attire, to pull the chairs back to the sides of the room, back into waiting-room mode. Then she passed out yet another form; Amber accepted hers with a smile. It looked like a quiz; there were questions followed by blocks of lines. The first one was, "What are three things you like about Origin Marketing?"

Amber didn't wait in suspense as Mike and Tanya began calling applicants for their final interviews. By then she was comfortable and even a little weary. It was dark out, she could see through the windows. She took her time on the questions; the second asked for three reasons the presentation was so effective.

At long last, Mike dismissed the last person from his office and came to the door. He caught Amber's eye and asked, like before, if she was ready. Amber followed him in and took a seat, this time not worrying about whether it had to be offered first.

The man had her application out, which he read over again with an air of restlessness. "Well Amber," he said. "You showed a lot of initiative during the presentation."

Amber nodded, without smiling, which would have been smug.

"So you worked mowing lawns?" he said.

It was a good thing Amber had chosen not to smile, because she suddenly felt persecuted. "Yes," she answered simply.

Mike nodded, not looking up; if he paused significantly it meant he expected her to explain more, probably, but he was busy reading the sheet. "What sort of pay did you get from that?" he asked. It was a vague question; Amber got the impression he just had to say something to fill time while he read. On her résumé she'd listed her grass-cutting employer as "Craig & Schartmann," which looked like the name of a business, while really it was the last names of the two old ladies who lived beside them. She couldn't tell Mike that her payment was a crisp twenty-dollar bill.

"Usually about twenty dollars each time," Amber said. Usually about, as though there were other complications that could change the fee, official things that would add cents and tenths of cents, like for a real job.

Mike went on through the other items on her résumé, asking more questions which might have exposed all the other half-truths and exaggerations she'd threaded in, but Amber was pleasantly surprised to find that she could side-step all of them. Then Mike got into the juicy questions, the main guns of job interviews. He folded his hands on the desk and asked, "So, what skills do you have that you could bring to this company?"

"Well," Amber answered, and an entire run-down of her virtues occurred to her smoothly and evenly, at the perfect pace to recite, all the while with gold-star eye contact. "I can follow complicated instructions, I'm able to work without supervision and motivate myself, I'm good at evaluating myself..." It wasn't hard to think up details like that. She'd never tried to enumerate them before because they were so pompous, like something off the back of a cereal box. But there, in the immediacy of her first job interview, all such inhibitions disappeared, and she was able to call up all the phrases she'd ever heard to describe perfect employees.

When she felt that she'd flattered herself long enough, Amber finished by trailing off, glancing into the distance and giving an abashed little smile to show that she was done. Mike smiled back, and asked his next question: "Why are you interested in working as an Independent Contractor?"

The wrong answer would have been that she just wanted money. Instead, she really liked the idea of setting her own hours and working in such a non-traditional environment, one that would force her to really take charge of her own career. "It would give me..." She grinned. "... psychological... and spiritual satisfaction."

Mike smiled back. She'd made him think he'd done her a favour. "What would you say might be your biggest weakness in the workplace?"

That was the big one; it was suicide to declare that she had no faults at all. The most potent way to answer that question was to put forward some negative habit that was really a positive habit in disguise: "Well, sometimes," Amber offered, "I have a hard time asking for help, because... I like to solve problems on my own." She effected a conclusory nod, but Mike looked unsatisfied. "That is, when I come up against a problem I can't solve, I want to just stick to it by myself, rather than running for help right away..." Amber had her hands curled in the air, gesturing along with her elaboration. "And that can be bad sometimes, because it means I use up a lot of time that would have been saved. If I'd just asked for help."

She couldn't have been less specific, talking about problems and help and time, in reference to nothing in particular. But Mike hummed with understanding. Eventually he sat back in his chair and said, lisping emphatically, "Well Amber, the hardest part of this job is having to decide who we can accept and who we can't accept. So it's my pleasure to say," he said, "you've got the job." Across the desk came his hand.

Amber's smile grew as she shook back. She'd done it; she'd pushed the right buttons. Apparently she was good at job interviews.

"Welcome to the team," Mike said, sitting back.

"*Thank* you," Amber gushed. Her smiling prompted him to smile even more. There were a few more details to discuss, such as the first training session being the very next day, for nine hours—in business attire, again, and Mike passed her an orientation booklet full of loose papers. Amber admitted that she was nervous because she'd never imagined herself doing work like this before; Mike said he understood perfectly. After all, he'd started out just like her, as an Independent Contractor himself. It wasn't that Amber was letting her guard down; that interview was just the beginning, after all. But she was hired; it was done. She'd done it.

Still in the midst of thanking the man and repeatedly announcing that she was very happy, she collected her backpack, stowing away the booklet, and then she left the office straightaway, walking through the waiting room without a pause, thinking that if she lingered a moment more she might ruin everything. She closed the door, and then it was behind her.

Nonchalantly she went back down the wooden stairs. So she was in, she thought. She had a job. That was that. And not a bland one; already she could imagine the little social brushes she'd have in the future: *I'm going to be busy tomorrow,* she'd say. *I'm working.* They'd ask her what her job was. *Selling knives,* she'd answer matter-of-factly, which sounded a little silly, but that was okay. It was interesting. If they were trying to work out a time to meet for something, she could add, *But I'll take tomorrow off if I have to. I set my own hours.*

Walking back out to the street, she looked up at the giant government facility buildings, lit up from within against the evening sky, modular, anonymous slabs that had never meant anything. But now, she could look up and see the ceilings of odd rooms, and think that someone worked in every one of them.

The streetlights were on, and there was a very light shower of snow, the kind that could only be seen in car headlights. There was a coffee shop on the way back to the subway, and Amber decided to reward herself. She'd earned it.

In the subway station she went to the gate by the booth, staffed by a man with black hair, overweight, the blue shirt forming a smooth, ironed slope down from his chin. He was reading a newspaper; Amber approached the window and stared at him until he noticed her.

"Just one," she said, sliding a ten-dollar bill under the window.

Silently the man slid back a five-dollar bill and the rest in change. Amber immediately pocketed the bill; there was a bit of a line behind her. She palmed the five dollars in coins. Half of it was to pay her fare, of course. Amber wasn't sure what happened then. She rooted through the coins with her fingernails for a second, as if to count them, then, perfectly blasé, she dumped all five dollars into the fare box.

The collector watched her do it, thumping his fists on the counter in bewilderment. "What are you doing!?" he cried. Amber's empty hand hovered over the box. It was too late; the box was sealed, welded to the counter, and the man's helpless screech pretty much informed her that he wasn't able to retrieve whatever went in there without a lot of trouble.

And there was a line behind her; "Never mind," Amber said, stuffing her wallet into her pocket, letting the fat man get back to his paper.

So suddenly a welt was slapped on the good tenor she'd brought away from her first interview. Her attitude before seemed absurd, as though if it had any substance it should have been able to totally deflect bitchy feelings from a random tiff like that. How could she go back to blissful daydreams about her future after pointlessly throwing away two and a half bucks? And it wasn't just the money, it was the attitude of that guy in the booth, him and his... So fuck it all; she wouldn't think about anything.

Standing on the subway platform, staring across the tracks at the engraved station name, Islington... *Selling knives. I sell knives, actually.*

Getting back to Jesse's house took another hour, but the trip back wasn't urgent. The time was relaxing. It was time to think. On the way some passengers had a fight on the bus. There was shouting, and the guy stood up in the aisle, grinning at everyone, though the girl wasn't letting him go, and she flung her purse at him over two rows of seats. The driver made an emergency stop, then the rest of them went on their way.

It was still snowing when Amber got back to Lowbank Court. The little particles churned like a fluid just below streetlights, the only place they could be seen. Already there was a film of snow on the ground, enough to leave footprints.

During the trip back, as it happened, Amber had decided how to handle her first sale. The only person in Toronto she could go to was Carrie Sykes. She was the only one with whom Amber could imagine treating the pitch with the levity it needed. Amber would play up the fact that she was "practising her schtick" rather than actually trying to sell something; afterward Amber would shrug ironically, they'd both have a laugh, and Carrie would triflingly sign the paper saying the pitch had actually happened.

Maybe she could do that for Jesse too. It was another $22.50, after all.

Could she make her brother sign off on a pitch too?

Jesse's car was at the curb, but with tire tracks still impressed in the snow, as though he'd gone out and just come back. Truthfully, Amber had looked forward to the possibility of him being out, of having to wait in the park again, in the snow. It would put off the necessity of calling Carrie and getting started. But she was also anxious to see her brother again and make sure he hadn't died in the four hours she was gone. She rang the doorbell, and through the fogged glass she saw Jesse's round figure charge up the basement stairs to let her in.

He said, "Hey, we were going to chill with some people for a while, but I thought we should be here in case you came back."

"Okay," Amber said, getting the message: her spontaneous outing had kept these people from enjoying themselves. They went down to Jesse's room; the smell greeted her once again, the smell of Jesse seriously needing to wash his sheets. Guy was lying on the bed, in almost exactly the same spot as when she left four hours ago. It was like he'd never moved, aside from taking off his sweatshirt. "Hey Amber," he said.

"Hey," Amber answered. She stood in the space between the bed and door, wondering what to do next.

"How did the interview go?" Jesse injected, bent over his computer chair.

"Pretty good."

"What place was it again?"

Amber resented the questions. It sounded like he didn't really care; he was just used to being nosy. "Some place," Amber said. Truthfully, the name had escaped her. Then she remembered: "It's a place called Origin Marketing."

"Uh oh," Jesse said. His voice was ominous.

"What?"

He didn't add anything; he just kept that stare on her, twisted over his chair. "Origin Marketing, eh? What'd they make you do?"

"They just *made me* go to an interview."

"You know about them, right?"

"I do now," Amber asserted. Of course Jesse was going to explain what the fuck his weird reaction was all about, but he was toying with her for the moment, making her squirm and worry, having fun criticising her.

"They're a kind of pyramid scam, aren't they?" he said.

Of course, Amber thought. Not that she agreed with him, but still: of course. There was just something apropos about the fact that Jesse would say that, that he would entertain such an image of the business Amber had visited in that creaky-floored building. Of course the system could be frowned upon. The whole Independent Contractor deal was after all so atypical, so that if Amber had found the whole experience, the entire hour and a half of interviewing and presentation-watching, saturated with a sort of surrealism, well, of course it was because of that. They'd given her an answer before she left. They'd booked her for nine hours of training before she left the office even once and had time to come down from the cloud. And the strange feeling she had about it, the way she was now remembering the whole evening, was somehow rounded out completely, bundled and tied, by the idea that someone, somewhere, would call it a *pyramid scam*.

"Well, take it easy," Jesse said at length, still in that ugly bent-over position. "Don't let them make you buy anything."

Guy had stayed out of it, quietly playing his video game. Amber tried to watch, but she couldn't sit down. She could barely stand in one place. "I've got to make a phone call," she said and walked out. She went up the stairs, but she didn't flow around the corner toward the kitchen and the telephone; she went straight out the front door. She wasn't running away this time, not like last night. She just went out, simply, into the street, and it was just like she'd left it, snowing and dark.

She hadn't changed her clothes yet. She was still wearing the sweater and bowling shirt. It looked retarded. She didn't own business clothes, and that was that. And in she'd paraded, her school backpack finishing the look, and they'd been so careful to emphasise, *business attire. Of course.*

In a bus shelter at Steeles Avenue was an ad for a newspaper, showing someone naked on the street with the words "Get the whole story" acting as a censor bar. She didn't catch the name of the paper, and she didn't look twice. She didn't want to catch it. That's what the ad was supposed to make her do. It was calculated to use her, to take her money, just like everything else. Were there payphones anywhere? Yes, there was a pair of them near the convenience store, under the awning. She *was* going to make a phone call. She'd put it off so much, but suddenly the delay seemed senseless, and dangerous, and she wondered how she'd ever managed to wait as long as she had.

It was after 9:00 in the evening, though. That was too late. If everything were fine—and she wanted to convey that everything was fine—she'd easily be able to put it off twelve more hours.

Fuck that.

She hadn't brought her homework journal, with her social worker's phone number. She'd scuttled out of the house without thinking; she'd have left her coat if she weren't already wearing it. But she thought she'd be able to remember, this time. That would help decide whether the call happened or not; if she could remember, it would happen. Otherwise, it wouldn't. Good. She'd already put in a quarter, but a recorded voice reminded her that she was making a long-distance call. She'd have to part with three more dollars. That almost deterred her—but, fuck it, fuck it. It wasn't like this call would cost her the last handful of change she had in the world. She picked through the pouch of her wallet, sending an army of coins down the chute, and hell, maybe Janelle wouldn't even pick up, and she'd get it all back.

The number communicated with Janelle's home phone, but Amber knew it wasn't her personal line. Her phone would be doing something different, ringing in a special way or somehow signaling that it was one of her clients calling.

Janelle said, "Hello?"

Amber had plunged into the call without thinking about what she was going to say. She was already tongue-tied, before even saying hello back. She was startled by how much she'd built up the momentousness of this call over the last few days, fretting about when and how it would occur. Now that she'd made it, the act seemed very sudden and slight. She panicked and jerked the receiver from her ear, almost of a mind to hang up—she'd thrown away three dollars for this, though.

"Hey," Amber said. She'd imagined that she'd work out an entire introductory speech to rattle off, laying everything out in easy terms. *Here's what happened, here's what I did.* For an instant she felt she could whip that speech out of thin air, like in the Origin interview. Words had come to her magically then. But now, incredibly, perversely, she didn't care. It was the moment to speak, and she had nothing to say. She just let the line sit, dead, waiting for Janelle's next move. Amber had called, after all, and that was what she'd promised to do so many days ago. She'd promised to pick up a phone and dial the woman's number; now she'd done that, and it was up to Janelle to make of it what she liked.

"Amber?" she said eventually.

"Yeah," Amber answered. A quick guess.

"How are you doing?"

"I'm a little tired. But I'm okay."

Janelle sounded very calm and officious. Apparently Amber had expected her to fuss like a worried relative. *Oh, thank God Amber, I was so worried—*

"Where are you calling from?" Janelle asked.

"A phone," Amber said, aware of what an evasive answer it was. She'd meant to say *payphone*, but some passive-aggressive impulse made her shorten it, turn it into useless information.

"Are you in someone's house?"

"No, it's a payphone."

"Well," Janelle said. "It's good to hear from you." She paused, and added, "... although I expected you to call quite a while ago."

The accusation went unsaid: *You disobeyed me.*

But she didn't say that. Instead she said, "I assume you've tried to get in touch with your uncle."

Amber felt tremors, being brought to face assumptions that she hadn't even known she'd made. Whoever thought Janelle would have been proactive, instead of just sitting and waiting? After that first evening had passed, the thing Janelle would have done—the thing she certainly *had* done—was to place the call herself, ringing up Uncle Ian's number on her own initiative. And an avalanche of implications poured out of that; if Ian had never answered the phone for Amber, he probably had never answered for anyone else. What would Janelle have done then, in the face of that bizarre, unsettling circumstance? Any number of things. Perhaps she'd called the landlord. Perhaps she'd also called the police.

"Yes," Amber said. "He's not there..." She said it timidly, wanting confirmation.

"Hm," was Janelle's response. "Well, do you remember, we agreed that you'd call the day you arrived in the city?"

And there it was, at last plainly articulated, absolutely inexcusable, and Janelle might have asked that expressly as reproof—in grade six on the school bus Amber and the girl in front of her were having one of those bitchy childish conversations where voices weren't raised but the air still burned, where the point was to get the last word, shame the other with logic. The girl was obviously the aggressor; she had to crane around in her bus seat, while Amber just sat naturally, arms around her backpack, minding her own business. The tiff had eventually come around, somehow, to a duel of math skills; bitchy-girl charged Amber with multiplication: "Six times nine," or something. Amber had announced the answer in an instant. Then it was time for her to return the challenge; she'd always found sevens and eights the hardest, so she said, "Seven times eight."

The girl's face had lost all life signs for a moment. "What?" she said.

Obviously the little shit was pulling a charade to buy time, pretending not to have heard a question spoken straight to her face. But Amber never called her on it; she just repeated, "Seven times eight." By then the bitchy girl had of course drudged an answer out of her head and spat it smugly, and then she sank back down into her seat as though tired of wasting time, but Amber knew she'd lost. She'd been out of her depth as soon as math happened.

Amber always wondered, why hadn't she spoken up, called the little princess on her bluff and forced her to confront the fact that she was retarded? She just hadn't, and it didn't matter any more anyway. It had been almost a decade ago.

Then, as the snow continued to fall in the parking lot, as Amber slouched over the payphone, digging her heel into her ankle, her social worker had asked her that incredulous question and Amber said, "What?"

What if she'd just admitted, frankly, that yes she did remember that her call was three days late? Because that would have meant that she'd deliberately broken their agreement, out of malice, inconsiderateness, some other ugly quality. And that wasn't true. She'd delayed the call, day after day, because she hadn't wanted to just throw her problems back at Janelle, as if the woman's job was to drag her by the nose while she did nothing but sob into the phone. Well, maybe that *was* her job, for other clients. But it wasn't for her, not for Amber Drinkwater.

Janelle took Amber's answer as a request for clarification; she listed all the details of their agreement, which Amber already knew. "Yeah, yeah," Amber said.

"Where's your brother?" Janelle asked.

"He's in the house. He's fine."

"Whose house?"

Amber distilled everything into the remark, "I'm staying with a friend of mine."

"Who?"

"He's—she's someone I know at York University."

At the last second Amber had decided that a female friend would seem less dangerous.

"Name?"

"Carrie," Amber said.

"Can you give me her phone number?"

Janelle was sure plumbing for information. Amber didn't think she was writing it down, since there weren't beats between her questions, which meant she was just demanding details to catch her lying. And indeed, confounded by her own lie, Amber didn't know which phone number to give, Carrie's room or Jesse's house. The lie might be exposed if Janelle called either of them.

"I don't know it by heart," Amber said. "It's in my address book—I don't have it with me. I could—I could find out for you... Just, like I said, I'm at a payphone right now, I just remembered..." Lies and excuses would fail her soon, but she didn't have anything else at her disposal. "I went all the way to Ian's house, but he wasn't there," she managed to blurt. "I went all the way there, myself..."

"Well, Amber, it's good to be in touch with you." Janelle breathed into the phone. "May I ask, how much money do you have left?"

That was a prelude to something. "Like, I think... five hundred dollars."

"I want you and Guy to come back to Ottawa. Tomorrow."

Amber tried to twist up the phone cord. Protected by a metal casing, it wouldn't curl very tightly.

"I'll buy your tickets for you," Janelle said.

It was a perfectly plain instruction, but—"But what about our stuff?" Amber asked. "It's going to be delivered tomorrow."

"I've had the delivery delayed."

"What about Guy's school?"

And of course Janelle had an answer to that as well, which she patiently explained. In light of Uncle Ian's vanishing act, the move to Toronto had to be aborted. Amber considered it a bit of a thoughtless request, considering the amount of footwork she'd done since Saturday, trying to settle herself. What did Janelle think she'd been up to? It was like getting called out of her room by her parents, as if they thought anything she did by herself was second-fiddle and could be shelved at a moment's notice.

At the same time, she would be happy to quit sleeping on the floor. It would be an end to the mystery and anxiety. She tugged at the sweater, the bowling shirt.

"Okay," she said.

Janelle would let them find their own way to the train station tomorrow. As far as Amber knew she could have sent police cars after them, but she hadn't. Maybe that counted as giving them another chance.

She heard a car drive through the parking lot. Some guys shouted at her, showing off for each other. She pretended not to hear. The car's engine howled excitedly. Amber could tell it was leaving, and she dared to look then. It was a little black car, and she couldn't see inside even though the windows were down.

Assholes.

Amber listened along while Janelle went to her computer and booked the tickets. She listed off the possible times, and Amber picked one in the afternoon. A concession reached, the phone call petered out with pleasantries. Janelle assured her that they would locate her uncle as soon as possible and admonished her to always keep in touch, no matter what happened. They said goodbye. Amber added, "Thank you," just before hanging up. It was timed, she hoped, so that the woman couldn't slip in an answer, so that Amber could have the last word.

CHAPTER 5

On Wednesday morning Amber slept in. First she woke up at 8:00; three days out of the week she had early classes, and she was used to it. The air was humid, smelling like bodies; Jesse's little fan didn't seem to do anything. Amber turned stiffly on her side, feeling her spine strain, glad that it was her last time sleeping on a floor.

She woke an hour later, on her back with a view of how the casters on Jesse's computer chair were wearing ruts into the carpet. As for an itinerary for the day, she didn't have one. She was happy resting, whether or not the room smelled like sweat and grease, whether or not the floor felt like cement. They had to be downtown by 3:30; they didn't have to get up until after noon if they wanted.

Once Guy had been watching a movie and had shifted on the couch during the scene where the main bad guy was having sex with his girlfriend. "Guy's getting comfortable," his sister had snarked.

"Hey chaps," said Jesse.

"Hey," Amber answered, over the sound of the computer starting. "What are the odds I can take a shower?"

"Uh, well, I have to take one too, you know. They don't like it when I run up the utility bill," Jesse added. "But, yeah, sure."

Guy borrowed a towel that Jesse obviously used himself, every day. Then Amber shut herself in the little basement bathroom until she'd got dressed and completely dry; it probably took longer than half an hour. But the boys didn't complain; when she went back to the room they were—surprise, surprise—playing games.

Amber figured she'd probably never see Jesse again, except if she stayed on speaking terms with Carrie and the two of them kept going out—but Amber didn't think Carrie cared much for her. At any rate, she wasn't moved to give the boy an extensive farewell. It was awkward. He'd put up with a lot from her, showing up day after day with her brother in tow, so she owed him *some* gratitude; at the same time, she didn't like him. He and his room were disgusting.

Her brother, though, had asked for Jesse's e-mail, and he supplied it on a scrap of paper. It wasn't until then, in fact, that Jesse even knew they were leaving Toronto. "Give me a shout when you're back in this part of the woods, eh?" he'd said. Good, then. Her little brother could patch up the relationship. It made sense. The two of them had been hanging out constantly. They'd watched TV and played video games while she went out and tried to fix their lives.

They climbed the basement stairs for the last time, bags back on their shoulders for the last walk, and Amber said goodbye. Jesse followed them to the front door. Then they went out to the street, and that was that.

It was raining. It had gone back up above freezing, and the occasional remains of yesterday's snow were brown and icy. By that time many of the trees had finished shedding, although the sugar maples across the court still held patches of yellow. One was awkwardly bare on one side, like half-eaten food. As for the leaves on the ground, they were flattened by the snow, swept off the road into drifts against the curb and under hedges, drifts that would stay soggy forever. Around sewer drains they were beaten into a brown paste. Without the voluminous effect in the sky, now that the tree branches were empty and black, the leaves looked desolate and dirty; they looked like a mess. They were mixed up with garbage, with paper coffee cups.

"So, that's Toronto," Amber remarked as they walked to the bus stop.

"Huh," Guy said. "I wish Uncle Ian would turn up."

He still wished that, even after all the effort his sister had made for him.

Never mind, she thought. *It's over with.*

Compared to Saturday evening when they arrived, Guy looked feverish. He was pale and callow in the cheeks. Or maybe it was just the light. Well, when they went back to Ottawa he'd hopefully have a proper place to sleep, maybe even access to real food. Would he be going back to his old school, for the time being? It would be awkward to see his friends again after saying goodbye, after going through the child's tragedy of having to move to a different city because of forces bigger than himself. Amber didn't know what they were going to do with themselves. Where were they staying? Their old house in Cantley? Sure, it was Janelle's problem; that was what she resigned herself to by following the woman's instruction to abandon her life here. What if they just repeated at the Ottawa train station what had happened here, Saturday evening?

Amber had also bid farewell to her own friends, and one friend in particular: her name was Kathleen, and Amber had really said goodbye to her months ago, in July, at the end of high school. She'd annoyed Amber considerably in her last few years. Amber had English first thing in the morning, and the classroom was in a wing that joined the rest of the school by one wide staircase, and every morning after first period Kathleen would be waiting for her there, whether Amber liked it or not, grinning, almost as though she knew how annoying it was.

They crossed to the north side of Steeles Avenue, technically waiting for the bus in Markham. According to the schedule, it was ten minutes late, but Amber had figured as much based on the number of people there. Good thing they were heading down two hours early; the TTC wouldn't fuck her up this time.

Guy asked, "Can I get a Nintendo DS?"

"No," Amber replied. Guy just looked up the road. "We don't have money," Amber added.

Still, Guy was quiet. Fine then, she'd drop it too. Apparently it wasn't worth fighting for; he put the question out, and when it came up negative he pretended he'd never asked it. She was being treated like a mom, Amber mused.

But she wanted to do something before they left the city, some frivolous thing with money. She felt like the entire stay in Toronto had been a holiday, to end as soon as they got on the train. With nothing to do that day, yes, she'd taken the liberty of sleeping in, but it was only a little after 1:00; even imagining that it would take an hour to get back to Union Station, they were still early. She'd been spurred as much by a desire to get out of Jesse's room as by a precaution against missing their train. Nevertheless, they were left with a little spare time before they had to be there with their tickets, a maddeningly moderate amount of time, not enough for something like a movie, but too much to just waste on a bench in the Union Station atrium.

"Do you want to do anything before we go?" Amber asked her brother.

"We could go fuck quadruple paraplegics," he answered.

Amber looked among the other people at the stop. They were all so polite; they pretended not to have heard. "What the hell's wrong with you?" she said.

Guy gave her silent treatment. If she didn't know, he wasn't going to tell her.

"Fine, you can have a Nintendo thing," Amber hissed. "Eating's nice too, though."

"It's not just your money," Guy said.

"Janelle gave it to me."

"They were my Mom and Dad too, you know."

Was there nothing he wouldn't blurt to a sidewalk full of strangers? He'd said it with such clarity that he'd obviously been planning it in his head for a while. Amber felt blood in her temples. "Shut your mouth," she said.

And Guy did.

It was strange to think that not too long ago Amber had unlocked the door to her residence room at University of Ottawa, carrying coffee and a slice of chocolate cake—study food. She shared a room with an art student, and was still expecting that, living together, they would get on speaking terms eventually. But the other girl had a swearing problem, and it turned Amber off every time she had to listen to it. On opposite sides of the room, their living spaces were both depressingly messy, the main offence being an acquisition of papers that kept getting shoved under their beds. Amber's calculus homework was open on her desk, fighting for space with her laptop. The message waiting light on the phone was blinking. One of the secretaries from the housing office had called, saying someone named Janelle wanted to contact her.

The bus arrived, spraying slush all over the sidewalk. The few closest people tried to hop out of the way, with varied success. Following Guy's little episode, Amber abandoned her plans to do something special before they left the city. They would sit in Union station until 3:30. After they found seats on the bus, Amber felt something wrong on her arm, and she realised she wasn't wearing her watch. Automatically, she said, "Fuck." She'd taken it off the night before and left it at Jesse's; the bus doors were closed, and they were already on their way. If she'd noticed less than a minute ago, before paying her fare—she couldn't be without a watch, not when they were catching a train—surely Jesse could mail it to her. She experienced a frantic fit of mourning. Why had she not remembered her watch, this of all mornings? Reflexively she checked for her wallet; it was in her pocket. But no, they couldn't go back now. It would cost another fare, not to mention the opportunity for her brother to huff and snarl like a little shithead.

Coming up from the subway, crossing a thin aisle, they entered Union Station, and Amber found herself in a place she'd never seen before. It seemed to be the hub for GO trains, and while it was technically an open concept it still seemed like a labyrinth. Expecting to discover a way up to the atrium, the familiar place where they'd waited on Saturday, Amber just walked straight ahead. Soon she saw stairs, but they were choked by a threatening "Fare Paid Zone" sign. They found themselves in front of the something called the Air Canada Centre. Did Union Station have an airport?

There was nowhere to go but back. Amber tried to backtrack; but they couldn't have made any different decisions that first night. Where the hell were they? Where was the Union Station she remembered?

Amber was waiting for her brother to speak up and call her on her ignorance. She dared him, silently, once she'd changed direction one too many times.

Guy said, "You want to get something?"

He was talking about the Tim Hortons in a little food court.

Amber said yes. Being in a train station, the line was spastic. At that moment it was long enough to give them time to think. The place piped the coffee-cake scent of its wares liberally; it was their marketing strategy. Indeed, there was even a poster reading, "Enjoy the aroma." The storefront was a peninsula jutting from the wall; through a door Amber could see the white kitchen, a desk with a shelf of coloured binders.

There was a short woman at the cash with a sing-song way of talking, and she wore eyeglasses that hung from the hinges of her ears, sliding down her face. She had a helper who was twice her height and never talked.

What Amber noticed was the print-out taped to the front of the showcase: "Now Hiring: Kingston Rd. Storefront." Things looked so wide open sometimes. That was the sort of job she should have been looking for; it was what she *would* be looking for, whenever the time came. It was her turn to order. The woman said, "And for you?"

Amber ordered coffee for her brother, not bothering to ask if that was what he wanted. "Any doughnut, any muffin today?" asked the woman. She was a good choice for that job, sounding so pleasant that she could force doughnuts right down Amber's throat without seeming pushy.

"Here, I'll get you something from there," Amber said to her brother, waving at the showcase.

"Are you sure?"

"Sure, I'm sure."

The cashier's nametag said "Sanzida." After splurging mightily for a cheesecake, Amber said, "And, you're hiring right now?"

"Cheesecake—yeah, you want a sheet?" Sanzida asked. She looked for an application form under the cash register. "You work here, help me?" she said, smiling. "You start right now?" Amber smiled back, and fussed with her wallet. "No, no pay for coffee!" Sanzida announced, pushing the form and the coffee across the counter. "You work here now."

Amber brightly said thanks and took her order away, wanting to escape before the corona of friendliness got to her. They sat down near the "Enjoy the aroma" sign; the spot smelled like cleaning chemicals. As soon as Amber looked closely at the cheesecake she knew it was a mistake. It was a puck of corn starch with some blue stuff on top. The smell was too strong and mellifluous; Amber salivated dryly, and her tongue swelled in her throat. She wasn't hungry, not for that. Why the hell had she bought it?

"You want to work here?" Guy said.

That sounded like a scoff. "Why not?"

"Aren't you going to eat that?" Guy asked of her untouched cheesecake.

"Yes," Amber told him, and she did, filling out the form meanwhile, noting her weekly availability as "free," drawing arrows all over the calendar to show that there was nothing else going on in her life at that time. What about a phone number, an address? Kissing her teeth, Amber filled in the information as it would have appeared last August, before she'd left home, except she pretended her street address existed in Toronto, not Cantley. It wasn't like they really checked up on that.

Amber wanted to check how much time they had before the train left, but she just reminded herself of how stupid it had been to forget her wristwatch. She was sure, though, that they still had the good part of an hour, much more than adequate time to find the big atrium and pick up their tickets. Amber got the attention of Sanzida and gave her the completed form. "I get the manager for you," she said.

"That's not necessary," Amber called, but Sanzida had already disappeared into the back.

A man emerged. "You're Amber?" he asked. He seemed nervous, the way he leaned forward, his arms bent as if to receive something. Amber stood up as he walked out to the dining area; he took her to a table and introduced himself as Ash. Amber understood that this casual sit at a Tim Hortons had suddenly turned into another job interview. That awareness came back, the conscious nonchalance, just like last night. Ash looked through her application, nodding wisely. What he told her was that they were hiring immediately, and when could she start?

"Actually..." Amber said. "I was hoping to start in at least... a few days."

"The stores are short-staffed now," Ash told her.

He spoke so emphatically, it bordered on begging. Judging by the specks of icing on his uniform, he had been in the back doing the baking himself.

"That's too bad," Amber said.

"So if you want I can hire you on the spot. You can come for training tomorrow."

And they were all set to go. Amber felt incredible shame, as though she'd just pulled a prank on Ash and Sanzida and all the other workers, a prank that had flown out of control. Ash had written "Thursday" on the back of her application and drawn a box around it; that was tomorrow, her first day. But there was no way that could happen. "It's just," Amber said, "I'm on my way home right now, and I'm not really sure when I'll be back..."

Ash traced the box around "Thursday" until there was a trench worn into the paper. Amber glanced at her brother. His back was to her; his iPod earphones had appeared on his head, by themselves, a signal to her that he wasn't paying attention.

"What time tomorrow?" Amber asked.

"Say, eight o'clock to one in the afternoon, just a short shift to start?" Ash's attitude became warmer; he described how simple the job was; it was just serving coffee. The owners of the Union Station store also owned another store to the east, on Kingston Road, where employees were trained, because it was a bigger store and generally a bit slower. Ash smiled. They were short-staffed there too.

Sometimes things happened that were out of place, and when everyone else acted like they were perfectly normal Amber felt a vaguely terrifying sense of disorientation, like when she accidentally had a heavy sleep during the day and woke in the afternoon, her internal clock flipped on its head. And there had been plenty of opportunities to feel wrong over the last few weeks, like there was something missing, something she didn't understand. But she knew one thing: she'd come to Toronto expecting a life that all came together, and here it was, coming together.

"Okay," Amber said.

Ash repeated 8:00 for the start time, and Amber agreed that it was acceptable. The shift would only be five hours long, an easy start, all fine. She didn't have any other plans for Thursday, after all.

"Can I just say, though, don't try to call me at this number," Amber said. "I'm getting a new phone number soon…" She tapped mildly on the application. "… so don't try to use this one. I'll give you the new one when I have it."

"But, see," Ash said nervously, "we have to be able to call you in case something happens."

"Yeah, I know. I'll have the new number by tomorrow, though. Can I just give it to you then?" Ash still looked uncertain. He circled her phone number, around and around until there was another trench of blue ink. As though he had to mark up the page to think. "I mean, that one will *work*, for now… If you want to call me before tomorrow… Will you have to?"

"As long as this is a good phone number," Ash said. "As long as we can call you."

"Yeah, that's a good number," Amber said.

"You want to see the back?" Ash offered, flicking his head toward the kitchen. "Come, I can tell you about the job—"

There were two problems. One: did they have time? They still had to pick up their tickets. And two: Guy. Amber could tell he was concerned. In spite of the fact that he pretended to be minding his own business, he made tiny movements of his head to check on her. He would wonder where this was going. Well, he could keep on wondering then.

"Guy, I've got to stay for a bit," Amber threw at him, briskly, as she strode away with Ash. He looked up, confused and resentful, seeing her escape without explaining herself.

Ash took her through the staff door and into the back room. It had white tiles on the floor and a strange plasticine-like material on the walls. He showed her the sinks, the walk-in freezer, and the little oven for doughnuts that he said worked just like an EZ-Bake Oven. Amber nodded along with everything. She could do it for a few days, certainly. But on Monday, she mentioned, she had to be in Ottawa, for her exams. She couldn't work on Monday. Ash told her to relate that to the Kingston Road manager.

And she had to find a place to live. She had to, she had to. They weren't hard to come by. She could just walk into the cheapest-looking place and wait until one of the tenants got shot, and then there'd be a free unit.

And she could always just climb the stairs, get their tickets, get on board and let Toronto slip away behind her.

Ash smilingly announced that there wasn't much else to show her, and that he had to get back to the baking anyway. Amber thanked him and let herself out to the dining area that smelled like chemicals. Guy turned to her.

Amber said, "So, you can make it back to Ottawa by yourself, right?"

He didn't answer for a while. "I don't know," he said.

At 4:00 Amber was standing in the Union Station atrium, looking up at the giant departure board. There was no more changing her mind.

At 5:00 she ran up University Avenue, looking for food. There was a promising place, a little restaurant close to Front Street, but it was too little, with only a standing-room counter along the window, and all the raw food was piled up behind the counter, behind the one chef who talked into a cordless phone while she chopped celery, not even acknowledging her arrival. Well, fuck her, and the restaurant could thank that girl for losing her business.

As she passed a cluster of orange cones on the sidewalk, Amber dared her brother to wear one of them as a hat. He did it, walking along in broad daylight among the University Avenue businessmen. They passed an awning that said "Private Residences." It reminded Amber that she'd have to make runs to apartment buildings again; cheaper ones, obviously, than the one in front of them on University, with the awning and the glossy pebbled exterior and the two security guards in the lobby, but she'd harbour no more illusions that even the dingiest place would cost any less than six or seven hundred dollars a month. Landing a job had singly made the cost of things a lot less intimidating.

It was also high time to crack open her notes for her physics exam. She had less than a week to prepare. She had so many things to do, but that was life. Life was about getting from morning to evening and handling everything. It was late afternoon and daylight was almost over, but there were still many hours in the day, poised before her like thick slices of bread and, anyway, it had been the sort of overcast day when it never really got light to begin with. It was astonishing to think how that very morning she'd considered sleeping straight through to the afternoon.

Additionally, she needed a phone number now for her new employers. Suppose she got a cell phone, before the end of the day. Would it be worth it, acquiring a new piece of equipment, creating a new expense?

She'd indifferently walked past a thousand cell phone stores before, and she imagined they weren't hard too find. Perhaps there would be such a store right on University Avenue, although storefronts in general were scarce there. It was a street of offices, generally smaller than the soaring towers on the next street over. In a way, being in the shadow of taller buildings was a boon for these ones. Relieved of the burden of defining the skyline, they were a bit quirkier. For example, there was a pair of boxy grey buildings with blue glass, both looking like barely-finished toy models. One of them had a column of rounded galleries, and above the column, on the roof, was a chunk of bare framework, extending the pattern of the galleries upward as though there had been three more floors planned. The other building had a grandiose Y-shaped detail up the middle, like the casement of a church organ.

And there was a Rogers store on the ground floor. Even though she was looking for a cell phone place, she didn't clue in right away that there was one right in front of her. Instead of crossing the street and going in, Amber kept on walking. She promised herself she'd go in the next one.

No. No, Amber. You're going back and you're doing this, now.

"Hold on," she said to Guy. "I've got to go do something." She said it like she just had to find a bathroom.

"What?"

"A phone. For me." The full term "cell phone" stuck in her throat, like it was something to be ashamed of. The amount of attention she'd given to telephones in the last week was astounding. She ran across the street, not bothering with crosswalks, and she sensed Guy hanging back, confused about this latest move of hers.

Amber prepared a dissertation of exactly what she was there for—just a cell phone, only the basic package please, the bare minimum necessary to get a phone number in her name. She wasn't one of the idiots who wanted cameras and Internet and all that. Directly inside the door was a shelf with some models: Motorola, Samsung, Nokia, Sony, Audiovox, pamphlets, pamphlets. The place had a serious hush, like an office.

Amber slowly stepped around the partition and saw a man at a round table. He was dressed in a striped black shirt, and he had an earring. Amber must have seemed solicitous; he looked up, asked if she needed help. "Yeah," Amber said. "I need to buy a cell phone." *Duh*, she thought. What a thing to say in a cell phone store.

An older man was doing some business at a counter, carrying a computer in an officious grey slipcase. Amber wished her own could have been on display at that moment, but it was stashed away in her giant, bulging hockey bag. And she wished she could have been dressed in polyester instead of a dirty white winter coat.

She was invited to sit down and chat, time permitting. The store had an alternate entrance by way of the building's small lobby; she heard the titter of the door opening as Guy went to wait in there.

"I'm really just looking for something basic," Amber said, sitting down, her coat collar bunching against her throat. "I need to get a phone for work."

"Something basic?" the man repeated.

"Yeah," Amber said.

Already the earringed man probably knew what he was dealing with, a young woman who didn't dare presume to say anything specific. She didn't know what to ask for and what could be taken for granted; she didn't know what a reasonable price would be. She was throwing everything at this earringed man, expecting him to tell her what she wanted, which was probably his job, but still. "Something basic" would mean whatever he wanted it to mean. So Amber would behave as defensively as possible, frowning shrewdly, giving vague, noncommittal responses, as though she wasn't an ignorant customer but, perhaps, a corporate spy, only pretending to be an ignorant customer.

"If you want just a really good, solid start-up package—" he said, getting up to visit one of the displays. Amber followed him, concentrating vaguely on what he was saying, mostly looking at his earring, a matte silver ball post. Call display? Well, that would be good, but not necessary. She wanted *basic*—He drew Amber's attention to a cardboard stand-up for Virgin Mobile. The marketing strategy was a play on defaced photographs, smiling black-and-white faces with scribbled-on devil horns, plenty of little scribbled hearts. The word "Virgin" appeared in fluid letters, in a red blob. The cheapest option was to get a mini mobile for $69; it was illustrated with the price in a little heart. She could subscribe by the minute or the day or the month.

As for customisation… Amber nodded quickly and said yeah, well, that wasn't a big issue for her. Skins and ringtones and display pictures, she wouldn't fuss over those. She could picture that group outside Carrie's window that night, one of those aimless clusters of student drunks, using their cell phones to call people standing next to them. Those people would obsess over things like ringtones.

She swallowed carefully, feeling a little feverish, uneasy in her stomach. Was this really so nerve-wracking?

"I guess I see no problem with this," Amber said.

That was too fast. She wished she could have asked about something, argued, found more details, but she didn't know what else she wanted; it was a phone, it would ring, and she could answer it. So the guy went to a file behind the counter and printed out a contract, faintly watermarked with a giant Virgin logo, the size of the entire page.

Amber had scorned cell phones before because she hadn't needed one; nobody in high school really did, and it was only a trapping of vanity to own one. Amber remembered when a girl in a black dress had made a call on her cell in the student centre. *Talking on your cell phone! Why don't you talk on your cell phone!* This was at the beginning of the decade, in a high school in Cantley, not exactly a metropolitan place. Amber had been with Kathleen, eating lunch, splitting a box of Junior Mints, and she didn't look to see what the girl had done then; the incident died out anticlimactically, as expected. But it was terrible to hear.

And now Amber was signing the bottom of this contract. The earringed man signed also, a giant loopy thing that went all over the place. He unlocked a storage unit and brought out a red box, her new phone. He ripped it out of the bag and activated it for her while she watched. And then it was time to pay. The hardware as well as the start-up plan would be sinking her almost $100. Amber picked through her wallet for her debit card, resolving to check her balance at the first opportunity. The man jammed the phone back into the box, they smiled at each other, and Amber left, in pursuit of her brother.

The building had a tiny lobby with nothing in it but a cut-rock fountain that had been brought to Toronto from Switzerland, according to the plaque. Guy was sitting on some steps beside it. He was watching videos on his iPod.

So, that was one thing out of the way. Next was what place to call home for that evening. There was no way they were going to find an actual apartment that very day. What were the other options?

- The gutter.
- A hotel.
- Jesse.

She couldn't call up Jesse again. Not after the snobbish way she'd left him that morning.

- Carrie.

Maybe.

- Uncle Ian.

As time passed Amber found she cared about her uncle less and less; his case was filed away in her mind with other nagging responsibilities, like flossing. Hers had never been a family in which relatives kept in touch. She knew Ian, and her mother's two brothers, one set of grandparents but not the other. Her cousins were dim figures to her; she didn't even know how many she had. Anyone further removed than that was a mystery. She was concerned about Uncle Ian, but it was like the concern for a stranger.

Why had she just blown a hundred bucks on a cell phone she didn't want?

Sitting on the steps in an office building entrance, Guy told her she looked like she was about to barf.

"Do I?" Amber said. "Huh." She wanted coffee again. And she was breathing through her mouth. Water trickled in the fountain. The elevator opened behind them, and a person stepped past them to leave the building. They were obviously in the way. Amber started the chore of standing up and hoisting her hockey bag.

"We need to figure out where we're staying tonight," she announced, and then she experienced a round of dizziness. The lobby disappeared in a cloud of black snow, and she felt her shirt, dingy with sweat, heavy over her shoulders. She touched the glass door. It would be best to give Carrie a shout, Amber decided, since she hadn't seen the likes of them for a few days. It was logic to the rescue again. Reassurance. And Amber realised that she could make the call from her brand new cell phone and never scratch her wallet for quarters again. It was a gift, a welcome gift. She started to feel better.

First, Amber led her brother farther up the street, continuing the search for eats. At the intersection of College Street—the edge of University of Toronto—a ghostly sound came from the west of a young man shouting through a bullhorn. At first it seemed like he was the only one, just one guy with a bullhorn. But it became evi-

dent, as they got closer, that they were walking toward a student protest. "Great," Amber mumbled.

A little group roved the sidewalk, but on the other side of the
street, mercifully. There were also a few sentries at the Kings Col-
lege entrance, with signs on wooden stakes that said "F$$K FEES"
and things like that. Amber wished she could have figured it out be-
fore it was too late to divert down another street—ridiculously, since
it wasn't too late, she could have just turned her brother by his
shoulders and gone back the way they came, but that wasn't the way
it worked. In other countries a student protest could be a war zone;
here, in public, the challenge was to act indifferent, to not let the
noisy kids get to her. Turning around, being seen turning around—
that was out of the question. So they walked right into it. Someone
carried around sandwiches, someone tried to sell them newspapers,
one for fifty cents or two for a buck. Amber's arm curled protec-
tively around her bag as it banged against people hitting drums and
wiggling clappers. She saw City News vans; bored-looking police;
and what day was it? Wednesday.

Guy was stoic, not looking around, not asking, *Amber, what's
this all about?* The students sounded like they'd learned to protest
from watching movies. They actually did an "I don't know but I been
told." They did a "What do we want? When do we want it?" The
hardest part was at the edge of the protest, as they just started to walk
away, the few hot seconds when someone could say, *Hey, they're
walking away.* Indeed they *were* walking away. In a few minutes the
chanting faded back into echoes, and Amber said, "That's a protest
for you."

Guy said nothing.

The protest had done its work on her; perhaps she was able to
act like she didn't care, but she did. She was angry at the protesters.
What was a university demonstration? Bored kids skipped lectures
for this, throwing away the very stuff they paid for—at an incredibly
serious price, according to the logic of their own protest.

Amber remembered, being poor had been a rather delectable
part of her whole university fantasy, living in a rustic apartment with
some other girls, bonding through the shared struggle. Students were
poor, plain and simple. If she'd already had a career that paid the
bills, she wouldn't have needed to be a student in the first place.

She regretted every second of walking with her brother in this city. She didn't know where they were going, their bags were heavy, and each painful step was just more thing to use against her later. They traversed the entire campus before finally finding things like stores and restaurants. "Finally," Amber huffed, into the void of her brother's silent treatment. Once she bought him pizza for dinner he'd have to drop the sulkiness, she figured. And he did, but only enough to give one-word answers to her questions. Then he put on the earphones for his iPod.

Fine. Amber stopped trying and took out her new cell phone.

It looked reasonably intuitive, but Amber unfolded the glossy instruction sheet anyway. The sheet was designed with the same motif as the Virgin stand-ups, the box, and the pamphlets: hearts all over the place. The language in the instructions was the same stuff: "You'll fall fast in love with its 'Look Ma, no hands' speakerphone, crisp colour screen and light as a feather design. Hot, hot, hot." Eventually, the instructions actually told her what to do.

The screen displayed Carrie's phone number as Amber dialed it, and then showed a sunburst radiating from the cell's aerial when she sent the call—fancy, and unnecessary. She hoped she hadn't paid for that. Amber held the phone to her ear timidly, partly because of brain cancer, and also because she didn't know where exactly the phone went relative to her face. She was just mimicking the position other people used with cell phones. Suppose the earpiece was away from her ear? Did millimetres matter?

Automatically, she looked at her brother. "I'm trying to call Carrie," she explained.

"Hm," Guy said.

Carrie answered.

"Hey Carrie, this is Amber again."

"Oh. Hi."

It was just like a regular phone. Amber leaned her elbows on the table. "What's up with you?"

"Just working, really. You?"

"I've been staying with Jesse the last few days."

"Yeah, I know."

Having been fascinated with her new toy, Amber had forgotten to plan what she was going to say. Sensing her brother watching, she pretended listen to intently to something Carrie said—as though

Carrie were saying anything—which didn't help, because the effort of pretending made it even harder to find words. "Look," Amber said. "I'm sorry to bug you, but—" *But what?* "Is there any chance—" *No, a reason first.* "Tomorrow—" *No, she couldn't lie in front of Guy. Yes she could.* "Tomorrow I'm going to be moving into an apartment," she said, looking out the window. "And I hope it—is there any chance I can stay with you, one more night, just…?"

Fabulous load of stuttering. Well done, Amber.

"You mean tonight?" Carrie said.

"Yeah."

"You can't."

"Okay."

"People can't stay over too many nights who don't live here, remember?"

"Aw," Amber said. "Okay."

There was silence while Amber waited for Carrie to make a token apology; when it didn't come, Amber apologised herself, she apologised for calling and bugging her. The rule about guests in Carrie's residence, as she remembered it, had been two nights in a row. Technically, she could come back after spending a few nights elsewhere, couldn't she? So what Carrie really wanted to say was, *I hardly know you and fuck off.*

"Well sorry," Amber said. "But that's okay. I guess I'll give Jesse a shout."

"He wouldn't be able to do anything. He's not going to be home tonight."

"Oh no? Why, what's he up to?"

"We're going out," Carrie uttered.

"Oh really? What are you doing?"

"Just seeing people. We're probably going downtown. I don't know. We'll see."

Amber was being annoying on purpose, wanting to make Carrie suffer a little for being priggish.

"Okay," Amber said. "Well yeah, though. I'm in a bit of a spot here. I need a place to stay again."

"I don't know."

"Hm."

Silence and breathing. They were trying to out-sit each other.

"Well, I guess I need to work something out," Amber declared.

"Okay."

"Bye then."

"Bye."

Amber searched for the disconnect button on her phone. It didn't matter if she took her time, since Carrie had already hung up. A clock on the screen had kept track of the length of the call: a minute and a half.

"Want dessert?" Amber asked her brother.

"What?"

"I don't know. Look at the menu."

She rooted through her backpack for her homework journal and found the number she'd copied off a poster the other day, the one for an apartment tenant looking for roommates, the apartment with street number 2468.

A woman answered. Amber said hi, she was calling about the room for rent, and she looked sharply to the side while she talked, as if interested by something in the restaurant kitchen. It was to avoid looking directly at her brother. He was turning out to be a distracting sight while she was on the phone. The woman's voice had a strange, quiet intensity, like someone speaking through an enormous smile.

"To whom am I speaking?" the woman asked.

"My name's Amber."

"Amber? That's lovely."

"Thanks."

"When would you like to come see this place?"

"Whenever," Amber said. "I mean..." She was expecting to be told. She was waiting for the woman to name the day and time, so she could accomodate. That's how it had always worked. "How about tomorrow?" Amber asked.

"What time?"

"Would two p.m. work?"

"Eh?"

"How's two p.m.?"

"Two p.m.?"

"Yeah."

"Yeah, that's good."

Amber wanted to thank her, as though she'd just received a compliment. She went to glance at her wristwatch and remembered, again, that she didn't have it.

The woman went the rest of the call without mentioning her own name, as she told Amber how to buzz her room from the entrance when she got there. Amber couldn't shake the feeling that the woman was amused by the whole thing, like a parent watching a school play.

Amber decided to call Jesse next. She didn't care if he wouldn't be home until 3:00 in the morning. One of the Dundas kids answered; Amber asked for Jesse, and before putting down the phone the boy hesitated just long enough to get Amber back into that disoriented what-the-fuck mindset with which she was so familiar.

"Hello?" Jesse said in his brisk, weighty voice.

"Hey Jesse. It's Amber again."

"Oh, hey."

"Do you really have to take all your phone calls upstairs?"

"Yeah, but they're going to put in another line for me. At least, they've been saying that since August."

"Oh yeah." Amber couldn't just say, *We have to come over again.* She had to wiggle her way into the request, obliquely as always. It was never a matter of just saying what she wanted to say. "I talked to Carrie. She said you were going downtown today."

"Did she?"

"She said you were going out."

"Yeah, it's a guy's birthday party. It's going to be crazy."

It was bizarre that Carrie hadn't known they were going to a birthday party. Or else she'd just lied, which wasn't bizarre at all.

"Okay, well, look. I'm so sorry about this, but… but we… but, I mean… I think I left my watch at your place."

She used her wristwatch to bail out at the last second.

"You did? Actually, good, 'cause I found one in the bathroom."

"Oh yeah?"

"Yeah, so I've got it."

"Okay. Good."

"So what, are you back in Ottawa already?"

"Actually, no," Amber said. "My brother and I actually... we didn't get out of Toronto today, so we have to... I'm trying to find a place to stay again."

"Really?"

"Yeah, sorry. I mean, I was hoping—"

"You want to sleep here again."

"Yeah. Sorry."

"What happened?" Jesse asked.

"Well." Guy was now watching her blatantly, like she was on TV. She was about to lie again. *Go back to your iPod,* she wanted to say. "Turns out our tickets were for the wrong day," Amber said. "We can't leave today."

Her voice rose absurdly.

"Oh," Jesse reacted. "Well sure, yeah, if you're still stuck for a place then, Amber... No problem."

"Thank you so much."

"Don't worry about it. But the thing is—Where are you now?"

"Where are we? Still basically downtown."

"What time were you going to be getting here? Because, this party..."

"Whenever's fine for you, Jesse," Amber said. "I don't care if it's late."

Jesse suggested, why didn't they head up that very minute? They'd likely arrive before he left, and they could hang out in his room. Amber asked if he was absolutely sure; after all, they'd imposed on him for three days already... Yeah yeah. No problem, he said. If he were in her place, he'd have wanted someone to do the same thing for him. See you soon.

Amber made the announcement to her brother: they were going back to Jesse's. He nodded, swirling his thumb around the iPod control. Amber wondered if he'd actually been watching her after all.

Jesse answered the door at 7:00, and his hair was wet and smoothed back, smelling like conditioner. He was wearing a tight white sweatshirt—tight on him, a giant bell-shape—with a green shirt over top of it, unbuttoned. He'd been sitting in the living room with Mr. Dundas, doing sudoku on the coffee table. As soon as Amber and her brother arrived, Jesse held out her watch, dangling it like a doggy treat. Amber took it, thanked him in spite of being annoyed at that treatment, and allowed him to usher them down to his room, saying that he had to go right away or he'd be late picking up his girlfriend.

"You can watch TV or play games, or whatever," he instructed them breathlessly. "You know where everything is."

Guy was wriggling out of his coat, and Amber thought about taking another walk. Ever since leaving the train station Guy had been sulky. She could put up with it while they were moving from place to place, but she didn't relish sitting in a room with him for the rest of the day.

"Is there any place to grab some food around here?" Amber asked, securing her watch around her arm and vowing never to take it off again for even one second. Jesse reached under his computer for a case of beer.

"Nope," Jesse chirped. "Nowhere that's good, anyway."

"Well, somewhere not good is okay."

Jesse still wasn't any help. Even the nearest fast food was a fair walk, he said.

"This isn't exactly a great neighbourhood, is it?" Amber said.

Not everyone's rich, Jesse lectured her in an annoying holier-than-thou voice. I'm not saying everyone's rich, Amber answered in a voice that was probably just as annoying. It was one of those vague peacekeeping efforts, not wanting to look bad for Guy, that made her pretend to care about this birthday party, asking Jesse where it was and whom it was for.

Perhaps it was a peacekeeping effort in return that made Jesse extend an invitation to her. "I'd be fine here," Guy announced, his first words that afternoon. Amber hadn't suspected that Jesse's invitation included him in the first place, but perhaps he wasn't thinking about the party at all. Maybe he was telling his sister to go out and leave him alone. After almost a full week of never leaving his side, it made sense. What a good idea. Amber asked Guy if he was sure he'd be okay by himself, but it was a needless question, considering the pile of video games in front of him.

"So you're coming?" Jesse asked. "Do you want a minute to change?"

"I think I'm good," Amber said.

Jesse reminded Guy that there was pop under the bed, and he led Amber upstairs, taking the steps three at a time.

They rushed out to his car, and Amber got in the front seat, defeating the impulse to take the back again. For a second she imagined that her coat was much longer than it was, and that she had to hike it up so it wouldn't be caught in the door. Jesse put the beer in the back.

His driving had never bothered Amber before, but her stomach was unsettled. She felt the flavour of coffee creeping up the back of her throat; yeah, she had to admit, perhaps she could have stood to drink less of the stuff that day. She could tell that she was on her way to a drinking party. It was true that she hadn't been to a party for years, not since she was underage. Was it so naive, then, to look forward to things like Cherry Coke and pizza? She didn't want to drink beer, and she bristled at the idea. Jesse asked her again why she hadn't been able to catch her train, and Amber was forced to expand on her story a little; eventually she just shrugged and said, "I don't know, I don't know," as if the system was just so damn impenetrable. Amber recognised the route they were taking and realised were going back into York University. Jesse parked on the lane by Carrie's residence, got out and told her to wait.

Oh, right, Amber thought, regretting her decision to come along. Carrie had fed her stories over the phone so she wouldn't have to be hospitable, but when the she saw Amber in the car she'd know she was caught. Amber was in the front seat too; the girlfriend would be displaced to the back. Suppose Amber moved to the back herself, before they returned? She had plenty of time to agonise over it, but hadn't moved by the time they came back. Just as Amber had predicted, Carrie got into the back with the beer. In a show of everything being fine, Amber twisted around and said hello, pleasantly.

Carrie smiled at her.

But a glare of heat hung over Amber, a sense of *doesn't like*. Jesse took his place in the driver's seat, and they were off again. He was happily ignorant of the lightning flashing between the two girls in his car. *Yes,* Amber told herself, *you are paranoid*. There hadn't been a spray of sparks as soon as Carrie got in the car, and there wouldn't ever be. The incident was over.

Jesse drove past the place they were going, pointing it out, but he had to park two blocks away, he said, because parking was terrible. Carrie brought the beer out with her. Jesse called her "honey" and kissed her. Then they strolled along the sidewalk, not wide enough for three people, and Amber wound up trailing in the rear, looking at store windows—clothing, comic books, coffee. She wanted more coffee, but that wouldn't be happening, not now.

The party was on Dufferin Street, a wide street lined with townhouses and tiny little yards. Jesse swerved up onto a porch where there were three doorbells, one for each floor. He hammered all three of them until a guy answered the door. They were some of the first people to arrive, he announced. The house was thin and tall and smelled like Lysol; there was the sense of everything slowly falling apart. It was an old house, but not old in the sense of having historic character; it was just old. The first floor was given over to a living room and the kitchen, staircases upstairs and downstairs. Jesse made introductions—this was Mark, one of Patrick's housemates—Patrick was the one with the birthday—then they went into the kitchen to be chummy. Carrie busied herself taking off her coat. She was wearing a necklace made of a dozen strands of tiny beads.

Amber wandered into the living room, away from them. She wasn't wearing a necklace or anything particular at all. She was in a sweatshirt with bleach stains and pants with frayed cuffs that tripped her when she walked in her socks. The couches looked inviting—threadbare and misshapen, soft like an old bed. She slumped on one of them, stretching out to give her stomach space to settle.

It was risky, of course, lying down in another room while people were social elsewhere. Being discovered would be awkward. Sure enough, there were crunchy wood sounds from the staircase as someone came down, and Amber sat up. It was Patrick's other housemate and, fortunately, he walked past the living room without noticing her, greeting the gathering with, "Hey, you awful bastards." Amber listened. Everyone was calling him Ian.

Eventually Amber wandered out of the living room, which was soon populated anyway as other people arrived. There was no cake in Patrick's birthday spread; there was a card, beer and a bottle of vodka, no pizza, no Cherry Coke. When Patrick walked in, everyone burst into applause. Mark, waving a cardboard tube, led everyone in "Happy Birthday." Patrick was twenty-four.

Someone put on music. And so, the party was started. Everyone had apparently brought their own drinks, and every one of them was alcoholic. Did these people drink nothing else? Mark had wine in the fridge; one of his female friends had brought amaretto whiskey, which they gleefully mixed with Coca-Cola. Amber was in the kitchen when Jesse demurely offered her one of his beers.

"No thanks," Amber said, waving. "I don't drink."

There, she said it. And she failed to hide the fact that she expected nothing but disapproval for her preference, shooting nervous glances all around the room.

What did everyone have to say about it? They were all perfectly supportive.

Jesse: His outstretched arm, the one holding the beer, collapsing back against his body while he nodded, grinning, proud perhaps that his offer was responsible for this admission.

Mark: Humming shortly, turning around to reach up to the top of one of the kitchen cupboards for shot glasses.

Amaretto girl: "That's okay," stressing the okay, oh-kay, overt reassurance.

Amber asked if she could have some plain Coke.

The fact was, Amber didn't drink, and she knew she never would; it was something she'd laid out for herself long ago, in the early habit-forming days of childhood. Drinking meant drinking problems; smoking and drugs were even worse.

The middle school body was escorted into the gymnasium after lunch and seated on the scuffed floor; a woman in a flowered shirt, the guest speaker, after being introduced by a member of the student council, introduced herself as an ex-convict, and explained that she was continuing to give these talks even after working off all her community service. She told the story of her life, how she'd started doing drugs, the first time she'd purchased them on credit, all the shit thereafter. She was a wonderful performer, patiently threading the story along, the sense of gradually mounting calamity, holding up the microphone with the cord that trailed way back behind the stage. She portrayed her dealer-slash-boyfriend, chillingly uttering, "That's okay." "You know what, don't worry." *Stop*, was the instruction that Amber called down upon the young woman in the story. *Get out get out get out.* Never get in.

Well, the ex-convict had done her job. Amber had promised herself that all those bad habits would always remain other people's, and hey, in the moment, waving away Jesse's beer, saying no hadn't been hard at all.

Of course, she also recalled that she'd included swearing in the list of despicable habits never to form. Surely it wouldn't be hard to avoid three or four words out of a language of three hundred thousand.

Now that the party was fully under way, Amber could count the activities taking place: lots of talking while drinking, playing music on the stereo while drinking, not much else. Amber wandered around with her cup of plain Coke, looking at people's backs as they socialised. It was good to have more faces around, Jesse had assured her, but her face didn't seem very important.

She explored upstairs. There were some papers taped to the bathroom door, a comic strip and a few printouts, all having to do with hating parents and baby boomers. One item provided steps on how to dispose of their bodies down a sink, using household cleaners.

In one of the bedrooms, some people were playing a movie trivia game. Ian was sitting on the edge of his bed, the bottom of his hoodie bunched up at his waist. "Um, *Sky Captain and the World of Tomorrow*," he said. "Gwyneth Paltrow."

"Shit," said the next guy.

Amber stood in the door, watching. "Want to join?" Ian asked her. "We're playing movie tag."

"Oh gosh, I'd lose," Amber sighed. She'd never seen that movie, or cared about that actress.

She let herself be persuaded anyway, sitting beside Ian on his bed. Every time it was her turn, of course, she'd sit there grinning and clueless until Ian started listing off options: "*The Butterfly Effect, Magnolia, The Big Empty...*"

"Let's go with Magnolia."

Then Ian had to list off actors: "Tom Cruise, William H. Macy, uh, Luis Guzmán..."

"Obviously I suck at this."

The game couldn't last forever, but after it crashed to a stop everyone agreed it had been particularly extensive. "No thanks to some of us," Amber added.

"Don't worry, Amber," Ian said. "It's probably good you're not a nerd." Some impulse drove them all to spring off the bed and leave, leaving Amber on her own. She took the opportunity to lie back on the bed. She felt tired, and her stomach still hurt as well. It hurt in a frustrating way; she couldn't feel out what she was supposed to do. Was she to eat more, not eat anything, drink some water? She just hurt, and nothing seemed to offer relief.

Once again she heard the crunch of the wooden stairs, and she sat up just as Ian burst back into the room. "They're opening presents downstairs," he told her. "I guess we missed it."

"Aw. What did he get?"

"Retarded guy stuff."

"What exactly might that be?" Amber asked, widening her eyes.

"You know," Ian muttered. "The usual."

He sat in a beanbag chair, looking bored. Amber knew that conversations went nowhere if people didn't appear interested, which was why she'd faked that reaction of horror, widening her eyes like a film actress. She regretted it.

Ian told her that if she really had no idea what he was talking about she should go down and see the gifts for herself. Right, Amber thought. She didn't need reminding of how ignorant she was. What she said was, simply, she'd rather not, with a humourless laugh, so Ian relented and described them to her: gifts on the order of licorice thongs and mugs from the It store. When Patrick pulled them out of the boxes everyone would let loose with a guffaw. Ian disapproved of these things. The twenty second fuss, watching Patrick hold them up, was the only reason they'd been bought, a fuss that was mainly in appreciation of the person who'd been so clever as to choose them. Amber nodded along mutely, except to say "Yeah." or "I know."

"It's just, you can sort of see it coming," Ian said. "It's like, oh, surprise surprise. Thanks guys."

That was a place to laugh. "I know," Amber said. "Real thoughtful of them."

"No one's going to remember the joke gift in thirty years."

"Yeah. Totally."

Ian was quiet and thoughtful, then he got up and went to his closet. "Hey, you want a Vex?" he asked.

"Sure," Amber said.

He produced two clear glass bottles and passed one to her. The label was black with a big 'V'. It was made of lemonade and vodka.

Ian clubbed his hand over top of his and popped it open with a tidy hiss. Well, this was new. Amber wedged a fingernail under the lid and wondered if a hard enough ripping-motion would do the trick; but, oh, they were twist-offs. The lid's metal teeth dug into her flesh, while she prayed that it would work the first time. That she wouldn't look like a little girl at her first drinking party. She made an absurd effort, a tortuous grind, and—it worked fine.

Bringing the bottle to her nose, she instantly identified the alcohol, the distinctive, saturating scent that traveled straight to the capillaries in her face. She took a drink, and it was fiery and sweetly flavourless. Some of Ian's friends tromped up and burst into the room. Maybe, all along, it had been for the wrong reasons that Amber had refused beer from Jesse, since among the group that entered was amaretto-whiskey-and-Coca-Cola girl, who had witnessed the scene in the kitchen. "Amber's drinking!" she cried, and Amber said, "Oh, right," for want of anything else, resting the bottle in her lap, like she didn't know she had it. There went her righteous abstinence. The party had spread back upstairs, like a fume—drinking, talking about drinking, telling stories about being drunk. *Parties.*

Almost all the other women had put on nice clothes, but especially amaretto girl, a redhead in an auburn suit with flare pants, and she actually had a shawl on top of that. Amber remembered, once again, the humiliating ensemble she'd thrown together for her Origin Marketing interview. Here she was again, the very next night, looking like this—at least this time she hadn't even tried. The girl whom nobody knew, the friend of a friend of the birthday boy, dressed like this, drinking but not drinking. She wanted to leave the room, forget the Vex on the floor by Ian's bed and go back downstairs, as though that would get her away from people. There were *more* people downstairs.

Parties.

She wanted to leave.

An hour passed with Amber wandering from place to place, finding spots to sit down that wouldn't be conspicuous. She wished there was somewhere she could seriously lie back; her stomach was very uneasy. The taste of all the coffee she'd drunk inched along her tongue. And that Vex—but surely one drink wasn't enough to cause problems.

Song after song wafted through the stereo speakers; voices started to be raised in that particular drunken way. Amber recalled that Jesse had driven here, and wondered why she kept seeing him with beer in his hands. Surely it wouldn't be necessary to do the Right Thing and force him to call a taxi.

In the living room they turned on the TV. A female rapper was on the stereo, and Amber decided she wanted to go to the kitchen for a glass of water. Alcohol had made her thirstier.

But when she started to get up off the couch, her insides flattened heavily. It was worse than before. She thought she'd be sick if she didn't stay sitting down. She plopped back and breathed, carefully.

Don't think about it.

In a vinyl chair, in the middle of the living room, amaretto girl was boisterously making out with her boyfriend, in full sight, as a joke, which had lasted for a few minutes now. Amber thought it would be okay if she leaned over, hanging her head between her knees, like someone who had passed out in a seated position. People would see her that way, but she didn't care. She just had to breathe. *Nice and easy.*

The regurgitation reflex was mostly mental. By not agonizing over it, by sending happy thoughts to her uvula, the smell of fresh air, it could be repressed. Not this time. A belch forced open her throat, the sound of an exploding ketchup bottle. She tasted bile.

Oh God.

It had only been a dry heave, but the *sound*, sickly wet, protracted and awful, louder than the music.

At a stroke, she was the centre of attention. "Uh oh," said the guy beside her on the couch. "We got a live one." Someone shoved a plastic casserole bowl under her face, but no one rushed up to ask if she was all right, to help her. Amber stayed hunched over, stunned and flustered, doing nothing. Where were Jesse and Carrie? Where was Ian?

"You want to hit the bathroom?" someone wondered.

"I think I'm good," Amber mumbled, counting the Cheezie crumbs in the bowl.

On the stereo, the female rapper asked if you wished your girlfriend was a freak like me.

Ian was there, in the living room door. She heard him say, "Shit." Finally he breached her invisible sick-person force field and crouched beside her. "What happened?" he asked. "Were you sick?"

"I wasn't actually sick," Amber mumbled. She sat up for his benefit, but didn't want to raise her head and see the idiots around her.

"You want to lie down somewhere?" Ian asked. "Come on."

She was lead away to another room, the exodus of shame. Amber didn't want it to be a big deal. She didn't want to be the one who couldn't handle it, the one who had to go lie down at her first party while everyone else drank and blabbed away into the night. It was too late for that, though; it was already a big deal. And yes, Amber liked the idea of leaving the living room, getting away from the love-stricken couple and that music, and all those people she didn't know.

The other guests gave them an aisle into the hall, and Ian started for the stairs. It wasn't far to go. But standing up had made it come back, the pressure of stomach gas, the rotten feeling. Amber hunched over in the hallway, grabbing a doorjamb. "Ohhh," she said. She was in the middle of the house, there was only the living room, the kitchen—"Hold on," she gasped. "Is there a bathroom?" But there wasn't time to find one. She lurched into the kitchen, heading for the sink, and saw the door to the backyard standing open. Better. She rounded the table, glass bottles jingling, stumbled outside. Cement patio tiles, then frosty grass. She'd found Carrie and Jesse. They were on the patio with Patrick, smoking joints.

Amber fell to her hands and knees, with awful relief, her stomach shriveling like something dead, and up came a fountain of yellow bile. Ian's drink, the acidic lemon and the sinus-burning alcohol, choking, over-sweet sick-taste, flooding her nose and mouth, all the shit she'd eaten. It steamed instantly. She gasped and threw up again. She barely choked in a breath, and it happened a third time. *Oh God.* She couldn't stop. Flecks of it splashed her hands and sleeves.

"What's wrong with her?" Jesse scoffed mildly.

Amber tried to breathe again, a sound like a sob—*No more.* "Holy shit," remarked Patrick.—*please no more*—again, another time—*please please no more*—

CHAPTER 6

The school bus always arrived at 8:15 am, and if the clock on the microwave started creeping past 8:10 and she wasn't ready to go, it was time to panic. In the dream she got the impression of hours and hours passing while she ran around, still in the house doing who-knew-what, and the bus still hadn't come. If it had gone by without her, while she watched from the wide kitchen window, well, that would have at least been the end of it. But it still hadn't come; she still had to rush around at the last minute, the last minute endlessly prolonged.

When she woke up, she shoved her palms into Ian's mattress to twist and stare at the digital clock, which shined the numbers 7:44 at her, which meant she had sixteen minutes to get to Tim Hortons for her training shift.

The light from Ian's window, filtered through the downy cotton blinds which had probably been there when he moved in, touched down on the corner opposite the bed, the corner with Ian's closet and his beanbag chair. Amber was sprawled in his bed, facing the wrong way, her feet under the pillows, a bath towel itchy around her waist. She'd slept for four hours, at most. After Ian had given her copious attention, offering cup after cup of tap water, he'd conducted her to his room and told her to sleep, which she did, in her clothes, listening to the muffled throb of the party music. At midnight, though, she was awake, feeling tightness in her throat again. She tried to ignore it, but rose acrimoniously and went to the bathroom, just in case. Sure enough, as soon as there was a toilet in front of her, Amber fell over it and threw up even more. Afterward she stayed hunched over the toilet bowl. The rest of her was burned out, but her gag reflex had been energetic as ever. She hadn't had time to put the seat up, and there were pink splashes everywhere. She cleaned up with toilet paper, flushed, and went back to bed.

At 2:00 in the morning it happened again. Amber stumbled out of bed again, feeling as bad as a person stumbling out of bed for that reason could possibly feel, and once again descended to the bathroom floor. By then there was barely any solid matter left in her, and she threw up just a muddy stomach-coloured liquid, like clam chowder. She had no idea if Jesse and Carrie were still hanging around by then, or if they'd gone home without her. They certainly hadn't been coming up to check on her.

Again, at 3:00. Used to the routine by now, but still battered from the effort of climbing out of bed every hour, she shoved past The Life of the Baby Boomer and assumed position. This time, there was a new surprise: she had diarrhoea in her pants, instantly fragrant. Amber stayed on the floor, ready to cry. But inevitably she had to climb up, clean up. She shut the bathroom door, stripped off all her clothes and dumped them in the sink. Her shit had left a puddle on the floor, which she cleaned superficially with vast amounts of toilet paper, but she knew it would have be really cleaned, with Tilex or something, later. She got in the shower and sprayed her legs with the shower nozzle. If they heard her downstairs, well, fuck them for caring. Trying not to see herself in the mirror, she took a towel off the door and wrapped it around her waist, peeked into the hall, and ran back to Ian's room. She left her clothes there in the sink. It was too fucking late to do anything about them.

Consequently, sitting up at 7:44, she knew not only that she was late, but that she didn't have anything to wear. She slid to the edge of the bed and sat, propping her head on her hands.

The house was like a grave. Amber crept out of Ian's room. She could hear a dripping tap. She checked in the bathroom; her clothes were where she left them. She sneaked back to Ian's room, although she probably could have stomped around without waking anyone up. She'd wear some of Ian's clothes. He wouldn't care.

Ian had an old wooden dresser in his closet whose drawers didn't open and close properly. They didn't have rollers; they slid directly against wooden rails, some of which were broken, causing the drawers to tilt backwards into the next drawer down. The guy could live with it, apparently. Amber managed to jam her hand into one drawer and remove a black T-shirt. It had a silk-screened picture from Resident Evil.

Nervously, she looked in Ian's underwear drawer. He only had tighty-whities and silk boxer shorts. Buried way back in the drawer was a bright pink pair of panties with lace trim. Well, she couldn't take those, because what would she say when she had to give them back?

Well, who said she had to give them back?

Blue jeans finished her off, and then she was left with ten minutes to get to her new job. Excuses and apologies propagated in her brain like bacteria. As for her own clothing in the sink, she decided she'd search the kitchen for a garbage bag and throw it all in a closet somewhere, and later she'd beg Ian to wash it. She charged downstairs and discovered him on the living room couch. *Help me. What do you do when this happens?* But she didn't want to wake him. She didn't want him to see her like this, running around in his clothes.

Amber wondered if she'd find Carrie or Jesse anywhere. Other than the living room couch, there weren't any other soft surfaces on the ground floor, but perhaps they were in the basement. Amber went down the stairs, but found nothing but the boiler room and a closed door. So she went back up and stood in the living room for a long time, thinking about shaking Ian awake. It would have to be him. He was the only person there.

The store's address was written in her homework journal. When Ash, the manager of the Union Station store, had explained how to get there she hadn't really listened—*why?*—because she'd planned to use the map service on the City of Toronto web site anyhow. Every time she'd used it she'd admonished herself that she had to learn, eventually, how to find addresses without relying on internet convenience, as though knowing how to do something on the internet didn't really mean knowing how to do it. And here she was, high and dry in the house of somebody she didn't even know, no internet in sight and no other options.

Amber let Ian sleep. She found plastic grocery bags under the kitchen sink, took them upstairs and shoveled in her putrid clothes, then ran back down to stash it in the least offensive place she could think of, behind the furnace in the boiler room. Then she grabbed her coat off the hook where she'd hung it eleven hours ago and ran out the front door. Her arms felt chilled right away; under her coat she was wearing only that T-shirt. As for which way to turn, Jesse had driven them, so she didn't know where the hell the nearest subway station was, but she had to choose a direction, north or south.

If she'd had the store's telephone number, she could have called them on her cell phone and got directions, but it was written in her homework journal, which was in her bag back in Jesse's house. The only possible solution she could think of—

"Hello?" Mr. Dundas said.

He'd answered promptly and didn't sound like a zombie. Thank goodness they got up early in that house.

"Hey, is Jesse there?"

"Jesse...? It's very early. He isn't up yet."

"Oh."

Amber had been wary of calling so early in the morning, but hey. It was a weekday after all, and the kids would have been going to school, and Amber had been up well before 8:00 when she was still in school. She kept walking, squinting to see what the big street up ahead was, conscious of her cell phone against her ear, since people who used cell phones while walking on the street usually seemed obnoxious.

"Sorry to be a hassle," Amber said, "but I think my brother's still there. Is there any chance you could call down the stairs and see for me?"

A pause. "Who is this?"

"This is Amber, I was—I stayed—I was staying over, with—" *Staying with Jesse*, a phrase that failed to make it off her tongue. "I stayed over a few nights ago. I think Jesse might be there, and—" *My little brother too*, another thing she couldn't say. There were canals dug through her explanation, full of details that she couldn't admit, because Mr. Dundas would have taken them the wrong way. "My brother Guy is probably downstairs, and I really need to talk to him. If it's okay ... If you can. Can you get him on the phone for me?"

There was no answer. Amber heard the sound of movement, though, and then she heard her brother's name shouted.

During the interval Amber started to cross a street. There was a Pickle Barrel catering van outside the church on the corner, and Amber walked past it just in time for a car to pop out of nowhere and squeal its tires at her. Amber finished an undignified jog to the other sidewalk. Obnoxious cell phone gaffe number one.

"Your sister's on the phone," Amber heard Mr. Dundas say. She heard a delay, a flurry of scraping sounds as the phone changed hands.

"Amber?" Guy had a sleepy voice.

"Hey Guy. Did Jesse come back last night?"

"No."

"Well, can you do something for me quick?"

"What?"

"Can you look in my journal for a phone number for me?"

"Where's your journal?"

Amber instructed Guy to go into her backpack for it; he read the number out to her, and Amber patted her coat pockets to see if she had anything to write with. Nope, she didn't. She stared up at the blinds of windows she passed, hastily committing the number to memory.

"Why didn't you come back yesterday?" Guy asked.

"Because," Amber said. "Why do you care?"

"I don't care. I'm just asking."

"Well, it got too late to go on the subway."

After a moment Guy told her that he was planning to go to a film screening that evening.

"What?" Amber said. "What film?"

"It's Salvador Dali. It's a surrealist film festival."

"Where did you hear about this?"

"I just saw it in an ad," Guy explained mildly. "While we were walking around downtown and stuff. I just thought, you know."

"You're going to go just because you saw it on an ad?"

"Well, sorry I tried to live a little."

"I'm not telling you not to go."

"Then I'm going."

"Fine, go then," she said, walking thump-thump-thump. "I won't be back until the afternoon. I have to go to work now."

"Okay."

"Well, bye."

Guy's blathering about Salvador Dali had almost made her forget the phone number he'd just told her. She remembered numbers by picturing the shape her finger traced over the number pad as she dialed; she was pretty sure, shit, it would suck to have to call the Dundases again—

Someone answered: "Thank you for calling Tim Hortons, how may I help you?"

"Hey," Amber said. "Uh, my name's Amber, I'm supposed to be working today at about eight o'clock, I think, right?"

"Amber? You training today?"

She had a heavy accent. Amber could tell, she said "you training" not as a colloquialism, but because that was her grip on English.

"Yeah. Um…" Amber heard the beats in her voice as she walked, a little shudder with every step. She *sounded* like she was hurrying, which was good, or maybe not. She got to the corner of Dufferin and the big street, and there was a subway station right there, lucky for her. There were two things she needed to accomplish with this call: find out where the store was, then grovel about being late for her first day there.

"I'm having trouble finding the store," she said. "I think I'm going to be late. What's the address again?"

"Three-oh-nine-one Kingston Road."

"All right," Amber said. Kingston Road meant nothing to her.

"Can you find it?"

"What?"

"Can you find it?"

Amber looked back and forth at the intersection. She decided to jaywalk. "You mean do I know how to get there?"

"Yeah."

Amber almost said, yes, of course, because she could find out, using a phone book, or an internet café. It would be a lie to say she needed to be told everything.

"You'd better tell me," Amber said.

"Where are you now?"

If Amber knew the geography of Toronto she could have made up some location, somewhere reasonably close to the store. If she said she was at Dufferin subway station, it may have been a confession of how late she really was. So she just said, "I'm on the subway."

Not entirely false, since she was entering the subway that very minute. The woman gave her instructions: Warden subway station, the 102 bus eastbound to Kingston Road, and then a little north on Kingston until she got to a place called Cliffcrest Plaza, and the store was on the opposite side of the road. Once again, Amber had to memorise it all. She said she'd be there as soon as possible and apologised once more, for good measure. The woman laughed, inappropriately, and hung up.

Well, there, she hadn't been screamed at yet. But maybe that woman had fallen for her half-truth and assumed she was only a short jog away. Or maybe the screaming was due when she actually got there. Maybe a hundred things. Amber checked the subway map, paying for her fare with change: she wouldn't have to transfer off the Bloor-Danforth line to get to Warden station, but it was way to the east, almost in Scarborough. First she was sent way to the west for the Origin interview, and now this. It would take her at least a half-hour to get there, if she was lucky, and for all that time she'd have her thoughts to keep her company. What was it with having to ride the subway to the ends of the earth?

The subway was too loud. All the sounds hurt, as a westbound train came and went and then an eastbound one careened up. It rattled on the track, the brakes hissed too much, and the front of wind shook her around abusively. Amber got on board, and there was nowhere to sit except for a couple empty seats around a giant guy with a garbage bag and plastic shop glasses on his forehead, but those seats were empty for a reason.

When the train got moving and she was securely squeezed in with everyone else, Amber closed her eyes and let her head hang. She was tired and only noticing now, in this idle moment. All morning she'd felt weak, and it only occurred to her now that it was a symptom of more than just the panicky way she'd woken up. She probably didn't have a speck of food in her. She actually fell asleep, standing up on the subway, or came very close, because she suddenly heard the conductor announce a station, and she had to hastily consult the map over the door to make sure she hadn't missed her stop.

Then she realised that she didn't have a transfer, which meant she had to have a whole episode of abandoning the train at the next station, all the while worrying about what would happen if she was caught since this was against the rules, since she was supposed to get a transfer at the station where she paid her fare. She imagined that the next train would come very quickly, and she'd be charging back to the platform to catch it, when she actually wound up waiting five minutes, time that crawled past like beads of water. Late again, just like for the Origin interview, thoroughly frustrated that her future would be determined by some anonymous subway conductor who would show up whenever he felt like it. It was already past 8:00; she was already late. It was just going to be a question of how late, exactly—something sort of reasonable, or would she be fired on the spot? *Good work, Amber.*

She spent five minutes looking at the posters on the median. Then the next train came, and the subway emerged to an above-ground track, and then a very high above-ground track as they crossed a wide valley on a giant arched bridge that must have been a hundred meters tall. There was not only a river but two six-lane expressways in the valley; then she was underground again.

When the train next emerged into daylight, the next station was Victoria Park. Out the window was an expanse of bare trees and snow-marbled litter. According to the map, Warden was right after that. The train went up a grade, into what looked like a station built on a warehouse roof. From the train she could see that this part of town was clearly less populous than the city to the west. There was actually space for a big parking lot. At Warden station Amber swept out of the car and looked at her watch: thirty minutes late. Classical music was being piped through the station speakers. Now she just had to grab the bus.

Which bus? Remember the number, you bitch. 102.

Signs in the ceiling said "Buses." The arrow pointed out through the turnstiles, so Amber ensured that the transfer was still in her pocket and strode through, the turnstile ratcheting around her waist. She saw that there weren't other people in sight and decided it was time to run. Pat pat pat, a girl in a hurry. She thudded down yet another stairwell and burst out the front doors.

Amber walked to the sidewalk and immediately knew something was wrong, since there wasn't a bus stop on the corner. A little to her left she saw the sign: No entry, TTC vehicles excepted, $500 fine for illegal entry. At Warden, buses were boarded from *inside* the station, like at Finch. *What the fuck.* The "Buses" sign pointed out the turnstiles. No, it had pointed *past* the turnstiles. Amber had seen another part of the station over there but hadn't thought anything of it because—*because?* Now she was fucked. She'd have to pay another fare to get back in.

Or she could walk. Maybe it wasn't very far, and all the time she'd spent strolling around downtown had convinced her that Toronto distances weren't all that intimidating. Amber ran toward the intersection, reconsidered, stood distressed and indecisive—No, she'd made up her mind. Which way was east? Across the street was a small forest, which Amber assumed to be a part of Victoria Park, and she used that to decide.

Warden Avenue sure wasn't a busy street, fortunately. With nobody else on the sidewalk she could run unselfconsciously, exploiting the first few moments when she still had energy and nothing hurt. Her phone and wallet bounced around in her coat pockets. Inevitably, her throat chilled from gulping icy air, and her chest started to fill with the usual sluggish cramps. Running. Shit.

With the few coils of her brain not engaged in worrying or feeling exhausted, she mused: the neighbourhood reminded her strikingly of her home in Cantley. It was an outlying low-industrial area, with mundane single-storey buildings on streets with No Exit signs, auto shops and small factories with ISO 9000 banners, stores selling boring things like office furniture, a few dejected cafés that looked closed. There was cold wind, blowing dry, powdery snow over the pavement in sheets. The sidewalk squares were uneven, littered with wood chips and small rusted things; scrub grew in the cracks, and the hydro poles were made of wood.

Her dad owned a warehouse in an area of Cantley like this. He had sometimes taken her and her friends to climb on the tall shelves of crates and to ride their bikes around the loading zone. Once he'd lifted them with a forklift to the top of the freezer, a twenty-foot drop, and then driven away while they all screamed and cried about being stranded. It was just a joke, though, and he came back a minute later with Guy perched on the back of the seat, laughing at them. He'd been five.

Amber decided to walk for a while. What street had she been told she was going to meet? She had to go north when she got there, that was all she knew. She decided to look at all the names of the streets she crossed, hoping one would jump out at her. But most of the streets didn't have signs.

Enough. Time to run again. If she just kept going, kept clearing ground—a bus drove past her. Thanks for that.

Up ahead was a large plaza with a Rona Home & Garden store. Was it Cliffcrest? What was the name of the street? It looked like a big one. How late was she? Only a little over half an hour.

That was acceptable, for someone in her position. She squinted ahead to read the street sign: "Eglinton Ave. E." The same Eglinton that skirted Silverthorne? The big thing about this street name was the 'E' at the end, since the only way she could come upon an 'E' street going crosswise to her was if she was actually running north or south, which meant she'd gone totally the wrong fucking way. Amber stood on the sidewalk, gasping, her heart hammering in her temples, traffic driving around her, with no clue what to do next. She was totally lost, in the middle of an alien city where she didn't know anybody and nowhere was close enough to walk.

She had to call the store again. There was nothing else to do. Thank God for her fucking cell phone. But she no longer remembered the phone number. Would she have to place another appeal back to her brother and the Dundases? No—because it was saved in the call history. Good, something had gone right for a change.

"Tim Hortons, how may I help you?"

"Hi, this is Amber again." She was trying not to pant into the phone. "Look, I'm so sorry, but I think I'm totally lost. I haven't been able to find the store."

"Amber? Where you are now?"

"I'm at the corner of... Warden Avenue and Eglinton Avenue."

"Where's that? Did you take the 102 from Warden?"

Fuck you Amber, you dumb motherfucking cunt.

"I'm not sure how I got here, really. Um... Where do I need to go now?"

The employee had a short consultation away from the phone, then came back with a confusing series of directions about catching this bus to this street, but Amber had already made up her mind: she'd walk all the way back to Warden, pay another fare, and just take the 102. She turned on her heels while the girl was still blabbing and said, yes, she got all that, she'd be there as soon as she could. She closed her phone with a smack.

Her throat was frozen and dry. Her face and hands were too cold, the rest of her was overheating. Since she'd already blown any chance of being even remotely on time, Amber decided that she'd take it easy and stroll back to Warden. That decision lasted about a minute, then she was running again.

There was lute music over the speakers when Amber got back to the station. She made a blank, macabre face as she passed by the booth to pay her fare, wondering what the collector would think if he recognised her. The bus terminal reminded her of an airport. It was a long gallery with benches and payphones; the buses drove underneath the gallery to load; stairs led down in different places. The lute music was interrupted by recorded messages admonishing her to use the garbage bins and not smoke on TTC property. It took five minutes for the 102 to arrive, and after unloading it delayed yet another five minutes before driving over to pick up passengers. By the time Amber got on, it was 9:00.

She wasn't going to take any chances, so she asked the driver, "Excuse me, is this an eastbound bus?"

He had a mouthful of something; he spread his arms in a what-the-fuck gesture.

"Eastbound to *what?*"

"I mean, is this bus going east?"

"Where are you going?"

"Cliffcrest Plaza."

"Yah."

"Okay, thanks." *And sorry to interrupt your meal.*

Cliffcrest Plaza went by out the window before Amber recognised it. It was smaller than she'd anticipated, a utilitarian little place with just a couple banks, a public library and a dozen other stores. Amber looked out the other window. There it went, her workplace.

She walked back from the next stop. She was tired all over, and her stomach ached, running on empty. On any other occasion she'd have dared to run to a convenience store to buy something, something light and fluid, a drink or a Nutri-grain bar, before going on, but not today. If she could just muster up a presentable attitude as she walked in the door…

It was Tim Hortons. It had the same decorating scheme, the same uniforms, all the same stuff for sale as any other one. Behind a swinging door, the same white-tiled kitchen, with the oven out front. Soft rock played on the store radio. There were a half-dozen employees looking busy; Amber didn't want to unduly disturb anyone, so she lined up with the customers.

Most of the workers were brown. Were they all related? This one was wearing a name tag: Tharani. She had a halting, constantly apologetic way of speaking English, all smiles and nodding. She dealt with the customer in front of Amber and then concentrated on putting away cash in the cash drawer, talking to herself. Then she looked up. "Can I help you?"

"Yeah," Amber said. "I'm actually supposed to be working today."

"You supposed to be...?" Her hand hovered over the array of buttons.

"I'm supposed to be training for work here, today," Amber elaborated. "It's my first day."

"Oh," Tharani said again. She looked over her shoulder and called for someone named Cynthia. A Chinese girl at the drive-thru window stepped back, speaking into her headset, one of the few non-brown people. "One second," Cynthia shouted back.

"She'll be..." Tharani said, and then a bunch of unemphasised syllables that essentially assured Amber that Cynthia would be right over, smiling and nodding. Amber nodded also and moved to a spot in front of the sandwich counter, where another brown woman was scraping furiously at the bottom of a metal casserole dish.

Cynthia swayed like a buoy to find someone to take her place; then she strode over and faced Amber across the counter. "Amber?"

"Yeah. I'm so sorry about all the trouble it took to get here—"

"That okay, no worry."

"Okay."

"Nagi!—Come around," Cynthia instructed, running to the back of the store.

Amber walked around the counter, uneasily watching the mass of brown uniforms walking back and forth from the coffee machine to the showcase to the cash. At the moment they were all the same to her, all anonymous, as they would be if she were a customer. She was so self-conscious, trying not to look around too candidly, but she couldn't help but notice things like one of Tharani's customers yabbering at her while she nodded and nodded, frantically sorting a mess of change in her hand.

Around the corner from the drive-thru was the store office, a little nook behind a thick grey door, a wraparound desk occupying three of the four walls, overhead cabinets with keyholes descending from the ceiling. On the fourth wall was a giant mural to Jesus Christ. A man was sitting in a swivel chair facing the computer, and he was old, with liver spots and drooping jowls. "Nagi, Amber is here," Cynthia said.

Nagi turned around slowly. "Amber?" He repeated it like it was a foreign name, which it probably was to him. No one here seemed to speak English with any ease. Nagi's eyes panned slowly over the spread of desk until he located a uniform, a shirt, visor and a pair of pants sealed in plastic bags, Amber's name written on the plastic in marker.

"She is late," he told Cynthia, looking over his eyeglasses.

"It okay, she got lost," Cynthia replied.

"She got lost?" Nagi gestured in the general direction of the street, as though he thought Amber had lost her way between the sidewalk and the front door. Amber licked her lips. Cynthia passed the uniform to Amber and looked at her shoes, saying that it was okay for today, but Amber had to bring black slip-resistant shoes as part of the uniform. Amber said she understood, and she went to change in the staff bathroom. The bathroom floor was stained with dirt, and Amber didn't want to drop any of Ian's garments, so she put them in the sink, and naturally she had to reflect on the appropriateness of it.

As she changed she observed the poster beside the bathroom mirror, illustrating some immaculately dressed employees. Helpful arrows identified each element of the uniform, like "no jewelry" and "pants." The brown pants felt thin and brittle, like paper. Amber checked the tag and was surprised to find that they were made of cotton. She'd never felt cotton like that before. They were also too short; she could see Ian's socks. As for the cream-coloured shirt, Amber hoped the material wouldn't chafe—well, chafing would be fine, if only the material were a bit thicker, to disguise—good lord. It was a naked-in-public nightmare. Ian hadn't owned any bras to go with his pink lace panties. Her nipples glowed like bloodstains. How long could she hide in the bathroom without being missed? Perhaps if she kept on the Resident Evil shirt... But the picture showed through, a man pointing a gun. Well, she'd rather Cynthia see a gun, instead of the other thing.

She put on the nametag, a re-used one with a sticker label. She tried to stuff her wallet into her pants pocket and discovered that the pockets were fake. So she stuck it back into Ian's pants, which she twisted into a ball and jammed in a locker. It was not secure at all; she'd remember to bring her bag next time.

Delaying was over. Amber walked out of the bathroom, through the break area, realised no one was waiting for her and that she'd have to wander through the store until she ran into Cynthia, who turned out to be back at the drive-thru, a legion of coffee cups spread across the counter before her. Someone had just ordered fifty coffees. Her helper was piling more cups onto the end of the line, jabbing at sugar and cream machines, while Cynthia poured coffee like she was watering flowers. The helper girl turned, holding a long stirring spoon, but Cynthia waved her away and packed the cups into a cardboard tray. Amber stood behind them, watching, rubbing her hands together.

After sending the tray out the window, Cynthia spun, her arms out like an orator. "Amber, come," she said, striding toward the storefront. "Today your first day, so you just learn to pour coffee. That okay? Tharani—"

And so Amber got put beside Tharani, who shrugged and smiled a lot while showing her how the cream and sugar machines were foolproof, there being a separate button for each size. Employees were not required to measure. The first customer was dressed in a Domino's pizza uniform. He said: "Coffee black." More like "bleck," the way he said it. And, well, Tharani pointed at the sugar machine with a big smile, and Amber said, "Okay," and while she fiddled with the cash register Amber descended to the cup dispensers—"Which is medium?"—but she found it herself, so then—the dispenser clunked loudly when Amber pushed the button, twice. And then pouring the coffee, carefully and timidly—not full enough? Now? And then taking the plastic lid, and—

There. She'd just served coffee.

In all the times she'd gone to Tim Hortons herself, she'd never noticed that they did cream and sugar with the big clunky machines. How long had it been that way?

The next customer, an old bulldog-ish man in a weird orange vest, ordered, "garden sandwich, just lettuce and cucumber, no mayo. Tell her—" Pointing at the girl at the sandwich counter. "—no mayo."

"No mayo, yeah," Tharani granted, nodding.

"*You* tell her," the man repeated. "Don't just put it up there. *You* tell her." Tharani looked confounded. "You put it in there, and you get it wrong all the time. *You* tell her—"

By then he'd attracted the attention of the sandwich girl, who had been surreptitiously clocking this all along. "No mayo, I know," she said.

The man kept up his rant anyway, for face, while picking and choosing coins. "I ask for no mayo all the time, and all the time you get it wrong…" Tharani smiled her smile, once up at him, and then again for Amber. The man got his sandwich—"No mayo?" with eyes probingly wide—and then came the next customer. Amber was a little stunned. That had sure been rude.

Tharani showed Amber the spot under the counter where the bags of coffee grounds were kept, and showed her how to brew a new pot. She showed how they wrote the time on the side of the pot to judge when to pour it down the sink.

"It not hard?" Tharani said.

"Doesn't look all that hard," Amber replied.

Tharani nodded and smiled sadly. After ten minutes Amber almost dropped a cup of coffee, passing it across the counter. She was so weak. Amber knew that she was still sick, and there would be trouble if she ate anything now. She had a perfect excuse to spend the day in bed. In high school she'd have exploited it cheerfully. If only it weren't the first day of her first job. Her shift was only five hours, one of which she'd missed, but the end of it still seemed outrageously distant, like the bottom of an ocean. How could she get through it?

She stayed with Tharani for an hour, and even after that much practice, it seemed to take an unreasonable amount of energy to remember where different sizes of cups were. The first few customers were treated to Amber groaning, "Uuhh," her hand quivering indecisively, and she poured coffee much more slowly than anyone else, since she was deathly worried about dropping the pot on the counter or the floor. Her aim was off with the cream and sugar dispensers too, not only in terms of positioning cups under them, but also in terms of sighting the buttons; often her finger would crash against the machine as many as five times before she actually pressed it in the right place.

The store was filled with a wilderness of beeping: the cash register, the monitors above the sandwich counter, the ovens, the steeped tea machine, the microwave and the big digital clock above the drive-through. Amber didn't use the cash register yet, nor was she allowed to touch soups or sandwiches, and any time Tharani had to leave and do something, Amber had no choice but to stand there and mess with the coffee pots until she came back. She tried leaning subtly against the counter to try and rest, just a little, since she felt like she could barely stand up. It was banal work, for sure, unskilled labour—but still serious business, because it was a job, it was work, and she'd get over it. Meanwhile she kept compulsively glancing at the clock. Her shift was done at 1:00, still terribly distant.

After two hours Cynthia called Amber to the back of the store. It was the first time in two hours that Amber turned her back on the counter. Although her body was accepting the fact that she was awake and had to do things, her arms still felt heavy and lukewarm, and she found it hard to look out the window at the daylight.

"How is it?" Cynthia asked. "Not hard?" She told Amber to take a fifteen minute break, during which time she was free to sit at the table in the back of the store, beside the training computer. She gave Amber a package of papers to take home and sign. The cover letter welcomed her to the Tim Hortons store, which was going to be an "exciting" place, apparently. Amber didn't have a bag, so she stashed it with Ian's pants. Apparently she could have free coffee on her break; that was the best thing that had happened to her that day. She tentatively filled a china mug, not believing that it was actually free, expecting to be stopped and challenged by someone with authority.

In the break area she put her head down on her arms. Her feet were hurting from the standing. Amber realised how long it had been since she ditched Janelle's train tickets, almost twenty-four hours. It wasn't too late to take Cynthia aside and say, look, this was a mistake.

Maybe later. On the telephone. After she called Janelle—*or before.* Which of them was the less intimidating? At the moment, the easiest thing would be to just finish her five-hour shift and get out of there. All bets were off until she got back to Jesse's and had a sleep.

After, *fuck*, of course, detouring all the way out to 2468 Eglinton West, to see that apartment.

Breaks were timed with a stopwatch outside the store office. Amber heard it beep in the distance. Two more hours. She hadn't finished her coffee; she poured it down the sink in the bathroom. Then she returned to the storefront, holding the empty mug against her stomach, like a treasure.

Expecting more counter work, Amber once again approached Cynthia at the drive-thru; instead, the Chinese girl took her right back to the computer in the break area to start on the training CDs. It was a black Dell, a desktop chassis that they'd stood on one side so that CDs loaded vertically; apparently it didn't break when they did that. Someone had renamed the C drive to "Begine to master rhymin."

The training CD series filled a rack above the computer. Amber was instructed to load disc 1. She balanced it on its edge in the CD tray—*sideways!* A matte appeared around the edges of the screen and a video started: acoustic guitar music and a long shot of some Tim Hortons store in a field somewhere, the neatly-framed fluorescent sign high up on its pillar. Someone walked past Amber, getting something from dry storage, and Amber felt an impulse to grab at the volume control knob; there was no reason other people had to hear her doing this.

Disc 1 was called "Always Fresh Orientation," all about the mission statement and stuff. Amber watched historical footage of the very first store, slow zooms on a photograph of Mr. Tim Horton himself. Random businesspeople appeared in interview, explaining that it was not about putting big stores in small towns. There was a montage of employees, or actors at least, passing plates and cups and bowls across the counter, smiling like school picture day. Amber sat with her feet together under the chair, grateful to be resting, thinking about what a crazy mess she'd made around herself. As soon as she got back to Jesse's...

The rest of the day looked like it would be bleak. After work, feeling the way she did, going all the way to an apartment in Silverthorne would be an impossible labour. At 1:00 she was finished work; if she went straight back and slept for an hour then that would leave basically the rest of the day to see the apartment; maybe she could call the woman again and put off her visit for a few hours, or to another day entirely.

No, Amber. No no no. Mommy's not here to take care of you now.

It took twenty minutes to finish with disc 1, and Amber wondered if she was to go ahead and do disc 2 as well, or report back to Cynthia. Amber looked in the direction of the storefront, hoping the girl would come back and tell her.

She could brazenly pop in the next disc. It was on Health and Safety.

The actors got a workout on the Health and Safety disc, portraying burns and falls. After that, Amber had been watching training videos for forty-five minutes. She pushed back the chair, nudged up her visor and went to look for Cynthia.

With less than an hour left to go, with the end in sight, Amber's feet seemed to hurt more than ever. When she got to the counter, a pair of women were—jokingly?—pressing upon Tharani, the short, morose-looking woman, the issue of why larger sizes of tea cost more, since it was the same teabag. Theoretically, they could buy a small tea and then just get a free cup of hot water, couldn't they? Right? Cynthia called Amber to the office to point out the work schedule for the rest of the week, her hours written in pen at the bottom. Her start time for that day was corrected to 9:00. So, she hadn't been screamed at, but they hit her in her wallet. *Fine, justice is done.* Her next few shifts, all overnight, were

Friday to Saturday – 11:00 pm to 7:00 am
Saturday to Sunday – 11:00 pm to 7:00 am
Sunday to Monday – 11:00 pm to 8:00 am

It took her a moment to comprehend all the days and times, just what they meant in terms of her immediate situation.

She noticed the extra hour tethered on for Monday morning, obviously because it was a weekday morning, and they needed that extra little bit of help. And precisely seven hours after the end of that shift she'd have to be in Ottawa, writing her physics exam. She'd never told Cynthia about that. Amber stared at the page, feeling blood creep up her neck, glazedly wondering whether some other interpretation would occur to her. What to say? Whatever she thought of, any way of mentioning this, it made her feel sick. Trying to put words together—*but can't sorry no*—made her feel like throwing up. Like last night, fighting down the Vex: don't think about it, don't turn your attention inward; breathe, look around, think about something else.

Not today. Not while she was sick. Tomorrow.

And then it was 1:00. The minute hand oozed around twelve, and Amber waited stoically for someone to relieve her. Ten minutes later Cynthia said, "Amber, you're done? Go, go!" And Amber obeyed, changing back into Ian's pants, relieved that her wallet was still there. It was too bad she didn't have her backpack. Amber folded up her uniform and the papers and wadded them all into one of the plastic sleeves.

"So, you're back tomorrow night?" Cynthia said as Amber walked through the storefront one last time.

"Yeah," Amber said.

"Okay, I see you in the morning." Cynthia got back to picking apart coffee filters. And Amber left.

It was snowing again in the street, on an angle, and the sidewalk salt was kicked away. Amber stood on the curb, looking to Cliffcrest Plaza across the street, wondering if she could remember how to get back to the subway from there. There was a bus stop at the corner, in front of the United Church and Community Centre, and Amber wished there were someone else there, also waiting for a bus, whom she could imitate—someone whom she could ask if it was even the right bus. She went into the shelter, waited ten minutes, and no one else showed. By the time the bus actually came, Amber was wondering if service had been cancelled for the day. She was on the bus and pulling away before she realised she didn't have enough change; standing beside the driver, trawling through her wallet long after she realised, she finally confessed that she had to get off at the next stop, sorry, sorry. She used the ATM in a Mac's and discovered that the convenience charge was $2. It was a wait for the next bus— ten minutes, again—and at last she was somewhat, kind of, on her way.

Idle again, holding her plastic sleeve of treasures, she felt terrified. *Get out, get out. Don't get in. Into what?* She wasn't going to quit her job, not on account of being nervous about experiencing something new, of having new responsibilities.

So she backtracked all the way she'd come that morning: back to Warden station, on the subway to the west, over the valley, all the way to Yonge. Just that much took fifty minutes; then it was time to transfer to a northbound train. Amber sat with her head bouncing against the window and her eyes closed, only opening them to look at the names of the stations. By the time she got to Eglinton she'd been going for an hour; it was already 2:00, the time she'd said she'd be at the apartment. Why did travel time have to fuck up her whole life, every little piece of planning shot to hell because of these indifferent TTC drivers? It was so tempting just to stay on the train, keep going up to Finch.

By the time the bus had deposited her at the corner of Keele and Eglinton, she'd been in transit for ninety minutes. Well, that was something she'd just have to get used to. She'd be making that trip eight times a week if she lived here.

At Keele Street the street numbers were around 2600. Amber looked around a little to confirm that the numbers decreased to the east, up the hill full of Carribean restaurants. She wanted number 2468, tasting the little pattern. She walked up the hill, counting down the numbers, wondering what kind of place it would turn out to be. She passed the pizza place. It was odd; none of the buildings in the area were residential, unless you counted the second floor apartments.

She felt a sense of gravity as she passed the pharmacy, and it wasn't just fatigue from climbing the hill. The pharmacy's street number was about 2500. She looked farther ahead... It couldn't be. It was the West Side Rehab building, its chemical green sign, the numbers 2468 plain above it on the red brick. It was, it definitely was.

The front door was tied open with a computer power cord. Trying to look like she belonged, like she knew at least as much about the place as the crowd of mainly-black school kids noisily letting themselves in, Amber found the lobby speakerphone and hoped it was more intuitive than the one in Carrie's building. She rang the woman's room and said sorry for being late, she just got off work and so on; her strategy was to just motor-mouth her whole explanation before the woman could interrupt. The woman laughed and said that Amber was lucky she wasn't any later, because she was about to leave for work herself.

A zapping sound came from the inner door, meaning it was unlocked. It was an awful sound.

A bulletin board was full of newspaper clippings and community notices. It seemed a bit condescending, like something a guidance counselor would put up in high school. There was a notice that tenants had to report any changes in their income within thirty days or they'd lose their subsidy. Did that apply to her? She'd never had an income until just a few weeks ago, until the pension plan had started.

The elevator had weird, cone-shaped buttons. Amber chose floor 14, as the woman had instructed, which was really floor 13, but for some reason architects still did that thing of pretending there wasn't a floor 13. Amber vowed that she'd never do that. Years of engineering training weren't supposed to make you superstitious.

She stepped onto floor 14, which was really floor 13, and started at how low the hall ceiling was. It seemed barely taller than a doorway, and it was reduced even further because all the utilities were exposed. Some drop panels were missing. There were stains on the walls and the cheap carpets, and the doors and baseboards were the same sickly green colour as everything else all over the building. Amber knocked at apartment 12. And even after all that, she was still unprepared for the fact that the woman in the apartment was black, and not just black, but solid landed-immigrant Caribbean black, wearing a brightly coloured jacket and a headdress. Amber was hotly aware that she shouldn't have cared. She shouldn't have. But she did... that bright, probing speech; her name was Simone. Amber grinned and asked to see the room.

The apartment was decorated lavishly, proudly, as though Simone expected to live there for another thirty years, as though she considered this rental above a drug rehab clinic to be her home, permanently. There were carpets and table lamps, a gaudy chandelier above the dinner table. A giant tapestry of horses hung on the living room wall.

The two rooms for rent were recently vacated by her daughter. They weren't even two rooms, really; it was one bedroom, with a tiny back room no bigger than a balcony, separated through sliding doors like for a closet. Maybe it *was* a closet. There was a desk and a dresser, but no bed. Simone said she'd taken the bed. She'd taken the carpet too; the floor was bare hardwood.

Amber nodded at the room, like it was something to be understood, rather than inspected.

"So, you have telephone here," Simone said, pointing at the jack with her toe.

"Do you get wireless internet?" Amber asked, sensing that it was a pompous question. What a thing to ask in 2468 Eglinton West. Simone prattled that, basically, she didn't know. And it sounded like a challenge to Amber, this black woman with her sonorous voice that bordered on being harsh. It sounded like, where do you think you are? Amber wasn't sure if Simone even knew what "wireless internet" meant.

The woman said that she was going out to work in five minutes, so Amber couldn't stay long. That was fine. Amber gazed around the room, almost as though she knew what she was looking for, and she asked how much the rent was. Simone said that her share of it would be $500 a month.

And in fact, if Amber wanted the room, Simone just needed a $500 deposit, and it would be hers.

"Five hundred dollars?" Amber repeated. "Now?"

As though Amber had been protesting the ethics of asking for a deposit, Simone said, "Well Amber, you just need to prove that you're really interested, eh?"

"I mean," Amber said, "I don't have five hundred bucks right now. Could I get it to you later?"

"You can bring it whenever you like, but until I get that from you, someone else could come and see the room and like it better, eh?"

"Yeah. It's just I'd need to get it in cash, I don't have a chequing account... Can I get it to you tomorrow?"

Simone repeated what she'd just said about someone else coming and putting down a deposit before her; then she'd lose her chance. Amber understood perfectly, so she said. She'd bring the deposit tomorrow. And she just might move in tomorrow as well, she added with a chuckle. With that, she excused herself quickly. Yes, she really liked the building. It was nice and cheap.

It took another forty minutes to bus back to the subway. In all that time, Amber had nothing to do but think about how terrible she felt. And from there, she still had to take another bus from Finch station to Jesse's house. She wasn't even sure why she was going back up there. *To sleep on his floor?* Waiting in the bus hub, sitting on the ground, leaning against the cold glass, she called Jesse on her cell phone to see if he was home. Nobody answered. The bus was a half hour in coming. Her life that day had been ruled by public transit. She'd got out of work at 1:00; now it was almost 4:30. It was getting dark.

She considered calling the house once more, walking into Lowbank Court. No one had answered before, but she was numb to the possibility of no one being home, already thinking about passing out on the swing set in Bestview park. A figure blurred behind the frosted glass.

It was Mrs. Dundas, wearing a bright yellow kerchief around her hair. "Hello," she said.

"Hi, I was hoping Jesse would be here."

"You've been around here a lot, haven't you?" *An accusation.* She stepped away from the door, suggesting that Amber could come in.

"So, Jesse's here?" Amber pressed.

"He may be."

"Is my brother here?"

"Who's that?"

"He's younger than me, he's... he's been here before."

"Might I know your name?"

"I'm Amber."

"Amber? Well hello. I just like to know who's sleeping under my roof."

"Oh, it's just for like a few days. Like, my brother and I just got to the city, and we're moving in with, like—"

Mrs. Dundas let Amber blather for a little longer, humouring her, and eventually offered her own name, Martina. The way she stood in front of the living room, clearly blocking off the house, it was impossible not to imagine what she thought of this interloper, this uninvited guest of Jesse's who kept turning up day after day. "Sorry, I'm pretty tired," Amber said, sloping her shoulders, sighing a giant sigh—then changing her mind, since she didn't want Martina to know she was there to sleep.

"Oh really?" Martina said. "Care for a latte?"

"What's that?"

Martina swished to the kitchen, waving Amber in. Amber was relieved at first—this was better than that strained civility—but, of course she knew what a latte was. It was something to do with coffee. So instead of curling up in Jesse's room for much-anticipated rest, she wound up in Martina's kitchen, back in that awkward limbo of not knowing if it was okay to sit down.

Martina's espresso machine was the stainless-steel gizmo that Amber had mistaken for a soda fountain. She poured skim milk into a metal pitcher and put warm tap water and beans into the top. "I like it strong, Amber," Martina announced. "Hope you're not averse." Amber had to think of her own mother; she'd never had an espresso machine, but if she did, and if she were to make it for her daughter, she'd never chat like that. Martina held down a button, and the machine made a harsh sound, liquid squirting too quickly out a tiny metal portal, a sound like swallowing. "Here, have a try."

The kerchiefed woman held out a bowl-like mug. "Thanks," Amber said, threading one finger through the handle. A landscape of white foam covered it; the drink itself came on suddenly and was really hot. Amber tried not to cringe.

"What do you think?" Martina asked.

"Hmm!"

"Are you sold? Never had one before, you said?"

"Nope," Amber admitted.

The woman chattered about the machine and how her cousin had bought it in the States, while Amber complacently continued drinking. It was definitely very rich, as she'd said, like a milkshake, but bitter. And meanwhile Martina kept up her chatter, a lot like what she'd been doing with her friend the other night—she'd made espresso then too—and Amber tried to pay attention, realising she was also being treated like a friend, a grown-up friend. "It's good stuff," she remarked.

"I know," Martina simpered. She turned around. "So, Jesse told me a little about you. Where are you going to school?"

"University of Toronto," Amber said. "The Civil Engineering program."

Somehow, she resented how many syllables it took to say that. A moment ago she'd been treated like an adult, but adults were never asked, *Where are you going to school?*

"What's happened to your living arrangements?"

Amber lowered the mug from her nose.

"Just some mix-ups," she said. "I'm moving into a place—I'm not sure when. Could be tomorrow, if I get the money together." She was too tired to explain any better.

"Whereabouts?" Martina asked. God, she was just like the social worker. *Details, please.* And the way the woman looked at her, hair tied back and brow high, it wasn't just making conversation any more. The message was, get out of my house. Stop freeloading. *Yes, I know*, Amber thought. *I'm sorry. I'll leave.*

"A bit away," Amber said. Suddenly, ridiculously, she didn't want to mention the building itself; there were lies more plausible than the truth, more likely to make this woman happy. "Closer to downtown. It's a new place near Eglinton station. It's pretty good. I don't have to pay for a parking space, so…"

"What about your brother?" Mrs. Dundas pressed, no longer Martina; the stint of referring to her first name was over. "Who's looking after him?"

Well, their parents, Amber said—since he was going back home to their parents, while Amber got an apartment in the city, for university—that made sense, really. *Now dismiss me, Mrs. Dundas.* Her generosity been exposed as a trap. She was testing Amber, feeding her grown-up drinks to gauge how grown-up she really was, and Amber had failed, completely. She hadn't proven herself in charge of her own life; she'd proven herself a freeloader after all. Amber wasn't even going to dwell on it. She was going to get downstairs and sleep. She was getting hot in her hat and coat, which she hadn't even undone yet, and she was still holding her uniform under her arm. The travesty was that she was perfectly free just to turn around and glide from the kitchen any time, but no, if she did that she would have to glide straight back out to the sidewalk, like all the other times she'd run away.

Amber laughed and said, "Okay, I'd better go see if Jesse's in," and walked off, wondering if Mrs. Dundas would storm after her, which didn't happen. Amber hurried down the familiar stairs, discovered Jesse's door closed, the door to the room she'd thought she'd never see again. She knocked and no one answered, so she went in.

Jesse could have been at a class, or somewhere else, but she didn't give a damn where Jesse went. She wondered, where was

Guy? He'd said he was going to a film festival; did it start in the afternoon? She didn't have the energy to be concerned. At least all her bags were still there, on the floor. Jesse would probably let them sit there forever. She pulled off her hat and coat and put them on the chair, catching the reflection of Ian's T-shirt in the dark computer monitor, yet another reminder of last night. Getting her plans in order, she opened her backpack to set Guy's school schedule out where she could see it. It wasn't in the cover pocket of her journal, even though she was sure she'd put it there. It wasn't loose in her backpack; she pulled everything out just to be sure. Maybe she'd been carting it around in her coat pocket all day. It wasn't there either.

Oh shit. She wouldn't worry about it now. The room was empty, and the bed was softer than the floor. Amber moved a pile of binders and paper from Jesse's bed and turned out the light. There was a blurry blue rectangle lighting the bed from the small window; other than that, the room was dark as night.

Amber was banking on the hope that Mrs. Dundas wouldn't get suspicious about the freeloader going downstairs and not coming up. She tried not to think. She didn't want to think about all the things teetering over her, this job, this deposit—or all the things crawling around on Jesse's pillow. She just wanted to sleep.

The first cup of coffee that Amber ever enjoyed had been at 5:00 in the morning, in July. Up until that moment, the few tastes she'd had of the stuff had been unpleasant—bitter, bland and grownup—but that cup was delicious.

10:00 the previous day: Guy was counting his money for a trip to Trois-Rivières. Dad insisted that he take his fanny pack, which Guy never wanted to wear because he thought it looked dumb, and then drove him to his friend Jason's house.

11:00: Jason's brother's friends came to pick them up in a Ford Explorer, long after Dad had gone home. There were five people piled in for the trip; Guy, Jason and his older brother, the girl who owned the car, and her boyfriend. Guy got the back seat, in the middle. He made the entire trip without his seatbelt on, too intimidated by the stranger beside him to hunt around in the cleft of the seat.

12:00: When they parked on the roof of a parking tower in Trois-Rivières, Guy felt like he was in an amusement park. It was the heat, the bright sun reflecting off the pavement, and the gardens on the sidewalk. Many of the music venues were admitting all ages that day, as promised, but not all of them; the unforeseen complication was that they couldn't go to all the shows they'd planned for with these minors tagging along. The driver girl made gloomy faces on the curb, in a shirt that showed all her back freckles. Jason's brother abandoned them with the instruction that they were going to be leaving at *one o'clock,* okay? Yes, one in the morning. And he walked away.

16:00: Guy and Jason returned to the car in the afternoon, but it was locked, so they screwed around on the parking tower for a few hours before going back into town.

19:00: They returned to the parking tower roof again, bored with the festival and out of money.

23:00: And then again. Now, however, the parking tower roof was empty; they stood around the spot where the Ford Explorer had been, scanning the skies as though it had taken off.

1:00: By one o'clock, the appointed meeting time, the Ford Explorer was actually emergency-braked ten kilometres north of Trois-Rivières with an overheated engine.

3:00: Guy and Jason were outside the bus station, seeing if they had between them the four dollars it would take to call home on a payphone.

It was an hour's drive from Cantley to Trois-Rivières. Guy sat with Jason on a wooden bench outside the bus station, the terminal being closed at night, shivering in his shorts and Grateful Dead T-shirt. He fell asleep with his arms crossed. The person who woke him up with a clasp on the shoulder, a long brown coat and corduroys, was Uncle Ian, who had been living with them on a cot in the basement.

5:00: It was a clear dawn when Guy got home. The air felt like 7-up. When he went into the house, he discovered the entire family up and waiting for him; it was vindicating to be the focus of so much attention.

For some reason his sixteen-year-old sister had put on coffee for him and prepared a cup with cream and five spoons of sugar. But Mom said no; so Amber sat at the kitchen table and drank it herself.

"Since when do you drink coffee?" Mom asked her.

"Since right now."

There was a clattering sound—the doorknob. Amber sat up, surprised and mortified. "Whoa," Jesse said, turning on the lights. Amber responded with a thoughtful hum, blinking, scrambling for her wits. Her mouth was coated with dry spit-slime, and she had a sore throat like she'd been snoring. Her stomach hurt like fuck.

"When did you get back?" Jesse demanded. "I was waiting all morning for you." Right beside the bed, like a nightmare.

"I had to work," Amber said.

"I called Patrick's in the morning, and he said you weren't there."

"*I fucking had to work.*" Too distracted to watch her tone of voice.

Jesse observed her. Bits of snow were on his hat and shoulders.

"You got pretty fucked up last night, eh?"

Camaraderie. Amber snickered in spite of herself. "Oh god. I had one drink." Then shame. "I'm sorry."

"Hey, it's not a problem. Shit, last night was..." He laughed too, searching for a word. "*Crazy.* Holy shit, you were there all night, right?"

"Yeah," Amber said.

"Were you there when Mark started waving his erection around?"

Seemingly, she was. In Ian's bed by that time, though.

"Okay, well, around midnight it turned into, what it was called was a two-pieces-of-clothing party..."

"What the hell is that?"

"Well, it's like... You have to take off all your clothes except for two pieces."

"Oh dear."

Jesse went on, "Anyway, so Mark came out of his room wearing just this silk housecoat and like, a leather pouch, right?" He cupped his hands around his groin for emphasis.

"Oh, yuck."

"With a zipper," Jesse added. "And then he was dry-humping people. And he got a picture of this one guy with his face right up…"

"And then he whipped it out?" Amber said.

"He totally whipped it out."

She'd definitely slept through that, and she wasn't sorry for it.

"Did you witness this?" Amber asked.

"No way, Carrie and I'd already gone. We left around midnight I think. But *then*—" His speech was interrupted with giggling as he stared over her head, eyes lively, approaching the next detail like a tantalising bite of food. There'd been an orgy in the other upstairs bedroom, he said, with the door open and everything.

"Aw shit," Amber replied through an incredulous smile, then she asked, "Is it snowing?" And then, "Where's Guy?"

"Guy?" Jesse said. "He said he was seeing a movie."

His film festival. Amber looked at her watch: it was 8:00 in the evening. She cross-referenced this with the view from Jesse's window: darkness. *Shit.* She shouldn't have slept for so long; she should have set the alarm on her watch, made it a quick nap. Now her brain was waterlogged, and she had to lurch to her feet—if she were at home in Cantley she'd have eaten some breakfast cereal, sitting in the kitchen with all the lights on. Instead she was in a tiny basement room with one harsh ceiling light and nothing to eat but pop and fruit cups, which weren't even hers.

"Hey Amber," Jesse said. "Martina told me to tell you to get Origin Marketing to quit calling them."

"Okay," Amber said.

"Serious, it's ticking them off. Don't you have your own phone?"

"Yes," Amber answered.

"Then get them to start calling that instead."

Amber fished her coat off of the computer chair, ensured her wallet was still in the pocket. She wasn't planning to contact Origin Marketing ever again. The solution to her groggy condition was to get up, go out, and buy something to eat. A distant, arduous solution, but afterwards she'd thank herself. "I've got to go out," she said.

"Where are you going?" Jesse asked. "You don't have to stay here again, do you?"

Not a shred of hospitality. "Yes—God—this'll be the last time, though, I swear. I'm moving into a place tomorrow. I just gotta go out now." She zipped her jacket and put on her hat.

"Whatever," Jesse said. "The Dundases are nice, I just don't want to step on their toes, you know?"

"Yeah. Sorry."

Amber lurched up the basement stairs, hearing the sizzle of a frying pan, smelling onions—the Dundases' dinner. *Food.* Amber hurried out the front door, planning, she guessed, to either get food at the plaza on Steeles, or else take the bus somewhere, as though she'd miraculously wind up finding her brother if she just went out with that intention. But she'd already seen everything along Bestview Drive so many times. A change of scenery would make her head stop clamouring. So instead she went to the park beside the elementary school, where she'd sat with her brother days ago, walking up the path, dark because there weren't any lampposts. She walked to the edge of the playground with the swings and the giant octahedron, looking grey and frosty. Then she went on to where the path branched off into a fitness trail, a dark asphalt swathe into the woods, and she looked down a minute, feeling certain that this was a place where criminals went at night. There were no lights, no people. She stood there for a long time, listening.

Signs told her that there was to be no golfing and no driving of motorised vehicles. There were tall, thin trees along the path; for a while there were also bright houses with backyards and chain-link fences, but the fences become covered in vines, and eventually disappeared. The trail got steeper. She'd left all the houses behind, and the air was like the time she'd visited home in October for Thanksgiving and slept in her old bed—the last time she slept in her old bed. She heard running water and found she could still see by the city light, as though the air itself were glowing dimly.

The grey of the snow stood out, describing shapes like in really old photographs. She looked over her shoulder, making sure she was still alone. This was quite possibly the stupidest thing she'd ever done. No one would be on this trail at this hour, at this time of year, unless they were rapists. Only an idiot would go walking alone in a place like this. And if there *were* someone following her, if would be one of those looks over her shoulder that set it off, whatever she had coming to her.

They made trails wander on purpose, of course. Something to notice would come at her, slowly, a snatch of wooden fence or a pile of rocks. Amber saw the moving lights of cars on a road bridge, elevated, oddly distant. The trail went under the bridge, through a few more twists, and then into a giant clearing, a stadium-sized aisle extending over the hills on either side of the river, arrow-straight, for the hydro towers. There were three rows of them, tall, weird shapes echoing from one end to the other, shapes like arms holding up the steel and aluminum wires, humming in the snow.

Amber could have rested more that evening, or busted out her physics notes to study, or she could have spent hours walking up and down city streets, looking for her brother, understanding that she didn't have a hope in hell of just running into him. Instead she was out in the middle of a dark field, in the snow, listening to electricity. Away from the path was a backhoe, parked and abandoned for the night, kept company by a pile of dirt and dozens of bags of gravel. Amber went toward it, off the trail and through the coarse grass.

She wasn't sure what sort of construction was going on, but they'd cleared a shoddy dirt road down from the top of the hill. Amber heard the sound of a motor and located a generator on a trailer hitch, pumping mud out of a plastic tube in the ground. Maybe they were building a road, but it was a weird place for it. The backhoe was locked up tight, looking a lot bigger up close: dirt-filled treads, hydraulics, the hitches connecting the shovel part to the boom. The shovel rested on the ground, claws down, creating a shelter. Amber crawled underneath it and hugged her knees.

She thought she might fall asleep again if she stayed that way, and she resolved to get back up, soon. The Dundas family had seen through all her excuses, she knew, and if they ever threw her out, which they would definitely do, possibly that very night... So she had to finalise the apartment thing. All her fears had a plain, straightforward remedy, as usual. It was a question of just going out and *doing* something, instead of lying around worrying about how important it was to do something. Tomorrow morning she'd call Simone about taking the apartment, and she'd go back and work out the deposit and move in on the spot. And in the evening she'd go to work. And years from now she'd have a funny university horror story about how she'd gone one night and hid under a backhoe because of how worried she was.

Driven by necessity, that was all. Nobody liked having a thousand things to worry about. And once she and Guy were living with Simone, once she was paying rent and buying groceries and putting away the little bit left over...

Suppose she just *never* called her social worker. What could Janelle do, besides put her face on milk cartons? Cancer victims sometimes reached a stage when they accepted that they were going to die; Amber seemed to have reached something like that, except in her case it was the death of a relationship with this government-appointed woman who had told her at their first meeting how happy she was that Amber was behaving so maturely.

Amber never humoured herself that she came from a broken home. Her parents were good. They were exceptional, compared to other families she'd heard of, compared to statistics like 65% of marriages failing, 25% of children being physically abused. She would never blame them for anything or make them watch her throw away what they'd invested in her. She appreciated everything she'd been given, or at least she wished she could, especially after moving out since, really, it was impossible to acknowledge these things while still in the middle of them, living under their roof, getting called to the dinner table.

There was a plane overhead. Amber listened. It was bad to sit the way she was sitting, her insides all crushed up. She was still starving, and only making it worse the longer she waited. Everything only got worse when she did nothing. So, enough reverie. She got up, crawled out from under the shovel, and walked the newly-hewn road up the hill, back to the streetlights and relative safety. Amber found herself back among houses, parked cars and Christmas lights. There, all that and she hadn't been mugged.

She emerged onto a larger street; it was the corner of Cummer and Bayview. Perfect: there was a restaurant called Coffee Counter in the plaza. Amber was starving, suddenly aware of the vast amounts of nothing she'd eaten with since upchucking a day ago. Her mouth felt bitter and dry. She strolled in, compulsively salivating, and waited at the counter. She surveyed the wares on display in the glass showcase; it was all variations on a theme, bottles of juice and pudding cups and pre-buttered bagels. She felt like she hadn't eaten in a year.

It had seemed like a good idea. She bought an egg-salad sandwich, and it tasted rotten and stuck in her throat. Everything had been good and fine until she actually had it in her mouth. The coffee tasted metallic and moldy, like paint was flaking off the cup onto her lips. She stirred in an assembly line of sugar packets until she knew she'd put in too much, and then it still tasted bad but with the added sting of candy-sweetness. It was like she had a chemical in her that spoiled food the second she tasted it. Suddenly the much-anticipated meal stretched out like chore; she counted bites on the sandwich, measured the depth of the coffee with her eye. She wasn't about to throw it away, though—she never wasted food—so she just sat quietly at the table, staring at the parking lot and listening to the radio, until she finished her dinner.

Then it was time to walk back to Jesse's, along the streets this time. And no, she hadn't forgotten about Janelle, but the prospect of calling her had soured along with the egg salad. She felt hungry again, almost as though she *hadn't* just forced herself to eat an entire meal. She wanted to go back and buy more food, like a donut, a chocolate one with toasted coconut. So she did; she turned on her heels at the corner, marched back into the coffee shop and did exactly that. She was out of change and had to break another twenty. She knew she'd just make herself feel sicker, but she didn't care.

Guy had used the money he kept hidden from his sister to buy bus fare Friday afternoon. Instead of going downtown, he first went to his school to drop off his signed course enrolment sheet. It had annoyed him to find it still there in her homework book when she got him to open it that morning. She made such a big deal about getting him into his classes, and then she forgot all about it herself. The signature was obviously fake, but it wasn't like he'd faked it himself. The secretary took it without a blink, as it happened. Then he walked around the school to find his classes, which was what he'd wanted to do the last time he was there, before his sister had made a beeline for the exit. It was last period, and he stuck his face up to the window of Canadian History 1. There were sure a lot of black kids.

On Monday he was supposed to be in there, but he had a premonition about this new building. In Cantley, living at home, he'd spent entire seventy-five-minute classes staring at the clock, wanting for it to be time to leave; but he felt sure that here, in this city, wherever he actually wound up living while going to school in Toronto, he'd dread 3:15. He wouldn't want to go home.

Then a teacher saw him in the hall and asked where he was supposed to be. He tried to say that he was just looking for his classes, but the teacher marched him to the office. He felt hot and angry; it seemed like he was going to get in trouble for nothing. Fortunately, the secretary to whom he'd just given his enrolment sheet confirmed that he wasn't officially in classes until Monday. After that he was asked to leave the building. *Fine, he was leaving.*

He took the bus downtown, standing in the aisle, looking around for anyone else his age. The cinema for the Salvador Dali thing had a Bathurst Street address, and was noted as being "below College". There was a subway station called "Bathurst" and another one called "College"; using those stations as co-ordinates he managed to walk out to the right intersection, and found the cinema by spotting the name on a poster board.

It seemed to be someone's house. He was nervous about going in, and he leaned against a street sign until a group of twenty-year-olds went in, and he tailed them. A girl at the door in pink denim took his $20 bill, and she looked charmed to see him, talking to him in a puppy-dog voice, as though it was a museum he'd gone to by himself, and it delighted her that he was interested in such things at his age, and as though he were five years younger than he was.

He didn't get back to the house on Lowbank Court until midnight. He didn't have trouble getting in, since Jesse was smoking on the sidewalk. The guy said his sister was passed out on his bed, but they could play some Station if they were quiet. They weren't quiet enough, it seemed. Guy heard his sister roll over when he sat on the bed beside her—not that she had anything to say to him.

CHAPTER 7

The drill was familiar. Amber would command herself to get up as early as possible, sleep in another hour anyway, then order her brother to pack up. They could move in with Simone when they arrived that day. Good thing they didn't have any furniture.

But she slept in again, until noon, deliberately, consciously, even after Jesse took off, even after her brother got up first and turned on the video games. She'd been sick, she reminded herself. And she'd landed a job, so she deserved some rest. At 11:30 she rolled onto her stomach, and Guy turned around and said, "Are you awake?" and she pretended not to be.

"What time is it?" Amber asked a half-hour later. "Oh, it's noon."

"A little after," Guy added.

"Ah shit," Amber said. "Want to go out for breakfast? I want pancakes and blueberries."

"I want pop and a frosty glass of semen."

"Well if they're serving that up today, I'll pay for it." She poked him in the back.

"Just a sec."

"But only if you get a semen glass."

Amber picked through her hockey bag, trying to remember which clothes were still clean, and she went to the musty downstairs bathroom to change. She was going to wear a sweater with mostly-gray stripes. She was hungry and hoped it was in a healthy way; nevertheless her gut felt heavy, and she sat on the toilet for two minutes. She stood in front of the sink and smelled her arms. As soon as they got to the apartment, she would have a shower. When she finished dressing and went back to Jesse's room Guy was still playing the game, but standing up now, frustratedly mashing at the controller, a display of finishing up as fast as he could.

"So, you're working now?" Guy asked.

"Yeah," Amber said, surprised that he cared. "I got a job at Timmy's."

"Do you make the doughnuts?"

"No, I don't make the doughnuts. I'm on the front counter." She poked him again. "Come on, we're moving into that apartment today."

Guy was quiet, a measured silence intended to drain momentum from the conversation. He probably didn't like the fact that his sister had arranged things for him again. "What apartment?" he asked, finally.

"The big one, near Uncle Ian's," Amber said. "Remember?"

She could have mentioned the rehab center, or the porn store across the street, and then Guy would have known instantly what building she meant. But she didn't want to remind him that they'd been laughing at it a few days ago.

Amber pulled at her sweater collar. "And we still got to get that form into your school."

"I did that yesterday," Guy said.

"You did what?"

"I took my schedule to school and gave it."

"What do you mean?"

"I mean, I took my schedule to the school and gave it."

"To who?"

"I don't know, I just gave it in at the office. Holy crap."

"Well, fine," Amber said. "So you know where you're supposed to be on Monday?"

"Yes."

The television burst into loud static, and Guy turned it off. They put on their coats, and Amber told her brother to pack his things, since they weren't coming back after breakfast. He'd spread himself out quite a bit; he had dirty clothes on the floor and books on Jesse's desk. A few more days, Amber thought, and his stuff would have been totally integrated with the fat guy's; he'd be living the same way, the same torpid smell hanging over him and everything he owned. Amber gathered up her bits of paper, her computer, her work uniform. She pulled her hat over her ears. Jesse would come home and find the two of them gone, without cordialities, along with all their stuff. Wouldn't that be a relief. The Dundas family would probably watch from the curtains, sighing. They hoisted their hockey bags, as in an old ritual, crept up the stairs and opened the front door.

The sky was like ice, and there were foot-high drifts burying all the yards in Lowbank Court, except around a metal box on the sidewalk. A giant cone of snow was plowed up in the middle of the court; kids were sledding down it.

"It's a snow day," Guy said. "Blows I'm not in school."

The trees all had white tops now; the willow on the other side of the court looked like a mountain. They walked down the middle of the road. Amber watched her breath steam. She could see Steelesview school around the bend, empty and benign on account of bad weather.

Guy asked, "Do you suppose we count as homeless now?"

"No, we have our own apartment," Amber said.

Guy accepted that.

But why would he even ask?

"It's okay, Guy," Amber said.

It was a snow day, indeed. Amber could see televisions on through some of the windows on Bestview Drive. She'd been aware, last January, almost a year ago now, that the snow day they had then would probably be her last one, since they didn't have school buses in university. Classes didn't get cancelled on account of a spot of snow early in the morning. And even if they were, it wasn't a holiday; it wasn't all the teacher's problem to work in the material they missed.

"Where the hell can we get breakfast round here?" Amber said.

"I don't know. You're the one who knows Toronto."

"I was just saying." She wiggled her fists in her coat pockets. "The only thing around here is coffee shops. There's one I went to the other day, but it's kind of a walk."

"Walking keeps you alive."

"I suppose it does."

Amber directed her brother onto Steeles. She'd walked it last night, the other way. Steeles was nice and plowed, a hedgerow of gritty snow covering half the sidewalk. The street lines were invisible, and cars just followed in each others' tire tracks, which seemed dangerous for a six-lane street. Amber asked her brother how he was finding the city, what he was doing with himself. Not much, he told her.

You're the one who knows Toronto. Your city, Amber, not mine; as though he resented being there, as though he thought they had a choice. And she didn't *know* the city; she'd just made more of an effort to get around and do things, instead of sitting in a basement playing video games. *I got a job,* she wanted to remind him. You handed in your schedule. Show up for your classes on Monday and get on with it.

And in the meantime, think about breakfast.

"You went to see a movie yesterday, didn't you?" Amber said.

"Uh, yeah."

"How was that?"

"Just really weird."

"That's it?"

"Well, what do you want to know?"

"What was it about, who was in it, was it any good?"

"It was surrealism. It was just weird," Guy explained.

Amber felt like she'd have to torture him to learn anything else. She shouldn't have prattled on with questions. But that was just the way she and her brother talked, blitzkrieg dialogue that lasted ten seconds. It was normal, and she was happy for it. There were spruce branches hanging low over the sidewalk, weighed down with snow, and it was taking effort to duck under them; that was a good reason to shut up for another few minutes.

She'd been facetious when she'd said she wanted pancakes and blueberries, since she knew Coffee Counter didn't actually have a kitchen. Nevertheless, the selection looked small and unpleasant when they arrived. They really just had bread and bagels and stuff to go on them. Guy could have whatever he wanted, she told him. As for her, well, was it all that coffee that had made her sick? Was this what a stomach ulcer felt like? She decided to avoid coffee for a while; they had six flavours of Fairlee and six flavours of Snapple.

It wasn't a bad place, Amber decided. It was busy at the moment, and Amber felt righteous for choosing it, for supporting the owners who had dared to open a freelance coffee shop in the same parking lot as a Burger King. They sat down with their bagel sandwiches, and a man in a windbreaker walked in the door. A card appeared beside the table: "Ladies and Gentlemen I have 4 brothers and my father is dead, Pleased spare money for food Any help Appreciated and God Bless". Amber tried to pretend she didn't notice, looking hard at her brother's face; the guy made a "Hunh" sound like a deaf person. Silently, Amber took out her wallet, not looking up at him, him with a white headband on, and goddamn she had a shitload of change, which she sorted through, trying not to give the guy a view of it; he was glancing toward the counter like he intended to buy something, but after Amber gave him some dimes and quarters he just said "Thanks," with a remarkably normal accent, and left the store. Amber watched him walking out of sight, through the windows.

And Guy could stop looking at her like that, searchingly, like something confusing had just happened. Amber lost her appetite. Something black and disgusting clawed up her throat, biological punishment. Fuck that guy. He'd probably been faking it, his clothes had looked totally clean, and now he was at the Smoke & Gifts buying cigarettes and fucking proud of himself, and there was Guy, having witnessed all of it.

"Aww," Amber said, laying her head on the table among the paper dishes.

Her brother didn't say anything. He finished his breakfast before asking if she was okay.

"Once we get to the apartment I got to sleep," Amber told him. She would have to be up all night, after all. And in spite of that, she still had to find time to take out her physics notes and study. *To study her notes which she'd been promising herself she'd do every single day since she got here you lazy fuckoff.* Guy tried to balance his carton of chocolate milk on her cheek; she sat up.

"So there," Amber announced. "Our last meal for a while that doesn't come from a grocery store."

Guy nodded.

"Want to finish my bagel?"

It was lucky, actually, that they hadn't gone someplace that served big breakfasts, because she'd definitely have ordered one and wasted way more money.

"I'm glad we're out of that basement. I'm sick of it," Amber said.

"I think it's pretty cool," Guy said between bites of his sister's bagel. "I might board with someone when I do university."

"Well, don't leave Toronto and you won't have to move any-where... What are you thinking of doing?"

Today his answer was, "That's something to ponder on."

"Ponder it up, bitch."

"Yo."

As for Amber going into into civil engineering, it wasn't like she'd known she would do that in grade nine. It wasn't like she'd been obsessed with Lego or some other childhood antecedent of con-struction. And it wasn't like she would look out over a neighbour-hood and be bursting with ideas for improvements. It was more a sense of awe, when she saw buildings like those two on Bay Street, those playful ones, or any of the big ones downtown, and she imag-ined that someone must have held designs for them in their head, and committed them to paper through the constraints of physics and live-ability. They were places where people went to work and passed un-knowing hours of their lives.

Even Ian's house, the tower-like house at the corner of Sil-verthorn and Dunraven, even just something like that, for a start.

"Well I'm done," Amber announced. "Are you?"

Amber gave Simone a call to tell her she was coming for the rooms. She imagined showing her brother into the lobby of the place, but it was hardly worth imagining, considering it would be happen-ing very soon. Whether he liked it or not, it's what they had to work with. She was glad she'd prepared him in advance that it was the Westside Rehab building. If he just discovered that when they got there, it would have seemed like a joke on him.

"Here we have it," Amber announced.

"This is right beside that bakery place," Guy observed.

"Indeed." Amber was happy to hear him focus on the bakery. "We're here," she said into the lobby intercom.

"Eh?" Simone answered. "You're the one looking at the room?"

A bit more than *looking at*, but, "Yeah."

"Good, come on up."

"Nice ceiling, eh?" Amber remarked on the fourteenth floor, remembering her own judgments of the low ceiling, the carpet and the walls; now she felt forced to unconditionally approve of it all, to make light of the problems, to sell it to her brother. In front of room 1412: it was her last chance to change her mind, before making it final and moving in. In a way, though, the last chance was already far behind her.

Simone answered the door in a grey silk suit, like a private school teacher. Her hair was teased out into an afro. "Amber," she greeted them.

"Hi Simone, this is my brother Guy... He'll be going to school." She realised she'd described him before as though he was much older than fourteen. "We're just going to put our stuff down."

"You're coming in?" asked Simone, nodding as though to confirm some deeper understanding.

"Yeah. Is that okay? We're just going to..."

"Come, come."

"Here we are," Amber said, showing Guy the room down the hall.

Guy was very quiet. His gaze seemed to travel the perimeter of the room, along the baseboards.

"And there's another room back here." Amber opened the sliding door to the back room. "You can have that one, I guess," she said. "Unless you'd actually rather have this one."

"You know, in Medieval times, girls would get rooms like this so that you had to go through the parents' room to get to them," Guy said.

"How chivalrous."

"So what are you doing about my deposit?" Simone asked.

"Okay, look," Amber said. "I've got the cash, I just wanted to know, is it okay if I give you a bank draft?"

"A bank what?"

"It's just that I don't have a chequing account set up yet, so I'll go to the bank to get them to write up a draft for you, for the five hundred bucks... It'll take about a day to do."

"What is this, Amber?" Simone said. "You said you could pay me today."

"Yeah, I can," Amber said. "I have the money, I just need to go to the bank and get a draft made, that's all."

"So you can pay, you just have to go get the money."

"Yeah... That's about it."

Amber wasn't sure what she'd just promised. It was bullshit, whatever it was. She'd pay, somehow, eventually, bank draft or not, just not right away, not that very second, thank you. Simone left them alone, going back into her living room and putting on loud music. And Amber comforted herself that she could always just walk away and never come back. She'd have loved to disappear for the rest of the day, sit on a bench somewhere until it was time to go to work. But she couldn't, because of Guy. She'd done so much to get him to this apartment; she couldn't leave now.

In fact, were it just her, she could sleep in a box and subsist on Kraft Dinner. But it was Guy, it was because of him; *he* couldn't.

Amber crawled to a corner of the room and took out her Introduction to Physics notes.

"Studying?" Guy asked. Amber nodded.

Measurement is the basis of physics. By learning how to measure physical quantities we make discoveries about the physical world.

"Are you just gonna be doing that?" Guy said.

"Yeah."

Guy went into the back room and thumped his knees against the wall.

"Don't you have a book or something?"

"No." Snappy, like it was her fault. Was her brother bored? *Of course.*

"Well, sorry. You know Janelle stopped the movers."

"Why can't we be at the house again?"

"Because Uncle Ian didn't have his shit together."

"What's that supposed to mean?"

"Guy, I'm trying to read."

Uncle Ian's fault. And Janelle's fault. It wasn't anyone's fault at all, Amber told herself. This was just the way shit went down for the two of them.

"I didn't even want to come to this stupid city," Guy glowered.

"Okay genius, what would have suited you?"

"Well…"

"Thought so."

"Fuck you."

That was his answer to everything. She moved his shit off the kitchen table because it was in the way: fuck you. She informed him that his sweatshirts stank because he never washed them: fuck you. And now he was saying it just because life sucked.

Well, fuck you too.

Even though he didn't deserve it, Amber let him have the last word.

Amber had let Guy use her computer, but he was finished with it. Her internet didn't work, and he was bored of the crappy games that shipped with Windows. He'd browsed her hard drive and internet history to catch her with porn, with no obvious discoveries. Her image folder was totally boring; mostly old pictures of her smiling, with friends whom he didn't know, and a scan of her own high school graduation photo; the nun-like robe, the funny hat with a pink sash.

She'd fallen asleep sitting against the wall, her white notebook spread out on her lap. Guy heard silence and realised the black woman had gone out, so he got up and walked around the apartment, discovering how old the furniture was. He entered the kitchen, so unlike the one at Uncle Ian's house; it had a tiny chunk of counter space, no bar into the dining room. It was dressed up lovingly, yes, with fridge magnets and wall decorations, and a clock with a pendulum, an old brass one that only grandmas would own.

But it was a stranger's apartment. Guy didn't buy it for one second. This wasn't home. They weren't living here. He was afraid of that woman, afraid of the fact that she was older than his parents, the icy way she'd demanded money. He looked at the knives, hanging from a magnetic strip, imagining how upset his sister would be if he stabbed himself in the stomach.

He put on his coat and picked up his hockey bag, taking care not to wake his sister. He took the elevator to the street and put up the hood of his parka. He knew he looked like he was skipping school, so he stayed away from George Harvey Collegiate Institute. He found himself in front of another high school, though, after walking down the hill with all the Caribbean restaurants. It was a different school; no one knew him there, so what could they do?

If he kept going west on Eglinton he would eventually approach Brownville Avenue, the little street where that Chinese family lived, the people who owned the Silverthorne house, his uncle's landlords. Guy didn't want to go visit them. He kept going.

Waking up at 4:00 in the afternoon when it was already starting to get dark, noticing voices outside the little room, Amber was glad the door was shut and the lights were off. It was like when Mom and Dad were mad. Maybe Simone wouldn't think there was anyone there. She'd been woken up by a sound like a grandfather clock; it could have been a big clock somewhere else in the apartment, but it had seemed rather close by.

She rubbed her face and set her physics binder aside. She crept into the back room to see what Guy was doing and discovered him gone. So she was in an empty room, empty except for Simone's daughter's unwanted furniture, her own hockey bag and backpack. She was hungry and thirsty, and her brain was fucked up from the nap. That was all well; she'd have to be up all night anyway. Her socks felt sweaty and cold, but it was too cold to take them off. *A laundromat: add that to the list.*

She couldn't study any more, not in the failing light, feeling the way she did. And she wasn't going to turn on the room lights and betray her presence. She was staked out then, with nothing but her computer, which Guy had left on like an idiot, which was displaying the low-battery warning.

Simone was in the living room. Amber waited and waited for her to go away. She didn't; Amber heard the microwave and dishes, the TV. How pointless to wait for her to leave her own apartment. She couldn't face that woman. She couldn't look her in the eyes again until she could pay, as she'd promised. If she were to leave the room, walk out into the hall, what sort of assault would be waiting there? What if she made straight for the exit; would Simone pounce like a soldier, not let her get away?

Well, it was after 4:00. Maybe the banks were already closing; it was Friday, and maybe that would be it for the weekend.

Whatever the case, she was bored and hungry as hell. She wanted to go out, and what kept her stuck in that room was intimidation from the loud-voiced deposit-demanding woman in the living room. She looked out the window. The sky was grey; it was snowing again. *Get me the hell out of here*, she thought.

Why don't you just go, Amber?

She had tears in her eyes.

Just *go*.

She couldn't.

She curled up in Guy's room, on the floor like a house pet, wondering: if she closed the inner door, maybe she could turn on the lights and study in *here*, make use of the time.

Get me out of here, she thought.

Prudently Amber assumed it would take an hour for her to commute to work. She left the apartment at 9:30, long after night fell, and betrayed her own promise to start eating out of grocery stores. She went to Caldense Bakery for sandwiches and bought some cake as well on impulse, telling herself she deserved a treat but not believing it. She didn't finish it. And she felt ridiculous because she'd worn her Tim Hortons uniform out the door. What a dumb idea. Thank goodness it was winter and she had her coat on; when she sat down in the bakery she didn't even unzip it. But the pants were distinctive, the colour, the tag on the side. *No black shoes, though.* She was stuck in her stained gray runners for another shift. She'd had all day to remember, but instead it was another mistake, another thing thought of too late. Surely they'd forgive her on her second day of work.

Her body was getting ready to go to bed, despite the hours she'd spent on the hardwood floor. She had to remind herself, no. *Not tonight.* And she was wrong about the commute taking an hour. When the bus ride along Eglinton to the subway took a good twenty minutes, she knew she was wrong. She called the store on her cell phone—she *tried* to call the store on her cell phone, made the discovery that cell phones don't work in subway tunnels, waited until she got on the bus at Warden and it was already 11:00, and then called to say sorry she was late. She hoped she could still use the TTC as an excuse. Then she fell asleep on the bus, woke up having already passed Cliffcrest Plaza, jumped out at the next stop and ran back. How many more times would that happen?

The evening manager was a man named Omar. The evening girls had already gone home, but he was staying late, waiting for her. Who would be with her overnight? The baker, and the night supervisor, Marie. Marie had long, wavy hair; she turned around, and Amber had to try hard to convince herself that this wasn't the same white woman from Keele Donuts, the one who'd been smoking at the table by the door, making the place smell like cigarettes.

Amber said sorry again for being late, and stayed at it until she was sure they understood she was really really sorry, then she went into the back to hang up her coat. She inspected her paper pants, the see-through shirt—today her nipples wouldn't be showing—the hairnet and the hat, the nametag with the label sticker.

"Sorry," Amber said when she went back out, "I was supposed to get black shoes today, but I couldn't get to it."

She shouldn't have said *sorry* again. Too many *sorrys* would make them all meaningless.

Marie said, "Well, get 'em tomorrow. I'll tell you now, Amber, I'm terrible at training. It's really not my thing." She said this grinning, right in front of Omar the evening manager, who tinkered in the office and left. That left just Amber, Marie the supervisor, and the baker to populate the place until 7:00 tomorrow.

"Soooo," Marie said, in a *let's conclude* voice, even though they'd just begun. Amber's training that night was to be answering the drive-thru and using the cash register. Marie's terrible training came in the way of brief, general instructions before she walked away, as though the details could be taken for granted. "So here we've got the cash register," she said, her tone of voice betraying how stupid she thought this training thing was. "You push the button of what they order, it tells you the price, you take their money and toss it in here. Pretty simple." Although, she had to concede that it would take a while to learn where all the buttons for different items were. "That'll come with practice," she added, and waved like she'd addressed the subject well enough. It was just as well, since the headset beeped just then. Amber could hear a car motor. "Want to take it?" Marie asked.

Amber reached for the cell pack. "Just like—What do I—?"

"Push the button and take his order!"

It was taking too long. "Hello?" said the customer.

Amber thumbed the talk button. Marie hadn't told her what to say. So she just repeated what she'd heard at drive-thrus before. Her eyes glazed, looking past her trainer's disinterested face. It was like having to read a script, an embarrassing script like for a kid's TV show, the shock of it. "Can I take your order?"

"Everything bagel with the butter, toasted, and a medium double-double with no sugar."

Amber stared stupidly at the cash register until Marie shouldered in front of her to punch in the order herself, her nail-polished fingers fluttering over the keys. "Two twenty-three please drive up," Marie said, and then, "I'll get the bagel." She started to leave and noticed Amber still looking at her, questioningly. "What you can do is grab the coffee and cash out."

"Okay," Amber said. But she'd already forgotten how the guy had wanted his coffee. Plaintively she looked to Marie; her back was turned. Fine, Amber got the picture. Car headlights moved past the window.

"Sorry," Amber. "How did you want your coffee again?"

The man rolled down his window. He had a round head, wrinkled eyes, thinning black hair. "Eh?" he said.

"How did you want your coffee again?"

"Everything bagel toasted with the butter, medium coffee, double-double with no sugar."

She hadn't asked for *everything* again. *Whatever*. She got him his medium coffee; double-double with no sugar meant, she supposed, not double-double at all? As Amber was passing everything out to him, he said, "No sugar, right? You always put sugar."

"Oh, no," Amber assured him. "There's no sugar in it."

"Good, because you always put sugar."

That was because he was an idiot who didn't know what "double-double" meant. Bitter words, but as he passed her three dollars he was smiling. "You are a new worker," he said.

"Yeah," Amber answered, smiling back. "It's my first shift. Well, my first night. I had a shift before but..." and she let it drop because she'd moved to the cash register and the window closed. He'd given her three dollars. How did you make change? Marie had wandered away. "Shit," Amber said. Time to do it in her head, math skills clawing up like drowning swimmers. *Two-twenty-three, so that is—so that is—*

"Here you go," Amber said.

"Thank you," the man said, smilingly taking his change. He did the *S'up?* movement with his head. "Bye now."

"Bye," Amber said.

Marie hadn't helped her with one word of that whole exchange. Apparently, though, she'd pulled it off just fine on instinct. She didn't need to be told how to talk to a customer; all she had to do was engage her sense of general politeness and consideration and respect, a sense which was apparently pretty rare among Tim Hortons workers. She'd made the man smile and talk to her, in spite of forgetting how he wanted his coffee.

Amber hovered around the front counter until Marie came back and described, in general, what had to be done overnight. It was a two-minute tour of duties that would take six hours. Amber nodded along with everything, studying the woman's short fingers seriously, each thing they vaguely pointed out. Basically, every little part of everything had to be sprayed or wiped, and every little commodity had to be replenished from the storage room. A beep would burst from headset every so often, or Amber would turn her head and discover a customer at the front counter. Some of them asked for bagels, and Amber consistently called on Marie to do them until the woman snarked that it wasn't hard—you cut it, you toast it, you put butter on it. So Amber learned to make bagels.

Hours passed, snow fell outside and turned slushy. Marie had some friends who apparently made a habit of visiting her overnight; she spent a lot of time smoking with them outside the front door. The machinery made white noise, the refrigerators and the oven, and the radio, tuned to a saccharine station that seemed programmed to put her to sleep.

By 2:00 Amber was feeling the effects of the unnatural sleep cycle. Her guts were languid; she found herself starting to breathe like someone asleep, deeply and serenely. Her feet were aching too.

"You look lost, Amber."

Marie and her friends were watching her through the window, communicating on the headset.

"Is there anything else to do?" Amber communicated back.

"Take a break, Amber."

The baker in his white uniform was going about his own private business in the kitchen. Amber asked him if it was usually okay to use the headsets to talk to other workers. He said yeah, he hated headsets by the way. He had a jock's voice and a wide mouth. Amber poured herself some coffee and went on break.

"Hey," said a voice. "You okay?"

Guy stayed on the ground. His eyes felt like they were weighted shut. *Go away*, he thought. Now that he was discovered, he certainly didn't want to get up, walk away, answer questions. Once in a store he'd reached and touched the bulb of a bathroom light on display. The man's shout was like the hot shock of pain.

Crunch crunch in the snow. "It's a kid." Different voice.

"Hey there, you okay?" Directly in his ear, *shaky shaky* his shoulder.

Guy moaned. His spit made dark trails over the frosty pavement to the curb. He'd just lie there until they got dissuaded. "Go away," he said. They realised he could talk, prodded him with questions: How did he get there? Where did he live? "Go away," he said again.

Ten minutes like that, and Guy revealed that he had a sister named Amber. "Go away," he said for the fiftieth time.

"Do you want to sit up?" They forced him. Spit had frozen to his face.

"Fuck off," he said.

He heard mention of calling an ambulance. *Fuckers*. They were all like his sister. A dozen clones of his sister.

CHAPTER 8

Marie suddenly appended another wave of duties onto the overnight list. Come 5:00, it would be time to start prepping for the morning rush. What was the morning rush? "It's fast," Marie warned, before sending Amber to clean the toilets.

The sky pinked a little, clear and still. And that was it, an entire night at work, the page turn of nightfall from beginning to end. Marie put Amber on the cash register at drive-thru to take orders. That beep would sound in the headset; "Good morning," Amber would say, since it was about time to start saying good morning. The buttons for different sizes of coffee, she'd basically learned. She instructed the customer to drive up please—and then the beep happened again, right away. Amber was scrabbling to separate two donut bags from each other; suddenly she was supposed to be doing two things at once.

"Hello?" said the customer.

Marie was on coffee, but she initiated the order herself, sounding weary and sour, very much like a middle-aged coffee shop employee. Frowning seriously, feeling the thump of shame in her temples, Amber finished it, and then the headset beeped again. *Again.*

"Uh," Amber said, "welcome can I take—can I take—"

"Okay," said another girl. "Amber can't just be taking orders." She was talking right to her but in third person.

7:00 was closing in, the beginning of the day and the end of the shift. Cynthia arrived, taking charge from Marie, who gladly dropped into the role of a coffee-pouring person who didn't talk except to guffaw, "No," whenever a customer phrased his order has a question.

With morning and a crowd of employees around her, Amber found she had her energy back. There were ninety minutes until the end of her shift. The end was in sight, until Cynthia went into the kitchen for some reason and cried, "Oh no, ohhh nooo!"

Amber had been trying to locate croissants on the cash register, and she heard the clinking of metal pots. She hadn't seen any significance in the mild scorching smell she'd noticed, and suddenly she knew not only that there was a problem but that it was her own fault. Thoughtlessly, she kept studying the cash register, looking for croissants.

"Amber, what happened?" Cynthia thrust a double boiler at her. The bottom was shiny and copper-coloured.

"What...?"

"Do you know how you are making soup, Amber?"

Amber stared, unsure of where this was leading.

Cynthia called for Marie, saying her name like "Maury".

"Hello?" chirped the croissant customer.

Flustered, Amber twisted back to the cash register. "Anything else?" she asked, still skimming for the croissant button. She found it but failed to notice that they had sold out of the variety he'd asked for. A confusing scene followed at the window where Amber had to apologise and ask if he wanted the other kind, and he indulged himself in a sigh, and Marie flicked Amber's arm to shoo her away.

Amber hadn't put water in the double boilers when she put on the soup. That was the big fuck-up. "Do you know what it is, a double boiler?" Cynthia demanded.

"Well yeah."

She was going to university, and Cynthia asked if she knew what a double boiler was. It probably would have been easier just to say no, though, since Cynthia started interrogating her on exactly how they had wound up dry and on the stove. Amber claimed she'd looked in them earlier—well, she looked in *one*, it had water in it and it was fine. And maybe the others weren't. She'd assumed. Amber demonstrated what she'd done, lifting up one of the soup pots, glancing in. It was all bullshit, of course. She'd put the boilers on dry and that was that, but god damn, the house of cards was under construction, since she'd learned her lesson the second she saw the shiny red bottom of the boiler, and she didn't see the point in weathering any extra discipline. Cynthia held it up again, saying it was ruined, hopefully none of the others were, and Amber thought it was idiotic how they were standing there staring seriously into the metal pot like there was wisdom to be discovered there.

"If you want to keep your job," Cynthia said in her version of English, "you ask how do you do something. If you are not sure you ask. If you need know how something works, you get a supervisor show you. It's okay to ask."

Amber nodded. Cynthia's breath was horrible.

Then she noticed that Amber didn't have black shoes yet and grilled her on that. I know, Amber said, I just haven't had a chance yet, I'm sorry I'll have them tomorrow. Let me know when it's time to do something right again.

With one hour left, Amber was sent to the bagel counter, and she prepared three toasted bagels before it was discovered that she'd toasted them upside-down. Another big delay, a mess of apologising, someone else hacking away at replacements. "We're training today," Marie said, her giant butt swelling as she leaned out the drive-thru. *No we're not, you cunt*, Amber thought. *If we were, these things wouldn't happen.*

And then it was over. No it wasn't. Amber was ready to put kilometres between herself and the store when Cynthia asked if she could stay another hour, just to do things like taking out the garbage, so she could see how they were done. Was that okay? Of course. She wasn't about to refuse.

Amber Drinkwater was into her first year of university, and she hadn't yet pulled an all-nighter, until then. 8:15 on Saturday morning, some reflex in her nervous system feeling the morning air and the dawn light, wanting to energise her with energy she didn't have. Amber commuted back to Silverthorne, nodding off a dozen times on the way. She had her hand on the glass of the Westside Rehab door before remembering she had to get the deposit for Simone. She stood like that for two minutes. Then she made up her mind that she'd walk to the nearest bank, perhaps resting on the first bench she passed, except the nearest bank was right across the street, a TD Canada Trust beside Caldense Bakery.

She recalled that she needed to buy black shoes at some point and resolved, in spite of her fatigue, to march over to Westside Mall right then and find some. It would have been nice if she were doing it out of firm discipline, but it was also a way of delaying having to face the apartment and the woman who lived there.

In Westside Mall there was a store called Westside Shoe Source. The manager was standing outside the storefront, dressed in an old-fashioned grey suit, looking impatiently up and down the concourse, broadcasting explicitly that he was waiting for customers. It was a bad idea, Amber had thought, since his presence and attitude were threatening, challenging, probably driving people away. Amber walked past him, in fact, hoping to find some other shoe store; then, feeling sorry, she went back. She saw the perfect style of black runner on display and summoned the man to say she wanted to buy it. They went through the steps of finding her size in the back and trying it on, getting Amber to walk thoughtfully around the store. She was the only customer, so she got the man's full attention; he offered her tip after tip, describing features that Amber really didn't care about and he'd probably read in a catalogue. It was a sickening kind of friendliness, the kind that hinted he was hitting on her, the kind that made Amber want to be totally morose to shut it all down; and yet the importance of politeness and generosity toward a shoe salesman in a shitty part of town made her smile back, laugh at his jokes, pretend everything was all right. The shoe didn't quite fit; he brought her another pair and then another, until Amber had to have been there for fifteen minutes. Finally she said they were perfect. They went to the check-out.

The shoes cost $72.50, a price which hadn't been marked, and which Amber hadn't thought to ask about until this point, after she'd gone through the whole dance and said yes, after he'd rung up the sale and stood waiting for her to pay. It was three times as much as she'd expected. It had never occurred to Amber that black running shoes could cost that much.

She paid with debit. It saved her the embarrassment of having to excuse herself to an ATM.

She went to an ATM anyway, the one outside the bank, to check her balance after paying for a pair of seventy-dollar shoes. And she didn't care to budget out how many days she could live on the $245.50 she had left. She didn't have enough to make that ridiculous deposit, and that was that, that building, that room. There were other rooms. There were other places she could go. But a place to sleep, right now, was what she needed.

Amber paused in stuffing a $20 bill in her wallet to wonder where it came from. She'd just made a cash withdrawal without realising it.

That did it. Screw Simone and her demands. She'd been feeling like shit for days now, and now she was so tired that she couldn't trust herself with her own money.

She dialed up the room from the lobby. The woman answered.

"Simone?" Amber said. "This is Amber."

"Yeah?" Simone said.

Maybe it was just the way Caribbean women talked. But that *Yeah?* was like a prompt, like *And?* or *Well?* As though there was something else coming up that she expected to hear.

"Is my brother up there?" Amber asked.

"Your brother! No."

"Okay."

"You coming up?"

"Yes, please."

The buzzer sounded in the little lobby. Amber turned to find the security camera. There it was on the inside, modest behind one-way glass. In case Simone was actually watching, Amber put on a show. She started to open the inner door—then froze—then patted her pants pockets—then huffed and turned, expressing the attitude of someone, she hoped, who had a sudden recollection in the lobby of her building and had to dash out for just a minute more. As soon as she was away from the doors, she took out her cell phone. There had to be somebody in the city she could call on.

Sitting on a garbage can outside Caldense Bakery, Amber called Carrie Sykes. *Please be there.*

"Carrie, this is Amber. I gotta to come over. I'm sorry, Carrie… I gotta come over. I feel like shit."

Amber hesitated, and she ended the call before she could say anything else. *There.*

As for Guy, she didn't know how to find him. She didn't know the first thing to be done.

She just had to make it to Monday and her exam. That was the big thing.

11:01. She got someone to let her into Carrie's residence, found the girl's room, and acted exhausted. She slumped absurdly on the ground with her back against the closet, feeling too tired to stand, her face hot with blood. I don't know what to do, she chanted.

It was a display she'd worked out in her mind before arriving, and now that she was in the middle of it, without the effect she'd wanted, the childishness of it blazed like fire. Carrie didn't know either. She stood in the middle of the room, awkward and ridiculous. Her roommate Ginger mostly tried to concentrate on her computer screen, but she had to glance over her shoulder. "What the hell do you expect from me," Carrie muttered. "Pardon me that I'm not your mom."

"You could show some sympathy," Amber sobbed.

"You could fix your own fucking life," Carrie replied.

12:22. "Hey, is Jesse in?" Amber asked the kid.

"*Mom! Is Jesse here?*"

Amber would have preferred not summoning the parents. "Good afternoon," said Mrs. Dundas.

"Hi there," Amber said. "Is Jesse here?"

Mrs. Dundas shook her head slowly.

"Okay." There was a picture of an Irish Springer Spaniel on the woman's sweatshirt, shaggy neck, big floppy ears. "Maybe I'll call again sometime."

"He's usually not in during the day," Mrs. Dundas said. "He goes to school." She said it in an ingratiating way, as though Amber wouldn't understand, never mind that she was in her first fucking year of university.

"All right."

"Good afternoon."

"Thanks, by the way," Amber called, but Mrs. Dundas had already shut the door.

14:45. There were three doorbells outside the townhouse, one for each floor. Amber rang just the middle one.

"Hey," Ian said. He was wearing pyjama pants. "How you feeling?"

"Fucked up as hell," Amber said. "Can I ask you if I could come in for a while?"

20:09. Amber had the opportunity to get up at 5:00. Rolling over in Ian's bed, the room and the sky dark, she could see the shining digits on his clock. It was brutal on the mind to keep waking up after dark and she was sick of it, and she rolled back over with her arm over her face. And just like that, it was 8:00. Muttering fucks and shits, she wiggled out of the covers. She hadn't eaten all day. Her stomach hurt again.

There was lamplight from downstairs, and the sound of television. Amber crept down quietly, wanting to survey the house before she was noticed. The TV was on the living room, but no one was there. Ian was in the kitchen. Something hissed on a frying pan.

"Good morning," he greeted her.

"Hey," Amber said. She settled into a chair at the kitchen table, blinking. On the table in front of her was a can of apple pie filling and a frozen pie crust. Ian was frying slices of banana in maple syrup. *Making dessert?* Amber almost asked it out loud, to make conversation. Instead she just thought the words. Silence prevailed except for the TV, the frying pan, Ian scraping with a spatula. There was an idiot gunning his motor outside.

Ian took the pan off the stove and brought the banana slices to the table on a little plate. They were golden, delicious smelling. He poured the apple filling into the crust and arranged the banana on top.

Amber remarked, "Yum."

"Want some?" Ian asked. "It'll be just fifteen minutes to bake."

He put the pie in the oven and set the timer.

"God, I think I haven't eaten in days," Amber said. She realised after saying it that it sounded like a plea to be fed, which it was; she just hadn't wanted to ask so blatantly.

"I've got bread if you're hungry," Ian said. "Or cold cereal or something. Or we can make pasta or something."

"Actually I wouldn't mind a sandwich, if that's okay."

Ian got out peanut butter, strawberry jam and white bread. Quaintly, he put regular butter on the bread before the peanut butter and brought it to her on a plate.

"Thanks a bunch," Amber said. She put her elbows on the table. "Don't suppose you have another Vex," she said, meaning to jokingly reference the fiasco two nights ago. But Ian stayed serious, which made her request sound actual, and greedy.

"No, I finished it all," he said.

Amber nodded, which Ian didn't see since he was washing dishes.

"How are you feeling?" he said, his hands pausing.

A lot better. Again, the words fired off in her brain but her mouth stayed shut, full of peanut butter and jam. She swallowed.

"I don't know."

"Ah."

Amber nodded again and kept on nodding into the silence, idiotically, a mute form of small talk.

Ten minutes left on the pie.

Ian unplugged the sink.

"So, any reason you slept in a Tim Hortons costume?" he asked.

"No. It's just... it's fucked up."

"Why did you have to come here?"

"Because." Amber paused. Unfeelingly, the way a hangnail fell off were it left to fall off on its own, she admitted, "I've got nowhere else to go."

Ian dried his hands. "You in trouble?" he said.

Amber guiltily took another bite.

"I guess. But... I don't know... I don't know what's happening..."

On Monday, Monday afternoon, she just had to be back in Ottawa.

"I don't know what's going on right now," she said.

She heard Ian breathe in, that *khhhh* throat sound that Dad always made when he was about to say something bitchy. Amber prepared herself to have to answer questions, defend her judgment.

"Hm," was what Ian said.

"This is good," Amber said about the sandwich.

"Well, wait for the main course."

Five minutes.

Once when Dad was grounding her in grade six, he'd suddenly added, "—*unless*, you have a date tonight."

"No," Amber had replied, bewildered.

All through school she'd maintained the same answer. Kathleen, meanwhile, started screwing some pathetic kid in the grade below her whom Amber barely knew. This was confessed to Amber in her bedroom, and Amber had laughed lightly, trying to make it a joke. It wouldn't remain a joke, though. Light laughter wouldn't be the proper reaction for long. It would become a topic of earnest interest, of keen, childish interest.

And Kathleen would become annoying as hell. Amber would no longer burst with joy to see her after classes, waiting. When she went to school in Ottawa, she wouldn't hurry to inform her of her new phone number. She wouldn't, in fact, ever talk to Kathleen again.

"I took some of your clothes, by the way," Amber said.

"Okay?" Ian answered. "I don't own Tim Hortons clothes."

"Well, I'm not *still* in them."

"You're fired."

Amber wondered if he knew about the surprise behind his furnace.

Ian stopped the oven timer at one second. The smell was delicious. Amber had picked just the right time to get out of bed, it seemed. Ian cut it into slices, served it onto two plates. He invited Amber to eat in front of the TV. She wrapped up in a blanket. They had seconds of pie, supplemented with potato chips and hot chocolate. It was a much different house than the one she'd thrown up in three nights ago. Ian hadn't known she was coming over, hadn't planned anything special, except the apple-banana pie, perhaps. Suppose he'd made it just for her?

After an hour of TV Ian said he was going to play video games. Did Amber have a preference? Amber mentioned that she came from a PC household and was out of the loop with these console thingies. Ian chose a *Final Fantasy* game, as if that narrowed it down. He loaded a game in some temple-looking place, but everywhere looked like a temple in *Final Fantasy*. Amber curled up on the couch and watched. Ian told her about a restaurant on Yonge Street that had an all-you-can-eat buffet. "Are you a vegetarian?" he asked, hesitating.

"No," Amber said.

"Well, they have a special after ten o'clock, you know. It's like, less than ten bucks… I was considering hitting that tonight."

"I work tonight."

"Oh, yeah."

For the first time, Amber was able to say that. For the first time, her job had entered the conversation.

And she regretted it. She wanted to stay there, on the couch, wrapped in a blanket. She didn't want to go to work. She wanted to eat Ian's food and watch TV and pass out right there on the couch.

"Ian," she said. "Can I stay here for a few days?"

Ian looked serious, twisting around the gamepad. Of course it would be more than a few days, she knew, but she'd wait for him to ask before she told him the truth.

He peered at her. It looked like he was going to ask right away.

"Yes," he said. "You can stay as long as you want."

The way he looked at her: who was this girl who'd crawled to his doorstep? He pitied her. *Good, let him.* He went into the menu screen, and when he rested the controller in his lap Amber knew things had finally crossed the line. He felt obliged. It was time to extend kindnesses, put things right.

"Is it any of my business what's going on?" he said.

"Nothing's going on," Amber answered, knowing that he was starting to suspect things—an abusive boyfriend maybe? Or her family? Some other token for sympathy? She could feel the bruises that he imagined around her eyes. No, nothing like that. Physical abuse was one thing that *hadn't* happened to her. But she felt perversely good, making him wonder.

"Okay, fine," Ian said. He closed the menu. "You know, you're very beautiful."

"Oh, thanks," Amber scoffed.

Ian didn't play it up as a joke, nor did he say something like, *no really*, pledging his sincerity, and in so doing demonstrate that at least the subject was comfortable enough to talk about plainly. He said nothing, which meant the subject was *not* exactly comfortable.

It was as though there were deadbolts in the room, like the whole house was a giant keyhole. And the whole place was turning on its side, certain things sliding into place, things like her having already slept in his bed twice, and eaten his food, and then pleaded to live under his wing. And here he probably thought of her as damaged goods. She'd have a lot of crying to do. She'd need hours and hours of attention.

And Amber was aghast at her own idiocy, the things she might have done, that she might have thoughtlessly walked through the whole script and not realised it until too late.

You know you're very beautiful.

When did anyone *ever* say that?

She heard a voice: *Don't get in, Amber. Don't even tempt these things. Don't even let them start.*

Ian's character ran around the TV screen.

And anyway, she looked at her watch and noticed it was nigh time to get on the subway. She was giving herself no less than ninety minutes to get to work tonight. "I should probably get going," Amber said.

"Okay, if you have to."

But she lingered on the couch, cocooned in her blanket. Good thing she'd worn her uniform all day.

Ian told her about his day tomorrow. He was going to get his hair cut at noon, and then later he had to buy groceries—an over-abundance of detail, exactly what times he was going to be home. He was desperate not to miss her. Amber got up and put on her hat and coat. She did up the snaps standing in the living room doorway. "I'll see you some time tomorrow then, Ian," she said.

"Yeah. See you, Amber."

"Thanks for the pie and stuff."

"No problem."

She hadn't told him about the bag of clothes in the basement. It was too late now. "Okay, bye," she said, and marched out into the snow.

It was disgustingly cold and windy. Amber squinted against the ice pellets blowing in her face. She rushed down the sidewalk with her hands in her pockets, her face buried low in her collar. *Hello, winter.* She glanced at her watch, compulsively. She had plenty of time today.

She remembered that she hadn't accounted for her brother since yesterday afternoon.

Well, God. If he wanted he could call her on her cell phone.

Speaking of which, she took her phone out to make sure it was on, and a giant question mark was filling the screen. She'd missed several calls that day, evidently, probably while she slept. It could only have been work, or her brother. They were the only people who had her number.

According to the screen, pressing a certain button would bring up information about who called. But when she did it, it said the caller and number were unknown. Oh yeah, she didn't have that feature. She hadn't wanted any of the special features.

She thought, just like she could grit her teeth against the wind, in the same way she could fight the sinking feeling, the thrashing of despair that was the reward for taking care of herself, for knowing better, for making the smart choice. The simple fact was, doing the right thing never felt good. And she would weather that, just as naturally as she hunched her shoulders in the cold.

So, that day had been pretty much a write-off. She'd spent the morning stumbling around for a place to sleep, the afternoon doing the sleeping. She was glad to be going directly to work from Ian's. He lived on the Bloor line, so Amber could just get on an eastbound train and chill out all the way to Warden station, no transferring, no leaping between lines. This time she wouldn't fuck up getting there. She wouldn't be *late*.

So.

- Suppose Cynthia were to give her a cash advance tomorrow morning. Just enough to satiate Simone, without forcing Amber to starve. And she could pay it back come her first paycheque.
- Tomorrow she'd spread out her clothes on the floor and get some serious sleep, first thing in the morning. Then she'd go somewhere comfortable to study, a coffee shop perhaps, but one where she wouldn't be tempted to spend a lot of money.
- As for Guy...

As for her brother.

Amber leaned over, leaned her head against the subway window, reassuring herself. Her little brother was smart. He'd once spent an entire night alone in Trois-Rivières. She closed her eyes to rest.

The train went over the valley, the six lanes of freeway, then darkness, a black seam supposedly containing railways and rivers, footpaths and power lines, but deep and blind, unlike the other seven lanes of freeway on the other side, and then it was underground again. Amber checked her watch. It was only 10:00. She was going to be early.

Forty minutes early, it turned out to be, which was too much, too long to wring her hands at the little table in the break spot. So she went for a walk. Amber crossed the Cliffcrest Plaza parking lot and set off to the south, toward the lake. The street was called Cathedral Bluffs Drive.

It was windy and cold, what one would call *bitterly cold*, with a dry, stingy breeze blowing onshore, and no snow in the air to cushion it. Amber cringed against it, wishing she'd brought a scarf.

All along Cathedral Bluffs Drive were perfectly ordinary single-family houses. Most of them had a second floor, but they were wide, flat-seeming. Many had Christmas lights on the bushes. The houses were all different, which was one way of measuring the age of a street. The trees were a better way, though. They towered; this was an older neighbourhood.

She imagined, though, that the houses on this street weren't just places she had to ask permission to enter. That was what other people's houses were to her as a kid in Cantley: places full of twists and turns, like caves or park paths, until the idea of property was driven into her. But no, houses weren't just land formations, there for discovery. They were the product of grotesquely vast investments of work and insecurity. Cars were in driveways; there were candles in windows. Imagine the time at the bank, the nights spent awake, wondering how it was to be done, how it would all be paid for. *But they did it,* Amber thought. *Look at them. In their houses.*

And she was walking down the street with her work shoes in a plastic bag. There was no sound except the wind in the trees, her own footsteps, the clinking of zippers on her coat. There was no traffic, no sounds of animals, not even the skittering of leaves or garbage across the road. Snow highlighted the cracks in the pavement like a wax rubbing.

The road turned into a crescent, and when the crescent swung back to the north, Amber kept going south, across a sports field. The field was dark, away from streetlights, and on the other side of it was a cliff, dropping down to the lake. The trees at the edge of the bluffs were indistinct, like an impressionist painting. There was a wire-rope fence, and a sign probably warning her not to climb over it, but she couldn't read it in the dark. She climbed over it and walked out to the end of a point, feeling the sense of vertigo and disbelief at approaching a cliff edge, having to reconsider again and again just how far a drop it was. Far down and in front of her was a beach looking horrible and cold, as any beach looked in December. Lake Ontario and the black horizon were blurry. A heavy sound rose up, the sound of the wind on the shore, perhaps the tide as well. To the east Amber could see lights from the next town over; there was a tiny cluster of city lights to the south as well, across the lake. Was it possible she was seeing all the way to New York state?

Meanwhile she checked her watch. Considering she still had to change, it was time to go. She wasn't going to be late again; she'd been late twice so far, and she'd only worked two days. So far, she had a 100% lateness record for her entire life.

At that distance, from that height, the beach down there didn't seem very big. But then Amber noticed a woman walking her dog along the tide's edge, having come from the marina, out of the lights to the dark sand and wind, walking her dog, a barely visible smudge. With the size of that woman for comparison: *imagine trying to swim across Lake Ontario, in this weather, right now.*

Somewhere under the roar of the wind she heard a fox bark. It scared her, reminded her of where she was. She ran back to the street and checked her watch.

The first thing Amber saw in Tim Hortons was the double-boiler she'd ruined yesterday. It was strung up over the cake counter, with a computer printout:

Attention: Everyone
180.50 $

And here she had to ask Cynthia for an advance. *Never mind.* She locked herself in the bathroom, even though all she had to do was change into her shoes and stuff her hair in a hairnet. It seemed like she'd barely left this place after finishing her last shift, and now she was back. Possibly the lousy sleep schedule was to blame, and wearing her uniform for eighteen hours. According to some, life was worthless when all of one's time was split between sleeping and working. This Saturday had been worthless.

Marie had a heads-up for her when she came out front. "We're out of large cups today. The delivery didn't come."

"So, how do we serve large coffees?" Amber asked.

"We don't," Marie smirked. *Gosh.* And in she settled for another eight hours. Amber looked up at the clock, a bad idea, and considered that the hour hand would be pointing more than halfway around before she got to leave, and it took some effort to fight down a feeling of exasperation. Eight hours: that was four university lectures. That was as long as a person was supposed to sleep.

"Now Amber," Marie said, "if you got any other questions you better ask them tonight, 'cause remember you're on your own tomorrow."

"Yeah," Amber replied, sensing that asking Marie anything would only earn her more smart remarks. One of the first overnight duties was to change over the cream cheese into new containers. Amber opened the sandwich table and piled all the casseroles on the counter. That was bad timing, because just then there was a customer at storefront, an old guy in a bright orange toque, the kind worn in the country to distinguish a person from game.

Because Amber didn't know how to make change on the cash register she had to do it in her head, and the guy noticed and took it to mean she needed to have every step of the transaction spelled out for her: now you give me my change; now you get me the donut. Good, thanks for the help. Amber pulled down the one he wanted, crunched it into the little paper bag and said good evening. Did he think she'd never set foot in a coffee shop before, that she hadn't the least idea what her job was? She went back to the cream cheese. But it would have to wait, since her headset beeped.

"Go for it," Marie said. Marie hadn't touched a cash register since Amber learned to use one.

ERIC HOPKINS

"Hellooooooo?" said the customer. It was a guy, with giggling girls in the background. *Great.* Amber greeted him as blandly as she could.

"Gimme… a turkey club sandwich," he said.

"Okay."

Marie shouted, "White or whole wheat!"

"White, girl." Giggle.

"Okay."

Amber had to remember where the sandwich button was.

"And why don't you toast that bad boy."

"Okay."

"And put some mustard on that bad boy."

"Okay."

"And gimme a large mocha." Giggle. "That's it."

"Nine thirty-two, please drive up."

"Nine thirty-two!?"

Amber didn't answer that; he was just showing off for the girls. She heard another holler from Marie: *No large cups.*

Amber stammered, "Oh sorry it looks like we've all—we're all—we don't have any large cups left."

"Whaaat!?"

Amber lifted herself from the till and saw that Marie hadn't started on the sandwich or anything, since a half-dozen people had walked into the storefront. So Amber had to fire off this order herself. Plastic gloves, white bread, toasted *right side up*—but the treadmill on the toaster wasn't moving. Why not? It just wasn't. Amber stared at it, bewildered, then decided she'd push the crusts through with the bread knife. Although after a few seconds Amber peeked in to see the bread spitting blue flame. She jabbed frantically with the knife; the crusts slid out charred and smoking like coal.

"Marie…" Amber said.

Her supervisor/trainer ignored her.

Amber held each half of the bun over the garbage can and scraped the burned bits off with the bread knife. She'd do the same for herself at home, with her own toast, so these guys couldn't complain. How to build a turkey club: the picture was taped under the sandwich counter. Where was the bacon? There were dregs left on the steam table from the afternoon, dry and brittle, although they had to be thrown out. So she trawled under the sandwich table for fresh bacon, folded a sheet in half, put it in the microwave for thirty seconds. Meanwhile she did the other stuff, the mustard on that bad boy—a bubble burst in the bottle when she squeezed it. Amber hoped the guy liked lots, that he was a bad enough boy for it all... Lettuce, the pre-portioned slab of turkey.

Beep. "Welcome to Tim Hortons I'll be with you in just a moment."

"Gimme three regular coffees and an Ice Cap—"

"I'll be with you in just a moment." *Thanks for listening, asshole.* Amber thought the cream cheese would be warm by the time she got to it.

She heard a scream from outside.

"*Heeeey!!*"

That's right, you stupid fuck, I've forgotten you. You only ordered all the most complicated items on the menu. Marie was still working at the storefront, at her leisure, it seemed. Scurrying back to the counter, *fuck,* she dropped the bacon on the floor. She couldn't just go on as if nothing had—fine then, the guy wasn't getting any club with his turkey. It was his punishment for being a bitch. *Crunch* as she pressed down on the top crust. She mummified it with wax paper.

When the drive-thru window opened a strong wind blew directly into the store, scattering a pile of napkins, and Amber saw what the guy looked like, the guy who'd ordered bad-boy mustard, a young brown guy with a round face and glasses, plain jacket, his friend on the passenger side, girls in the back. "Where's your helper?" he snapped.

"She's busy with storefront," Amber said.

"Why don't you get more people working at night?"

"It's because, nobody comes. Up to about one o'clock people come—" Amber was bullshitting all this. "—but after that, *nobody* comes."

"You should have more workers, lady."

So this was the part where he tried to be reasonable, the follow-up discussion to the caterwaul when he thought he was abandoned. Too late for that; he'd irreparably announced himself as a pompous prick. Amber just prayed that he would pay up and go before he discovered the ingredient missing from his sandwich.

No, they wanted more. The guy in the passenger seat leaned over to order a toasted bagel with this and this and this—way, way over, into the driver's lap, to look Amber right in the eyes, to make sure she got everything just right. Meanwhile, turkey club man was unraveling his sandwich, and Amber disappeared from the window as soon as she could; storefront was empty now, and Marie was dicking around the counters with a cheesecloth, but Amber knew better than to ask for help. *Ya toast it, ya put butter on it.* Her second try with the broken toaster went better; the bagel didn't actually burst into flame.

Mercifully, turkey club man wasn't aware that his sandwich was missing bacon, since he didn't say anything. Perhaps he didn't even know what a turkey club was. It wasn't out of the question for a Tim Hortons customer. "There you go," Amber said, handing over the bagel. "Goodnight."

Now drive away.

And they did.

"Sorry about that, I can take your order now."

"Yeah," the man said. "Gimme three regular coffees, and an Ice Cap—"

Amber asked, "What size are the coffees?"

"Large!" He sounded pissed to be interrupted.

Amber squeezed her eyes shut and said, "I'm afraid we're sold out of large cups this evening."

Huff. "You can give me an extra large for the price of a large."

"Okay," Amber said. *Fucking wheely-dealer.*

She poured his extra larges for the price of larges and mixed up his Ice Cap, wondering why people ordered them at night in December. The guy pulled up; he was a white guy, with bright red lips like they were dry and swollen. He said he wanted a cardboard tray for the beverages. Amber got one out, but the cups didn't want to slide snugly into the little bays. They dimpled dangerously as Amber tried to work them down, and what fun it would have been if the plastic Ice Cap cup cracked right up the side. She pushed them down as far as they would go and left it at that. The guy paid, and she wished him a good night.

Now drive away.

It was time to manhandle the cheese.

As if it would be that easy. *Bang bang bang*; swollen-lips was banging on the window, staring her in the eyes, presenting a tray of almost-empty coffee cups splattered with brown specks. "Think you could get me some new ones?" he grunted.

"Uh oh," Amber said. "Spilled?"

"*Ya* it spilled, all over my car you fucking idiot. Think I could get some paper towels?"

Amber got them and replacement beverages as per the request. Everything had fallen out of the tray, apparently. *Poor baby.* She should have removed the lids and sloshed him herself. Instead she stood in the window, attentive like a puppet, the freezing wind slapping her face, while swollen-lips fussed over his car with paper towels and sent the soggy mess back to her. "Get me some more," he said.

Amber got more. She muttered, "Here you go," and waited for him to disappear.

Marie had elected to start the throw counts. Good, Amber didn't want to talk to her. If there wasn't any more shit going down at drive-thru, she'd get on with the cream cheese. She put on a plastic glove and drove her fingers into one of them. The top surface was gummy and dry, since it was the least popular kind, and it probably hadn't been used all day.

And then her headset beeped. *Christ.*

She wouldn't have a free hand until she got the cheese mashed down into a clean container. "Hello?" said a voice. *I'm coming*, Amber thought. *You've been waiting two seconds.* Marie decided to help out; without turning around she greeted the man and asked for his order. "Everything bagel toasted with the butter," said the man, while Amber ripped off the glove and sprinted for the drive-thru. "Medium coffee, double-double with no sugar."

It was the double-double-with-no-sugar guy. Marie clearly thought she'd pulled her weight by jumping on the radio, since she went ahead fiddling with the throw chart. Round three with the broken toaster was another disaster. Scraping the ash into the garbage, Amber made the executive decision to tell people that there would be no more toasting tonight. Mentioning it to her supervisor would certainly make no difference.

"Here you go," Amber said.

"Thank you kindly," the guy said, flashing a smile. "How are you tonight?"

"I'm good," Amber told him.

"You're good?" he said. "Are you going to be here every night now?"

"No, I get days off," Amber said. "Here's your change."

"Thank you, Amber."

Right, her nametag.

"Okay, good night."

He lingered to smile at her before driving away. Amber's hands were freezing from reaching out the window. Now that the customers were gone, Marie came over and told Amber that she was finished the counts, so they could start putting together save trays and throwing out the rest of everything. Then she gave Amber probably the only useful piece of instruction she ever would: "Don't let a few bad customers get you down, Amber."

Amber nodded and played with the bill of her visor. Phrased in a hundred different ways, it was advice she'd been hearing for as long as she could remember. She saw a man across the parking lot, peeing on the YWCA building. He noticed her looking and waved.

Amber considered, she could always change her mind about Ian, go to live with him after all, in spite of all the stories and warnings, in spite of all her hard-earned common sense.

She knew she wouldn't.

CHAPTER 9

After all morning sticking them out the drive-thru window, Amber's hands were numb with cold. She couldn't pick change out of the till. Her face was cold, too. Her cheeks were stiff, and she hadn't smiled for several hours. Marie had told her to watch more training videos around 2:00 in the morning, and for thirty minutes she'd had to look at so many smiling faces that the expression itself had lost meaning; it had become just a weird and unnatural thing to happen to a person's face. From inside the store with its yellow lights, the outside looked strikingly blue, silent and artificial like an old photograph, the colour of a bleak landscape.

At 5:00 came the phone call from a girl who'd slept in and consequently would get there as fast as she could. At 5:10 Amber was basically shackled to the drive-thru register, Marie stuck at the front counter, the baker still doing the morning bake, which was supposed to have been finished. Someone actually let fly with their car horn, and Amber wanted to rush out and give him a medal for figuring out how to fix everything.

Human beings never looked so stupid as when viewed in their cars from a drive-thru window. Amber hated how they slyly tasted their coffee before driving away, to make sure it was made right. She hated how they not-so-slyly pressed their thumbs over the steam hole and shook it outside their cars, since she couldn't be trusted to stir properly. She hated the woman who insisted "from a *fresh pot*" after each of her orders, and she hated the woman who waved, panicked that she was about to be served steeped tea when she really wanted bag tea. A drowning person could hardly have been more frantic. And she hated how the one thing that united everybody, across all boundries of race, sex and class, was that if it took her longer than two seconds to answer the speaker they called out: "Hello?"

Amber felt like there was a fine glaze of grease all over her body. Perhaps there was, from the coffee machines steaming away night and day. She pressed paper towels against her face, and her cheeks and forehead left behind dark stains. She also had the faint taste of blood in her mouth, as though her gums had started bleeding for no reason, and her feet ached as bad as the last time. She needed insoles for her seventy-dollar shoes.

Cynthia arrived for 6:00. Amber was nervous to stir the waters concerning the double boiler, so she was extra pleasant when she said good morning. As for approaching her for the advance on her rent, how about she did it... never. *Well, no. Just not right away.* But she had to do it, and the sweetness of 7:00, going-home time, was dulled by the anticipation of the ordeal. Amber rehearsed and rehearsed in her head different ways to approach it, different oblique angles she could take, making it seem as though the issue just came up naturally instead of being something that she rehearsed and rehearsed. She had ten minutes left in her shift, and then five, and Amber made up her mind that she would start by calling Cynthia aside to talk about it privately and seriously. Cynthia, she'd say, can I talk to you a minute? In the world of minimum wage work, where managers were feared and hated, it was a rare thing to find an employee who actually *started* a conversation with her manager. She thought that was to her credit.

One of the other girls named Sujeeva walked up and said, "Are you Amber?"

"Yeah," Amber said.

"A guy just called and said that the girl at the window 'skimmed,'" reporting his exact word, "two dollars from his change."

"Really?" Amber said.

"He said he was *furious*, but by the time he got home and looked up the store's phone number he calmed down."

Sujeeva was smiling a little, and Amber grinned back, a goofy lopsided grin, hoping that they were laughing it off. "Well, geez," she said. "I might've made a mistake, but it's not like..." She sneered and shook her head.

"He said to 'keep an eye on that one.'"

Amber scoffed and looked to see if Cynthia agreed that it was laughable. "I didn't notice if I gave any wrong change," she said.

"Okay," Cynthia said. "You are off at seven?"

"Yeah," Amber said.

"You can go now."

"All right."

Amber went.

A snow plough accompanied her to the bus stop. She leaned her head against the glass. The whole night shift thing wasn't getting any easier. The ad on the bus shelter was for Gap clothes, a woman and a man with dreary Gap faces, in cowgirl position, in their underpants. In winter, looking at it made her shiver.

Maybe the bus had actually been cancelled because of the snow. Amber waited and waited, forgot she was waiting and remembered again. She waited for twenty minutes then checked the schedule and discovered that on Sunday mornings the first bus didn't come until almost 8:00. So she decided to walk to Warden subway station, plunging her hands into her pockets.

Her bowels suffered because she was tired, and she'd eaten barely anything but coffee and free donuts all night. Coffee was brutal. Apparently it woke up and energised people; in her case it was like firing adrenaline into a paraplegic, all that electricity dry and sour in her chest, under her eyeballs. If she shut her eyes for even a second she felt like she'd collapse, but her eyes were so dry she had to shut them constantly against the wind.

What she did was she stopped in at a Coffee Time on the way and bought another coffee. She didn't care that it would make her feel even sicker. That was the point. *Fine, get sicker, get sick until you can't get sick any more.* As she walked along St. Clair, blowing water off her nose, she considered stopping again; there was *another* Coffee Time in a Loblaws plaza, across the street from a cemetery. But she was on the cemetery's side of the street and didn't want to bother waiting at the intersection, so she went into the cemetery instead, wandered around until she found a spot to lie down, a spot out of the wind, and she fell asleep and had a being-chased dream.

It started out absurdly enough, hanging out with high school friends in a place that looked like a summer camp she'd gone to years ago. Something happened to make a man pissed at them, so he killed everyone, and went after her. She had the sense of running for hours and hours, through a huge variety of settings, thinking she'd lost him, then seeing him round a corner, still coming. She kept screaming, *it was a joke, it's okay, you don't have to do this*, all her powers of placation. But he'd become amused. It was outrageous that he would care so much about catching her that he would chase her so far, and if it was just a joke to him it was outrageous that he would pursue a joke for so long when his victim clearly didn't find it funny.

Whenever Guy made Kraft Dinner, he always looked through the spice cabinet for extra flavours. He couldn't imagine eating it plain, with just ketchup, although he remembered that he used to. He based his find on smelling the lid, a two second wave under the nose. And it was more of a "find" than a "choice"; he didn't know the origin of any of the jars or shakers in the cabinet. Mom had bought them, not him, and damned if he knew how long ago, or what they'd eaten that day, what recipe she'd had in mind when she brought them home. It didn't bother him when he didn't even know what some of them were called, the ones in plastic jars without labels.

He took the plate to eat in the den, watching TV, fingering the batteries back into the remote every time they fell out.

He should have been doing his homework, but he suspected that extenuating circumstances allowed him a few days to goof off.

When the front door opened, there was only one person it could have been. Guy sat there on the couch, waiting to be discovered. He heard her walk through the kitchen, almost tip-toeing, going all the way upstairs. He thought at first that she wasn't even looking for him; no, it was more like she thought he was sleeping in his room. The TV was turned down.

She came down at last and appeared in the doorway. Guy waited a few seconds to glance at her, since sometimes she thought she could command his attention just by popping into the room like that, and he didn't want her thinking that now. When he did look at her, she was staring at the TV too. She'd taken off her shoes and stood there in sock feet, but her coat was still done up to the neck, shiny with rain, her hat covered in little beads.

It was one of those moments when the only words were the usual ones, the ones that sounded vapid even on a normal day. *Hey. How's it going.* This was an occasion; he thought that something would have to happen that reflected its significance, placed it in the big scheme of things, something that defined the attitude the two of them would be carrying on. He didn't want to say, *Hey, how's it going.* So he waited for his sister to talk first.

"Uncle Ian's coming over soon," she said, panting. "I think he'll want us to live with him."

She went back to the pantry to hang up her coat.

And Guy wanted to get up for more ketchup, but not now that she was home. In fact, his entire body turned to stone in anticipation of her joining him on the couch.

When she tried to open a can of Devon custard she had trouble with the can opener. Guy couldn't see her, but he heard the clatter of the thing as she shook it in the air. Guy didn't move a muscle.

Daylight just disappeared. The entire day was over in a flash. Amber had slept under a tree, undisturbed by a caretaker or anyone else, for six hours, she discovered after digging her watch out of her coat sleeve. It was insane. Stumbling along St Clair East, stupid with tiredness, why had she decided to crash in a cemetery? It was too much work to finish the trek to the subway?

In order to go where? Nine hours, and she'd just have to be right back for her next shift, so why waste time thrusting herself into some other part of the city?

She'd been looking for someplace to sit down that wasn't a bus stop or a restaurant. A banner on the cemetery fence had announced that the Mausoleum of the Risen Christ was now open, indoor crypts available, and the idea of an indoor crypt had sounded safe. Amber wound up wandering way to the far end of the cemetery, across the river, to an area full of Asian families. She'd found a granite bench, dedicated in loving memory to someone named Alice Song, and sat down as though to pay respects to the Song memorial—a set of headstones, one with a cross, one with an engraving of Christ, romantic, eyes upward. Amber hung her head. After a minute she decided the spot was safe enough and curled up on her side in the snow, under one of the trees marking the plot. She figured she wouldn't accidentally lie on someone's grave if she stayed under a tree. And just like that, it was afternoon.

All she had to do was go to Simone's and get her stuff, and then she'd be fine. She could study in a public library, even a coffee shop. She'd hack through that exam tomorrow, and then she'd have a whole month, thirty long days, to figure out all this other stuff before the winter term started at U of T. It was adventurous, but she could easily go a week or so without living in a place that cost money. She'd just proven that by sleeping among the dead.

As long as she moved around and didn't make a presence of herself in any one neighbourhood, people wouldn't start to recognise her, wouldn't notice that she never went to any kind of home.

Really, that's what she'd been doing ever since coming to Toronto.

The main thing was that it wouldn't last. It was student poverty, not real poverty; it came with her age and her vocation. It was like a trial. She had one up on all the actual homeless people: she had a job, a bank account, and a place to be next year, once her winter courses started. Already, having finished three shifts at her work, doing the math in her head, she was almost two hundred dollars richer. As long as she didn't piss on herself and kept all her teeth, probably no one would even notice.

Never mind hiding under a backhoe. *This* would make a university horror story, years from now.

She heard a sound like a grandfather clock chiming, the same sound she'd heard several times in Simone's apartment. It was coming from her cell phone; that was the sound it made to warn her that the battery was running low. She took it out, and there was a message on the screen saying that she'd missed several calls. Caller ID unknown, since she didn't have that feature. Fuckers couldn't call when she was awake.

She climbed out from under her tree, cracking her spine. A quarter inch of snow had fallen around the gravestones, the wind had stopped, and it was curiously warm. Amber felt compelled to linger there on the ground. It was like getting out of bed on a weekend.

It must have been Guy calling. If only she knew where from. But fuck it, she was hungry, in a dry, sick way. And she had to pee somewhere. The graveyard had a river running through it, fortunately, with a stone bridge that she fit underneath.

She found her way out, passing the Mausoleum of the Risen Christ, a surprisingly modern building: flat roofs and vertical windows, like the front of Guy's school, she recalled. There was that Coffee Time across the street. But she wasn't going to another coffee shop. She was going to the Loblaws and buying groceries, like a sensible person. With great seriousness she went in and walked up and down each aisle, sort of the way she'd gone through her university course calendar in May, considering the value of every single item, whether or not it was of any use to her, whether or not she actually believed she'd use it for years to come—rice, scouring pads, rubber gloves... She visited the frozen food section, looking at Swedish meatballs, thinking about when she'd be able to afford them. She looked at cakes at the bakery, imagining that she'd buy something like that for Guy's birthday—or her own, or for Christmas, something to celebrate. There were whole turkeys on sale at the butcher, but those would be intimidating for another decade or so.

Breakfast cereal: now that would feed her from one end of university to the other. But even there, she'd need a bowl to eat it out of, cutlery to eat with, and a fridge, if she expected milk.

All these prerequisites, extra rules. How could a bowl of breakfast cereal seem so distant?

So she wouldn't look like a thief, Amber bought a chocolate bar on the way out the express aisle. The woman ahead of her was buying tuna and *Cosmopolitan* magazine. Eight sex positions never before published, your holiday hairstyle, something about astrology, and Amber chucked down a Hershey's Cookies n' Cream. "That's it."

And that being by no means an adequate meal, Amber went to Coffee Time after all. She swore that she'd spend no more than a dollar. She told herself she'd settle with just a buttered bagel, no cheese, sat by the window, chewing and staring at the napkins, sensitive to how sad and dumb she probably looked, eyes blank with the lethargic intensity of a battered girl.

She felt like she was making all the same decisions, learning the same lessons, over and over. How long would it be until she started rising above episodes like this? Strolling into the grocery store with lofty expectations, leaving with nothing but a chocolate bar she didn't want. Why couldn't she start into anything that didn't disintegrate? Why did the ground fall away before the foundation was in, before the land was even sounded out?

Before she knew it, her food was gone. A plain bagel wasn't a meal. She went back to the counter and bought coffee and rice pudding, and then a chocolate muffin. She took out twenty bucks from

the ATM with its $1.50 convenience charge. *Fuck you*, she was say-
ing. *Fuck you, you bottomless sponge.* It wasn't the sating of hunger
that made her decide when to stop, it was the recognition that she'd
spent almost ten dollars. And then when she walked out the door she
felt bloated, like she'd been mouthing spoonfuls of pure yeast. The
body was a liar. Girls her age were in a stage of asking questions,
like, can I eat this kind of food, in this quantity? Can I stay up this
many hours a night? The body's answer was a dreamy yes. Then
they wound up fat and cancerous. What the fuck was her body telling
her? What was she doing wrong?

Amber kicked a piece of garbage in the parking lot, a Subway
bag with the wrapper in it. It had weight and skidded across the
pavement like a hockey puck. Amber chased after it, took it around
the side of the plaza to investigate. Yes, for some reason someone
had left an entire, untouched subway sandwich in the parking lot.
Perhaps it had been dropped or thrown out a car window, as a joke,
and the person had been too squeamish to eat it after that, even
though it was totally wrapped in plastic and wax paper. Well, lucky
for her. She ran across the road to the bus stop, dug into her nickels
and dimes, and waited to arrive at Warden subway station before
eagerly unwrapping the paper, digging into the sandwich she'd found
for free. She sat on a little red seat, under the TTC wall map, bathrooms to the left of her, buses to the right.

It was a BLT with cheese, not exactly the cheapest sandwich
to leave in a parking lot. Amber didn't know how old it was; it was
certainly no longer warm. The bacon and lettuce and everything was
still sound, but the bread was soaking wet, like it had been in a puddle. It actually made her gag; it ruined everything. She had to concentrate like an athlete not to spit it on the tile floor, eyes full of absurd tears. She crumpled up the plastic and threw it away.

It was nothing to get upset about, she reminded herself. It
wasn't like she'd paid for that sandwich.

Amber went back to the West Side rehab building to pick up
her stuff. She'd barely woken up, and already it was dusk out. Night
shifts in winter were going to be brutal. Amber had only a vague idea
of what she'd say to get Simone to buzz open the building, but some

kids let themselves in just as she got there. She trailed after them, piled into the elevator with them, stood among them as they talked really loudly about some popular thing that she didn't recognise in the least. Amber left them at the fourteenth floor, thumped down the low-ceilinged hall to 1412, and knocked. She prepared a world-weary face, tired and humourless. It would be easier to push her way in and out, avoid a discussion.

Simone didn't answer the door. Instead it was another black girl, older than Amber, but much younger than Simone. "Hey," Amber said, understanding immediately what had happened, that Simone hadn't wasted a single drop of sweat waiting for Amber's deposit; she'd gone ahead and taken in another tenant, someone who could put down the money. And here Amber had expected to have to tell her, world-wearily, to go ahead and do just that. "I just have stuff here to pick up."

The new girl stood back, still too much of a newcomer herself to question the goings-on in the building. Amber looked in the bedroom; it was already full of the girl's stuff, including a terrarium of lizards on the dresser.

Was Simone even home? Amber would have liked it fine if she wasn't, but she heard that music from the living-room, the music that went along with the kitchen sounds and lamp light.

"Are you looking for this?" said the new girl. Amber's bags had been stuck in the back room. "Yeah," Amber said. "Uh, I don't suppose you'd know if my brother has been back here."

"I don't know who's been by," the new girl said. "I just moved in yesterday. Why don't you ask Ms. Clarke?"

Amber lowered her voice. "I already asked her."

"Okay, well."

Amber nodded. She was done with talking. There was nothing else to keep her. She hefted her bag, heavy as always, and said thanks. Then she turned to the door and screamed, "Oh God!" at a giant red snake, climbing up the wall.

"Oh, there's Ophie," the girl cooed. "Holy shit. What's she doing?"

Amber didn't answer.

"I'm getting my camera."

Ophie the snake was braced in a zigzag between the doorjamb and the wall, stretching her head upward, her scales shimmering as she ascended another few inches, a very slow oscilloscope. "This is so weird," the girl gasped, taking pictures with an old film camera. "Corn snakes are supposed to be arboreal. Does that explain this behaviour?"

Oddly fascinated, Amber stayed. She'd noticed things about the black girl, or mostly, things she hadn't noticed, like Simone's clearly Caribbean accent. She wasn't supposed to care about that woman and her English, her sharp voice, her music and her furniture, but it intimidated her, it had hung like a spiked ceiling in every room of this apartment. But this other black girl had probably been in Canada longer, was at least second-generation; her accent was perfectly domestic. There was less about her to not notice. She said her name was Candice. Amber did her spiel about being in first year civil engineering at University of Toronto, and Candice fussed supportively, asking how she liked it. Amber played it down, as though it were not terribly exciting.

"I didn't do college yet," Candice said. "I've been working with a mission called *Common Ground*, it's an arts education project that works between Canada and Guyana."

"Oh yeah?" Amber said.

"I do correspondence, I've directed some arts workshops, performance art, some classes…" Amber nodded along, wondering if in the course of this talk she'd be tested on her knowledge of Guyana. She didn't even know what continent it was on. Wherever it was, Candice had certainly much more to say about it than Amber had said about her university program, as though studying civil engineering was a shameful privilege, as though to mention it conversationally was like rubbing it in the face of Candice and everyone else from Guyana. Ophie had finished her ascent, with her front half stretched out along the top of the door frame; Candice plucked her down, and she coiled up around her arms. Amber felt an impulse to ask if she could try holding the snake for a while, but she didn't. She stayed at a respectful distance.

She said, "So, you're sure my brother wasn't here."

"Well, I told you. You'll have to ask the lady about that." A jerk of her head toward the other part of the apartment, her hands busy scratching Ophie's throat.

"I guess so," Amber agreed mildly. "Okay." She drifted toward the door. Amber noticed Candice wasn't wearing any socks or slippers, even though the floor was cold hardwood. "See you," she said.

What was she expecting from Simone Clarke? A torrent of re-crimination? At least some cold-shouldering, because she would be embarrassed for giving the room away? The woman was wearing what anyone would call "traditional" clothing, a bright patterned dress with puffy shoulders. Ultimately, the woman turned and noticed Amber, and she was cordial. Perhaps because Amber had her bag; she was getting her stuff and getting out. All was right with the world. She asked Amber if she felt any better, having observed that she was exhausted and hungry the other day, and she banged a nail into the wall, hanging up a calendar for next year.

Amber said, "Hey, do you know—do you happen to know when was the last time my brother came by?"

"Last time I see him he was with you," Simone said.

"Was that yesterday…?" Amber pressed, but Simone was getting icy and obstinate.

She insisted, "He's with you last time I see him here." And no wonder, since Amber had basically admitted to having lost him with her questions. Amber sensed it was time to go. She thanked Simone and, as soon as she stepped out the door, she knew she would never talk to her or the snake lady again. She left the Westside Rehab building behind, asking nothing, hoping that at least her intrusion hadn't irritated those women very much.

It had only been a little over a week ago that she'd first arrived in Toronto, bouncing off the train with her brother. At that time she'd expected such a predictable life, going to school and coming home to her uncle's house. And then her plans had changed, but far too glamorously; she'd expected to be as franchised as someone in her thirties, with some self-motivated career where she set her own hours and came home every day exhausted but happy like a TV character.

But now she was on the right track, slugging it at a coffee shop, which was the best work for a nineteen-year-old, really. At the moment she had a cash flow problem, sure. She'd be without a bed for maybe a few weeks. But the way she looked at it was this: didn't other kids sometimes stay away from home for days on end? Occupied with crazy hi-jinx like fucking and doing crack? And at the end of it all it was an awesome story for their friends. Well, her story would be even better, because at the end of it all she'd have a life.

Now:

- Find another place.
- Find your brother.
- Find something to eat.

The first item was being shelved.

As for the second, her cell phone was always on; she couldn't call him, he had to call her. Why the fuck didn't he? Except he had, apparently, and she'd missed it, sleeping in the cemetery. Other than that, she could wait around somewhere he was likely to go, like George Harvey Collegiate Institute. Tomorrow was Monday morning, his first day of school in Toronto.

Amber had been walking toward Keele Street during these ruminations, and she decided to pay George Harvey a visit, not that she'd really be there to meet him tomorrow. At 8:00 a.m. she'd just be leaving work, and she'd have to go straight downtown to catch a train to Ottawa. She'd only seen the front side of Guy's school before, the front of the building and the lobby. Today she walked around to the back.

The sports field was enclosed with double-height chain link fence. There were a few brambles growing up against it and pieces of garbage poked through the snow. The goal posts were violently rusty. The school itself was made of tan bricks with banks of identical windows, like a warehouse. Everywhere there were bizarre, heavy barricades that looked like they were for stopping vehicles. They were an awful, bright cyan colour, as though the school hadn't cared to paint over the factory colour-code.

Janelle was sending her brother into that?

Amber didn't care that it was close to their uncle's house. Let him walk an extra ten minutes or take a bus. In fact, she'd seen another high school just up the road, a much nicer-looking one. Why couldn't he go there? Someplace with enough funding to repaint their goalposts?

For the first time, she considered that her brother was in a shit-load of trouble.

More or less trouble than herself? That didn't matter. He was too young to be faced with something like this. He was only in high school.

What the fuck could she do about it?

Call my fucking phone, Guy.

For the first time, she considered getting the hell out of Toronto.

She walked up Dunraven Avenue to her uncle's house, the three-storey tower that had excited her the first time she saw it. The stones were highlighted with frost now. Amber climbed the hill and looked through the second-floor window. All her uncle's things were still there, precisely as they had been a week ago, the first time she peered in at them. There was clutter on the kitchen counter, the light left on in a back room that had been burning away, day and night, throughout her whole visit to the city. She was through raging after Uncle Ian. He was gone.

She stomped up the wooden stairs, icy black, to the third floor. There was no window near the door to see through, so she knocked and waited. There had been a chance that Guy, or someone, would answer. She tested the handle; it was locked.

What if her brother was gone too, now?

She looked down to the street, leaning on the balcony. It was quiet and snowy, white Christmas weather. Suppose she never heard from her brother again. Like an article lost in the subway, he had got away, and that was that.

She'd leave her phone on.

What she had to do was get through the ordeal without help. If she gave up and threw herself upon public services it would be all over. She had such a record of fuck-ups over the last week that it probably amounted to something illegal. Not an in-and-out crime like theft, but the kind that piled up: negligence, vagrancy, whatever the word was to describe her. And the longer she waited the worse it would be when she finally fell through. So what she had to do was *not* fall through. If she stuck it out to the end, when she was finally working, with a fixed address and actually saving money, then hey, who could complain?

With only 86,400 seconds in a day, she couldn't waste time daydreaming on a balcony. It was time to eat. Without having to take another twenty out, she had five bucks and some change. That was enough to go to a coffee shop. There was no point, unfortunately, in going to grocery stores when she had no place to put groceries. She conceived of buying a loaf of bread and peanut butter that would fit in her backpack, and that was a fine plan up until the point where she would have to open it up and butter bread in a public place. What better way to look like a vagabond? So, coffee shops it was. She didn't even have to have a full meal, since she could drink coffee for free on her break at work. That sounded like a good plan.

She went to the cheapest coffee shop she could think of, Keele Donuts, with the multigenerational Korean staff, the black man with tourette's syndrome and the chain-smoking woman who could have been Marie, the night shift supervisor. Who was there today? No one except some kids chilling in the parking lot, cardboard snowmen in the window.

Having set limits for herself, Amber felt, she was free to indulge within those limits, one of the liberating things about planning ahead. As long as she didn't try to have a meal, she was fine. She bought coffee, naturally, ignored the sandwiches and got another apple fritter, which turned out to be just like the last one, raw in the middle. She sat down at a table, eased her bag off her shoulder, and only then realised how it would look to pull out a laptop computer in this place, where gangsters did business on their telephones. It would be just her notebook then.

After ten minutes Amber was finished all her food and no longer concentrating, when she suddenly heard fluffy pop music. It was her cell phone. She'd never actually heard her own ringtone before. She scratched at her pants pocket, got the phone out. *Okay, okay so*—she opened the cover, haltingly pressed the wrong thing, and rejected the call instead of answering it. She stared at the LCD for a long time, the big question mark and the message saying Caller Unknown.

Amber hopped cafés for several hours, alternately eating food that wasn't a meal, staring at her notes and laying her head in her arms. She wasn't going to be ready for tomorrow. She was only halfway through her notes, and even that was mostly because the first few lessons had been on mechanics that she already knew from high school—cars, bullets, tennis balls. But there was crazy new stuff, and lots of it. She would flip ahead in her notes and be startled by a lesson that she'd forgotten entirely—of course she'd remember it again, that was the point of studying, but it was frightening in terms of judging how much further she had to go.

She could seize another hour perhaps, on the subway to work, and there would be her breaks as well. She'd have to forego doing any practice problems. At this point, the best she could hope for would be to quickly scan over the rest of her notes. At 9:30 she started feeling like it was time to pack up and head out east, but she lingered until 9:45, when she looked at her watch again and was suddenly filled with self-reproach. She ran to a bus stop, another matter of sweating and fuming, staring down the street to watch for a bus. She stepped right out onto the street for a better view, walking into the slow lane when there was a break in the traffic, scampering back when more traffic came. Of course it was a stupid exercise, and the bus wasn't coming any sooner for it, but she just had to know, because as soon as she knew, even if the bus were still ten minutes distant, at least then the rest of the wait would be measurable, not some aped act of faith where she wasn't sure if anything would come at all. Her shirt and underwear constantly felt sweaty, so that she never warmed up while standing around outside. She checked her wallet for $2.75. Surely she had that much change after buying all those donuts and cookies.

Her cell phone started again. *Take it easy this time, Amber.* The button with the picture of the red telephone had caused the disconnect before. So how about the blue one?

"Hello?"

"Amber?"

"Yes."

She knew who it was. Still, she waited for him to say it.

"This is Guy."

"Hey."

"I don't think that phone of yours is very useful."

The first time hearing his voice in two days, and he had to be a critic.

"I'm still figuring out how to work it," Amber said. "So you've been trying to call me."

"Like all the time. Where the fuck are you?"

"Where the fuck are *you?*"

"I'm lost."

"Have you been lost for two fucking days?"

"Yes!"

"Well I've been going crazy you know," Amber said. "Where are you?"

"If I knew that I wouldn't be lost, would I?"

"Well, I can't really do anything if you don't know where you are, can I?"

"Well, if you don't care then go fuck yourself."

Amber wanted to hang up, press the red telephone on purpose, teach him to be a little bitch. Instead, she just gave him silent treatment. Silence stretched on to five, ten seconds. She'd waited and waited for Guy to call; now he'd called, and she wasn't sure why she cared so much.

"Amber?"

"Don't talk to me that way."

"I'm sorry."

More silence, of a different kind.

Up the road was an old railroad bridge, the kind from the eighties with green panels masking the structure. Underneath it, at last, she saw the boxy figure of a TTC bus, which wouldn't have been there one second later or sooner for all her pacing and worrying.

"I didn't sleep anywhere last night," Guy said.

"Neither did I."

"Where are you?"

"I'm just getting on a bus."

Amber knew that didn't answer his question. She meant only to imply that she was busy; he'd called while she was in the middle of something. Even now, talking to her own brother, relieved to hear from him after two days, she had to be evasive. If she didn't tell him where she was, he couldn't criticise her for being there. It was how she talked to the social worker, her employers, her parents, anyone who felt license to come down on her with advice.

"If I told you where I was," Guy said, "would you be able to tell me how to get home?"

"Depends where you are."

Guy told her. He mentioned street names she didn't know, stores and landmarks she'd never heard of. They'd been in Toronto barely more than a week, but Amber had the feeling she'd got around in that time, visiting corners of the city that she'd never expected to see in her life. They should have counted for something, all the bus rides and squirrely little errands. But here her brother was trying to tell her where to find him, and she didn't recognise a single thing he said.

She also didn't know how to interpret "home".

"Could you call a taxi maybe?" Guy said.

"Why don't you call one if you want one?"

"I don't know the number."

"Then you open the yellow pages." The bus came to a stop. She queued up.

"Amber!" Guy's voice was strange. "Where are you?"

"I told you Guy, I'm getting on a bus."

"What are we doing here, Amber?" Guy asked. "I want to go home."

"We're going to school. And I'm going to work. Right now."

Pinching the phone with her shoulder, Amber stepped up and paid her fare. They were useless, pragmatic answers. But what did he expect? It was the truth.

"Does that answer your question?"

The phone made the grandfather clock sound, the low-battery sound.

"Look," Amber said. "I'm busy 'til tomorrow. You have to be at school tomorrow, remember?"

"Yeah."

"Just grab any bus and you can ask the driver if it's going to the subway. Once you're on the subway you'll know where to go to get to your school, right?"

"What am I supposed to do tonight?"

"You can just sleep anywhere. Today…"

Mention of the cemetery died on the way out of her mouth. She didn't want to say it on the bus, surrounded by other people listening. How could she calmly suggest to her brother that he curl up in the snow in a graveyard?

She had nothing else to suggest. So she pretended he hadn't even asked. "Just, do that and tomorrow after school we'll meet up, okay?"

"I want to go home." He was crying.

"I know. We'll think of something. Just make sure you're not late for school tomorrow, okay?"

"Okay."

"What's your first period?"

"Gym."

"Really? First thing in the morning?"

"Yeah."

"Shit. They'll probably want you to have gym clothes for that."

"I can just wear some shorts, can't I?"

"Maybe just for tomorrow. I don't know, I guess you'll find out. We'll get it settled later, okay?"

"Groovy."

Snow.

"Thanks for calling, Guy."

"Well, gosh."

They said goodbye.

Afterward, it was like every bit of blood in her body were flash-frozen. *Lamenting over gym clothes? You're one hell of a sister, Amber. Good for fucking you.* She hadn't known what to tell him. She sensed that he'd wanted her to drop everything and do something for him, right then, find him somehow, never mind that it would be a hopeless effort. That hadn't been fair. Here she was on her way to work—to *work*—and, what, she was supposed to ditch it? Blow off work like a punk, to join him in tears and confusion? He didn't know shit. When he was her age, he wouldn't be able to keep a job to save his life.

She could have told him to come to her store; he could have slept at a table in the dining room. Why hadn't she thought of it? But no, even that was too much of a chance, inviting someone to sleep over in her workplace. With her record so far, she had to walk on glass or she'd lose everything.

She was early, for the first time, by ten minutes. It felt great. There was no panic, no flurrying with her uniform in the bathroom. No one seemed to raise a stink about her bringing her hockey bag, since the store would be populated by only two people for the next six or seven hours, and her stuff wouldn't be in anyone's way if she left it on one of the break chairs.

So, here she went on her first solo shift at storefront. The $180.50 pot was still on display. Additionally, the evening girls showed her a letter the store had received, a two-page printout stating that there wasn't "an ounce of intelligence" in the store, in a round sans-serif font better suited for a birthday invitation. The author happened to own a temp agency and offered to replace the entire staff. The evening girls said goodbye.

Nine hours, to boot. Amber looked at the clock and pictured the hour hand three-quarters of the way around. She put on the headset and considered where to start.

There was a smell, like the mop used for the bathrooms. Maybe it was the steam table, which she'd emptied to clean—no, it was the customer, the newest one who'd walked in that night. *Of course.* And now that Amber was looking, her purse looked mighty threadbare, and her jacket. "I want..." she said. "I want... I want..." She was having trouble getting that sentence started. At the same time, she was summing up how every customer sounded. *I want I want I want.*

Naturally, it was getting easier. She was learning things, like never to make eye contact with a customer until the second she was actually taking their order. Her original inclination toward friendliness and respect had tempted her to give smiles to people waiting in line, but then they had instantly assumed that it was time for them to bark out their desires—even when she was clearly still doing something else, even while someone else was still at the counter—and there had to be an ugly mess of pleasant apologies. So she learned to carefully skirt her eyes around anyone waiting; she learned to ignore them, basically. If they noticed and felt upset, too bad. It was their own bitchiness that had forced her to do it. She'd started the job thinking that she could get by on that old kindergarten lesson: be pleasant and polite, and people will be pleasant in return. Amber looked at the clock again and despaired. She couldn't bear the idea of coming back here, riding the subway for an hour here and back, for months, years to come. Was it possible to be through with something after barely a week of it?

One thing that she realised, however, was a comfort: no matter how horrible a customer was, no matter how ugly the interaction, all she had to do was give them their change and wait for them to leave. And then it would be over. Every time a customer drove away or stomped out the door, the slate was cleaned. The next guy to come by wouldn't have any idea what had just happened.

And she'd have an opportunity to try again, being even more careful, expecting even less.

She wouldn't have it any other way.

That was, unless they went home and typed up a two-page letter offering to replace the entire staff, since obviously people were so spiritually delicate when buying a buck-fifty cup of coffee that she deserved to lose her job if anything went wrong. On the store radio a soaring female chorus told her to release her inhibitions.

For example, a man walked up to the drive-thru window, even though the storefront was open. He was on a coffee run from some overnight factory, and he spoke English so badly that he had to hand Amber a written list. There was a smile frozen on Amber's face—frozen, since it didn't go away even when she turned from the window. It was pretty clear, when there was an order of croissants written down on the list but thoroughly crossed out, that the man didn't know what the hell was going on.

"So you want everything on here *except* the croissants?"

"Yeah."

"So, this, this, this, but *not* this."

"Yeah."

He probably didn't understand a word she was saying. His response was just a sound. "H-yuh."

Ten minutes later he was back, making a *pssh* sound to describe how his boss had hit him in the face and knocked the coffee on the floor, sputtering that this was why he'd had it written down for her. Amber burned and decided not to charge him for the replacements, since it was all getting thrown out soon anyway. H-yuh, he said, and went off into the snow.

She should have at least told him sorry, even if it wasn't her fault, and maybe even made some cursory suggestions about workers' rights, not that she knew anything about that. She'd known him for about sixty seconds while he bought coffee—who the heck was he? What kind of a place did he work at, where his boss could hit him like that? Where did he come from that he had wound up at a job like that and couldn't quit?

Suddenly it seemed a very easy thing, making the effort to be cheerful to her customers.

Then a man cruised up and threw a bagel back at her because she'd only cream-cheesed one side.

And then it wasn't so easy.

Beep.

It was 1:00, not even a quarter of the way into her longest shift yet. Her face felt greasy again, and she snatched at the paper towel dispenser, ripping off little triangles. A song came over the radio, something she remembered from the nineties. It was something her mother had on tape, and she used to play it constantly in the car.

It was probably her favourite song, and she didn't even know the name of it.

CHAPTER 10

8:00. Amber took off her visor and wiped her forehead with more paper towel.

She took some clothes out of her hockey bag, ones she hadn't worn for a while, and changed out of her uniform.

Units of time were rarely counted in physics; they were the denominator, this and that per second. Even her salary was in dollars per hour. She'd never counted hours and seconds as much as she had in the last week. The next payday was the coming Thursday, but it turned out that because of some bureaucratic bullshit she would get paid two weeks *after* the end of each pay period. That was nice, that the company would hoard her salary for two extra weeks.

She wrote down her schedule for the coming week and said goodbye.

She went out to the sidewalk, nonplussed as a bus drove past her and pulled away before she got to the stop. No matter, she'd get the next one. She stood there as other morning people walked up in their business suits and winter coats. It was five minutes before another bus came, and by then a line stretched down the sidewalk. Amber felt the short-lived vanity of being at the front, on display as the senior member of this line of people from all walks of the city. But the bus pulled up, bewilderingly, the driver's reasoning a mystery, so that the doors opened at the *end* of the line. The crowd surged like iron filings toward its new locus, transforming almost beautifully from a line into a clump, and everyone pressed forward with that self-absorbed, mutual resentment of a bus crowd, that attitude that made people switch to driving, no one offering so much as an inch to someone else, because if they did that they were out. An old guy stretched his arm way, way out, since if he got his fist into the bus he was officially inside. Woodenly the driver said, "Watch the doors," and shut them on Amber's face.

So she was still at the front of the line.

Maybe she should have done something, like sticking her foot in the door, *how about next time you*—but what would that have accomplished? The driver would have just gone home and snarled to his family about this crazy cunt who hated missing the bus.

She waited for the next one.

It was showtime, time to execute the big plan. Next stop, Union Station and a train to Ottawa. Maybe she'd only have to sleep for part of the ride, and she could use the rest of the time to cram some more. She didn't know if her cell phone had enough juice left to last the day, so it was staying off until about noon, which was when she figured her brother would have the first opportunity to call her during school, if he wanted to—if he was even there.

She rode the subway to Yonge Street and went south for a change, instead of north to Eglinton or Finch, which had been her usual trajectory. South straight to Union station. She knew her way around now. She knew the way up to the ticket desks in the atrium, pervaded by people with briefcases and luggage. She looked just like one of them with her giant-ass bag and backpack, full of clothes and books and stuff, everything a person would need for a trip somewhere, basically the same package she'd brought to Toronto a week ago Saturday, all leaving with her.

She had to consider, as she waited in line, whether she thought she was proving anything by buying her own tickets after turning down Janelle's free ones. *Poor Janelle*. Imagine the panic, the professional fear. What if social work was just like fishing, and if one got away that was just too bad? Of course it wasn't like that. Maybe her *own* career was in jeopardy now. It was people like herself, Amber thought, who ruined social work.

But that was something *not* to worry about. Her immediate concerns involved the woman in the nice suit selling train tickets. Amber walked up and asked for a round trip to Ottawa please, same day return.

She should have known it wouldn't be that easy.

Apparently the last VIA Rail train to Ottawa had left a half-hour ago, at 9:30. The next one wasn't until 12:20, scheduled to arrive in Ottawa at 4:30, an hour and a half after her exam started.

"Oh," Amber said, hearing blood in her ears, horror pounding in her chest. Was it to be like this, after all she'd done? "Are there any other—I mean, is there any other train service I could check?"

No, that ticket booth only serviced VIA Rail trains, of which there weren't any to Ottawa earlier than 12:20. GO trains? Greyhound? I told you, this ticket booth is only for VIA Rail service. Besides, GO trains didn't go farther east than Oshawa, and a bus wouldn't be any faster.

"Fine, I guess, that's fine, then," Amber said, taking out her debit card.

After tax, it was $154.76.

What—

That was student fare, right? Cheapest class?

How could—?

How could it—?

She read the figure back aloud, from the debit screen, to make sure. Just to make sure. She pressed OK on the keypad, thumbed in her PIN.

She was terrified, wondering if she even had that much in her account.

The transaction was accepted. Thank you, said the screen. The woman slid the tickets under the window and wished her a good day.

Amber walked away, feeling dazed, wondering if maybe she were to just run fast enough from the Ottawa terminal—or if there was a chance her train would get there super early—

What the fuck.

The last thing she needed was for the homeless guy, the same guy who'd stalked her at the payphone the very first evening, to march up and demand just another fifty cents so he could get a coffee, glaring and spreading his arms in a *what's your problem?* attitude. She shouldn't have looked at him when she noticed him coming, since the only people who would ever walk up to her on the street were homeless fuck-offs, and they only did it because they wanted her money, which made them just like everyone else in a world where no one was out to help and the only surprises were bad ones. *A hundred and mother fucking fifty dollars to sit on a train.* Did she have anything left in the bank after that? She'd expected to pay eighty, maybe ninety dollars. How the fuck could fucking train tickets cost so much, tickets for a train that wouldn't even get her to the fucking place in time?

She knew that if she'd planned ahead, checked the train schedule beforehand, she could have simply requested not to work that extra hour this morning, for a damn good reason, easily made it downtown for the early train, not been shocked out of her mind by the price and presently be on her way, pure and simple.

Instead it was shit like this, always like this and always brought on herself because of these invisible rules that she was expected to know without asking, and she walked out to the edge of the sidewalk with her backpack on and her hockey bag over her shoulder.

Look at you now, Amber.
What are you going to do?
What are you going to do now, Amber?
She looked up at the CN Tower.
And she considered:

The exam was three hours; she'd only be missing half of it. Maybe she could call ahead and beg for permission to start late. If she didn't finish that was too bad, but at least she wouldn't forfeit credit on account of non-attendance. Her professor's phone number was right on the first page of her notebook.

She dropped her bag right there on the sidewalk, in the middle of Front Street, piled her backpack on top, wrested out the white notebook. She turned on her cell phone. Hopefully it had enough juice left for this one last call.

As it happened, she got his voice mail. Amber said hi and gave her name, stuttered that due to "a mix-up" she wouldn't be getting into Ottawa until after the exam started, not saying where from, and she wondered if there was any chance at all she could be permitted to start a bit late, or something. She gave him her cell phone number, and while giving it realised that she'd just committed herself to leaving her phone on.

That being done, she had nothing to do for two hours until her train left.

She was back downtown among the bank towers with their coloured glass and twentieth floors, but in no state to go for another inspiring walk. It would have suited her to slump on a bench.

There was only one thing to do that she could think of: she went to a coffee shop. On the ground floor of a building called One University Avenue there was a Second Cup, nested in a corner of the glass lobby. First Amber went to the bank machine to withdraw $20: the bill popped out for her, and then she waited for the receipt, with her balance. The piece of carbon paper emerged with a clatter. Amber held the $20 bill in her hands, the green Queen Elizabeth, reading on the receipt that it was the last bit of money she had in the world.

So, what would it be for coffee?

Something nice. She ordered a latte.

They had a special at the moment, actually, for Belgian chocolate lattes. It was a bit more expensive, but it came with marble chocolate biscotti. Amber had never tried biscotti before.

She sat by the window. Every seat was by the window; it was a glass lobby. She stuck her bags on the seat across from her. She could look out to the corner of University and Front Street, the corner of Union Station and the hotel, the elevated train tracks to the south, Lake Ontario. It was like Ian's building, in a way, the sense of perching in a tower, observing. It was incredible that they'd achieved that feeling with a ground-floor coffee shop.

There were two other women there, in business attire, chatting business-y things. Amber opened her physics notes and took a sip of the chocolate latte, the steaming hot latte with Belgian chocolate stuck right in it.

It was heavenly.

One of the girls behind the counter held the title of Manager, but they were both the same age, and both of them were too timid to shake Amber's shoulder. If it had been one of the business women, forty years old with permed hair, a powder-gray jacket and black shoes, sling-back with just the stub of a heel, then the sight of her with her head down, face buried in the crook of her elbow, would have been so silly that they could have easily tapped her awake in good humour, treated the nap as an accident. But Amber was in a dirty white winter coat. She hadn't washed her hair in days, and her running shoes were cracked and gooey with slush. Waking her up was a gritty chore that one of them would have to face eventually, soon. They couldn't just let her stay there.

It fell to the Manager. "Miss," she said. "Excuse me."

Amber sat up, sensing the lines her coat sleeve had left on her face. "Oh shit," she said, understanding immediately. She'd opened her physics notes just in order to drool all over them, apparently. She packed up while the manager mumbled polite things about a time limit on using the tables. Amber said yes, she knew. And yes, she felt okay.

Back in Union Station she studied a train schedule, trying to learn how to read it, as though it would yield information contrary to what the clerk had said, some alternative argument to the numbers on the big clock above the departure schedule. Her ticket was still in her coat pocket, and she still treated it delicately even though it was worthless.

She hadn't known the train schedule; there was a fuckload she hadn't known.

That didn't matter.

She shouldn't have assumed that these things would all just arrange themselves for her.

She walked out to the street.

I've told you over and over, Amber, and it just doesn't work.

I'm through telling you, Amber.

This is why, Amber, you're fired.

You fucked up for the last time.

Get the fuck out before I kill you.

She still had enough money for the subway. She considered, if she rode the subway all the way out to the east, right to the farthest subway station in Scarborough, she could walk from there to highway 401, which wound like a beach along Lake Ontario all the way across the province. Every step would put her one step closer, one less step to go, even if it was insane, even if it wouldn't help—but it *had* to help, somehow. And she would meet highway 416 in Johnstown, turn north for Ottawa—

And she could even make her way across the Rideau Canal into Quebec, onto highway 307. It was a route she knew particularly well. It would take her back to Cantley. It was driving along the 307 that her father had told her how proud he was that she was such a smart young woman, and not just in terms of grades and universities, Lord no. She was respectful, she had a heart. Typically, Amber had hummed at this and shrugged it off. *What's something I do that's so great?*

Well, Dad said. *For one thing, you don't swear.*

Back to a dark and locked house that belonged to the bank or the government or whoever was in charge of these things, full of old furniture and duck-taped boxes. Break a window and sleep at least in an unheated house, while her brother froze to death in an Ontario city.

It had the plausibility of a dream.

She could go for that walk anyway, though. She could take just as many steps, without leaving Toronto. She could walk up and down every street, one after the next. There were only so many of them, after all. Starting right there on Front Street, on the sidewalk in front of the train station.

Amber finally found a phone booth outside a mall, closed, surrounded by a snow-drifted parking lot. She'd been marching for almost twelve hours, and without a cup of coffee she felt like she'd freeze to death.

Just as soon as she made the call she'd wait right there until the mall opened and treat herself.

But the Bell telephone voice told her that it was a long-distance call, asked her to deposit another $3.10.

It was so cold it burned. Tonight of all nights, the wind had been against her. Her shoulders ached from clamping her hands over her ears. Her shoes were full of snow from stumbling through drifts at every intersection, because they plowed the streets but never the fucking sidewalks. Her ankles were covered in ice. They felt like they were stuck in bear traps.

She counted out her change on the ledge of the phone booth, into her quarters, then nickels. She knew that pennies weren't accepted. She didn't have enough, she just barely didn't. Maybe she'd find some money on the ground in the parking lot if she looked, in spite of the inch of snow covering it, even though it was so cold she could barely stand to bend down—

A miracle, though—one more little coin in the fold of her coin pouch.

Was it really enough? The phone added it up for her, tediously, coin after coin. It was.

The phone rang the special ring that would let Janelle know it was a client calling. Amber waited, seeing her breath frost up the plastic windows. Janelle would be pissed, crazy pissed, and not just for being woken up in the middle of the night. Or else she wouldn't be. Amber had no idea how the vampire-haired woman would act. But Amber was going to shove ahead, no matter what, and call in a favour. She was going to tell the truth, try to explain where she was, beg for someone to come pick her up. She didn't care how stupidly she came across, how clumsily it all spilled out. She would happily wear a brand on her face for the rest of her life.

The phone rang and rang.

It seemed, again, that in spite of all her grim resolutions, something was going to happen that had never occurred to her. Janelle didn't answer at all, and her voice mail kicked in. Amber's money clattered down into the phone's vault. *You've reached Janelle sorry I can't take your call leave your name and number after the beep.*

It had never occurred to Amber that Janelle wouldn't answer the phone at 4:00 in the morning.

Somewhere in a house in Ottawa, or in a mainframe in another country if Janelle used a voice messaging service, an answering machine or a computer had begun recording a creaky Toronto phone-booth, the wind, the beeping of the wee-hours snowplow. What the hell kind of a message could she leave? No matter what she said, it would sound farcical, like something out of a stupid black-humour movie. *Sorry Janelle, I don't know when you're going to get this, but I'm freezing to death by some buttfuck strip mall where I don't know where I am, anyway—*

What the hell was she supposed to say?

I don't want to fill your voice mail with details, but I've basically abandoned my brother and wasted all the money I saved in my life, I feel stupid just saying all this, it's four in the morning and I don't know when you're going to get this, but don't try to call back, since I can't be reached, like, anywhere, so.

I fucked up, Janelle. I fucked up big-time.

What was she supposed to say?

Janelle, it's me.

This is Amber.

It's me, Janelle.

It's Amber.

This is Amber.

She hung up.

www.ingramcontent.com/pod-product-compliance
Lightning Source LLC
Chambersburg PA
CBHW071836020726
47502CB00004B/1387